The Light Attendant:

A Canadian Bluebird Novel

Part 1

Wendy Fehr

Shifterspress
Saskatoon, Saskatchewan

Acknowledgement

This is a work of fiction. The reader will not find real people or real proceedings in this story. The characters I have created are purely fictional and serve only as a means through which the reader might glimpse some insight into the Great War. While the happenings in this book are based on actual movements of real army units and real hospitals as outlined in army diaries, I have taken great liberty with their situations for the benefit of my characters' development and the plot of my story. That said, I have tried to impart some measure of reality by inserting small doses of factual information.

The foundation of this book is built on the stories of people who went to war. I wanted the reader to benefit from the re-telling of these stories so that they might know of the horrors and of the beauty found amidst the horrors; the inhumanity and the nobility seen side by side; the wreckage and those things that sprung forth anew from that wreckage. To do justice to their stories I felt it important that the reader know the *lived* experience of the *people* there, not simply the facts of the war's happenings and the politics as told in history books. In order to adequately convey these experiences, I felt strongly that some ideas, situations, and events portrayed in this work ought to be told through the voices of the people who lived them—and I found many such voices in the course of my research—voices which told their stories in poignant, beautiful words of their time. This was particularly important where the veteran's thoughts, emotions, and observations provided the reader with an understanding of their lives which could not be explained or described in any other way or which would lose meaning if described in other words.

Toward that end, I have paraphrased a limited number of sections, giving credit to the original authors in the references at the back of the book. This was done in those particular parts of the story in which I found the original authors had such refined and clear voices that I dared not debase them by a poor attempt to describe that which I did not know first-hand and therefore had no right to describe. I felt such a method of reference would be understated so as not to stall the flow of the story for the reader while still allowing the reader to know which parts of the book bear more reality and inviting the reader to seek out the original works.

In the writing of this book, I have stood on the shoulders of giants, incorporating some of the ideas and experiences of those who have previously shared them with the world, mixing them together so as to share them anew with a new audience.

Above all else, I wish for the reader to be inspired by this work, not only to remember, but also to honour, those whose sacrifices have made our lives possible—sacrifices that serve as the structure on which our present society is built. My goal is to present their experiences so that we do not forget what *real* heroism looks like. I invite the reader to seek out their stories, for their lives were so much *more* than the simple story told here.

–Wendy

Proem

My family has, of late, been rather persistent on hearing about my time as a Nursing Sister in the Great War. I suppose this is the natural result of them bearing witness to the slowing of my steps and quietening of my voice. They are anxious, I suppose, to capture some part of me hitherto unknown to them so that they might have a "complete" image of me after I am gone. That would be impossible, of course, for they have not walked in my shoes over those hours, days, weeks, months, and years before their existence.

However, toward that end, they have asked me to review my diaries from my time as a Nursing Sister as well as Henry's journals from his life during the war, requesting I add any details I can still recall. Perhaps they believe my mind to be dimming along with my interest in this life. It is quite possible I have let go those details of life that are not worth carrying to the grave. I can assure you, however, I recall with a clarity that is infused with all light, every moment of my life spent in Henry's presence. Reliving those moments—each one playing in my heart daily—is all I have left since my dear Henry has gone. I will relive those moments until my end, savouring the bitter-sweet taste of each one.

Adding to my diary is not something I am particularly keen on doing. Oh, I don't suffer to any great extent from the recollection of the war—not like some of the men who fought in the trenches—but the entirety of it seems so out of context in this day and age as to be little understood, I think, even with all the details explained. The war was not an event nor a part of history that can be told. It had to have been lived and breathed and felt in all of its horror and splendor in order to be fully comprehended. The filling in of the details—more words in a book—will not afford my family any clearer image of who I was or what the events truly meant to me and did to me. No words can offer that—only the surviving of the thing will truly do.

Regardless, I will do what I can for the poor dears as they watch their mother and grandmother, their great grandmother fade, taking with her the knowledge and wisdom some 92-odd years of living will afford a person. I suppose I can understand their need.

I have never shared my diaries nor Henry's journals and I will not show my writings while I yet live. The extreme dichotomy between the words lying in stark contrast to the knowledge of the actual events—between the theory and the practice of it—would make me seem absurd or perhaps truly bizarre. To find beauty, fulfillment, and even love amidst the savagery (the word does not do justice) and destruction (also a vastly insufficient word) would make me appear to be dull-witted at best or disturbed at worst.

I will review the diaries and journals and write an accounting of them here so that the entries might be better explained and have some context given them which my family can peruse at their leisure upon my passing. I have told them I would do my best to write down the details of it all and, while there may be some things I choose not to tell them, there is no <u>forgetting</u>.

July 1, 1915

War Diary

Private Henry Ryzak

July 1, 1915

Volume 1

Diary Text: 8 Pages

[July 1, 1915]

A sledgehammer fist connected solidly with my jaw, snapping my head to the side and sending me reeling as I tried to keep my feet under me. I met with little success. I landed hard, my shoulder taking the brunt of the fall. I lay there on the hardwood, trying to scrape my raw egg thoughts up off the floor. I blinked and shook my head, trying to clear the muddle.

A mountainous shadow fell across me, cast by the dim, yellow electric lights.

Huh—those are new. When did Frank get electricity?

I looked up at the colossus looming over me, taking in his ham sized fists and his ridiculously large forearms.

Can't let those reach me. Could outrun him—he doesn't look that fast—but I didn't cheat!

AND he still has my money…

I decided to take the adage "keep your friends close and your enemies closer" literally. In one quick movement I heaved myself off the floor and launched myself into Goliath's midsection, grabbing him around his waist. At the same time, I hooked my foot around the back of his legs and pushed hard. The man toppled, landing with a room-shaking thud that rattled Frank's new chandeliers. The back of Goliath's head bounced on the floor and he paused, groaning, just before lowering it back down slowly.

I used the ensuing three seconds to grab a nearby wooden chair and dropped it on the man, pinning his shoulders and chest to the floor. I straddled the chair, planting a foot on each of his wrists to keep his hands where I could see them. One of them still held a fistful of cash—*my* cash.

I waited.

Another three seconds and the big Swede opened his eyes.

"I didn't cheat," I said slowly. He said nothing. He cast me a look that I could only interpret as a desire to kill me. "I did not cheat." I repeated more quietly, but more firmly.

"I can't give you all my money," he bellowed. The chair underneath me heaved and resettled on the floor as Goliath tried to get up. He let out a breath as he settled back again.

"Then you shouldn't have bet it," I said, planting my booted feet more solidly on his wrists.

The man still looked like he wanted to kill me—if not for thinking I cheated at cards then at least to get his money back. "Now give me the money—I won it fair and square."

"No. I need it to get my lumber to town."

"Fine," I said, folding my arms along the backrest of the chair and resting my chin on them. "I can do this all night."

The Swede growled and, despite the limited mobility of his wrists, he managed to loose the bills he clutched in his large hand, spewing them on the floor beside him.

"Take it then!" he roared.

"Thanks, I will," I said. I stood up off the chair, pushing my step just a bit to make sure I cleared the chair—and the reach of the man's hands. The chair wouldn't hold him after my weight was off it. I snatched up the pile of bills on my way.

I straightened the bills in my hand as the Swede sat up, pushing the chair off him with a clatter. He glared at me, looking sullen but slightly less like he wanted to murder me in my sleep. He sighed heavily and shook his head. If I had thought it possible, I would have wondered if the brute was about to cry. I considered that a moment.

I scraped a few bills off the top of the pile in my fist and dropped them on the floor beside the human mountain.

"This should get you down river. You can still get your lumber to town and make your sale."

The man looked up at me in surprise then looked down at the floor where the money lay. He slowly reached to pick it up.

"Frank," I said, turning to the barkeeper, "sorry for the trouble." I gestured to the overturned card table and tossed a few bills onto the bar. Frank ducked his head in a silent "thanks".

I retrieved my jacket from one of the barstools and walked out of the bar. I stepped out into the cool night, my boots sounding too loud on the newly paved main street as I started the long trek home.

Don't be too hasty in your assumptions: I'm not a *nice* guy. I didn't care enough about the Swede or his problems to help him. I didn't even care about the damage we'd done to Frank's bar. The money I left the Swede was to buy me time to get out of the bar in one piece and I only left Frank some money so he would allow me into his fine establishment the next time I needed a drink.

That's it.

Besides, I hadn't set out to start a bar fight that night—few of the fights I had been in had been started intentionally, despite what might be heard on the gossip mill in town or held as general small-town popular opinion. Really, I simply tended to get caught up in events beyond my control—frequently. That evening's fight was merely the culmination of many factors that were seemingly "ganging up" on me that day. In fact, the whole year was rapidly heading downhill—I was only waiting to reach the bottom figuring that would come soon. After all, it couldn't get much worse.

The economy was bad and had taken another blow when England had declared war against Germany the year before. Men went off to fight for Britain, abandoning jobs and families to enlist. Government contracts had been cancelled and the railway was laying off men—men like me. It wasn't my fault I'd lost my job and no matter how much my father badgered me, I couldn't find another—there simply wasn't any work. So I was stuck helping my father on the farm. I needed the money I'd won just as much as the Swede did. I had no intention of staying on the farm any longer than I had to.

That particular day was the July First holiday. Planting was done and after spending many days in the field working alongside my father and brother, I felt I had earned some R and R. My father hadn't seen it that way. He said it was a day to celebrate with family—and my mother insisted I go to the church social with them.

So I went to the church picnic with my father, mother, and older brother. I knew my mother had ulterior motives for suggesting that particular outing: it was a perfect venue for scouting out eligible young women and doing a little match-making. Lately, she had been talking non-stop about my brother and I getting married. She said I, in particular, was in need of a good wife to settle me down.

Settling down was the last thing I needed to do—moving on was the first.

I played along for her sake—and for the food. The church ladies always served up their finest at those sort of things. The chicken soup they had for lunch was good, not to mention the pies. The pies were painstakingly deliberate in their quality—an all-out effort on the part of the ladies to distinguish themselves and draw the young men's attentions. There was a lot of talk about which young lady had made which pie...a LOT of talk about pies. An unnecessary amount of talk about pies.

Despite some of the men trying to coax me into joining the afternoon baseball game, I eschewed playing ball in favour of drinking a beer in the shade. I didn't mind playing ball—I had played before and I had a good swing and even better aim when I was pitching—but the beer was more enticing and, truly, I wasn't keen on being surveyed, appraised, and deliberated on by the ladies, young and old alike, as though I were some prize horse up for bidding.

I did stay for the supper following the game—cold fried chicken and biscuits went rather well with another beer. However, I had no interest in the dance that followed, during which all of the ladies would be doing their level best to draw the men into dancing and conversation. I sat on a bench along one side of the church hall as the music began, watching the couples pair up while I sat quietly, working out my best escape plan.

My brother dropped down beside me. "Aren't you going to ask anyone to dance?"

I scanned the room. One or two of the girls garnered a second look from me, and several more were looking back at me, but there was something so…suffocating about them. Not *them* exactly, but the *idea* of them that smacked of reliving the same life I had watched my parents live every day for my 20-odd years of life.

Since when had settling down ever made anyone happy?

"Nope," I replied, shaking my head, "that's not for me."

"Well, more for me then," my brother said with a grin and he launched himself off the bench and over to a dark-haired girl with a slight figure. Within thirty seconds he was dancing with the girl—an admittedly tolerable looking woman to be sure.

I got up off the bench, flipped my jacket over my shoulder, and left.

I had no particular intention of ending up in the local "watering hole" when I walked out of the church. I simply arrived there out of long habit and familiarity. The evening did not feel particularly portentous. Sometimes I wonder if I would have done things differently had I known that evening would set off a chain of events that would change my life. Would I have stayed to dance and found some nice girl with whom I could settle down? Would I have intervened in Will's conversations of the evening, fending off our doom?

Likely not.

"Well, hullo, Henry!" Frank called from behind the bar when he caught sight of me. "If it isn't my best customer. Surprised to see you in here on the holiday. What'll it be tonight?"

"Anything cheap and cold," I said as I went up to the bar. Frank poured me whatever he had on tap and slid a mug of the dark brew over to me. I tossed a coin onto the bar and it immediately disappeared into Frank's pocket.

I sat down on a bar stool and turned to watch the poker game presently in play at a nearby table. A giant of a man held sway there with three other men seated around the table, all of them with cards in hand. Given the Giant's heavy boots, unshaven face, and multiple layers of muscles, I had no choice but to assume he was a lumber man.

"Hah!" he yelled suddenly, slapping his cards down on the table for the others to see. A smile split his face open like a jack-o'-lantern. The others at the table jumped in their seats and cringed back from the wide swing of the Giant's arms as he raked the pot toward him, still grinning.

I studied the man as he shuffled the deck. He glanced up and saw me watching him. We regarded one another for a couple of seconds.

"I am Tove," he called over to me with a heavy Swedish accent. "What is your name?" he asked as he deftly dealt the cards to the others at the table.

"Henry," I replied, taking a sip of my beer. I wasn't entirely certain why I had answered him. Perhaps it was the way he announced himself: as though he were the only one in the room.

"You look strong. What is your work?" Tove asked.

"I used to work on the railway. Now I help on my father's farm."

"Ahhh—a settler's son!" Tove said, nodding as though this bit of information told him all he needed to know about me. The idea rankled me somehow. "I like settlers. I make much money from you."

"What work do you do?" I asked.

"I am cutting logs and taking them to the towns," he replied with another nod. "Business is good. Much money, *ja*. From people like your papa who need houses for their families."

"Hmmm…" was all I said.

"Henry," the Swede said with a grin, "come. Join the game. I could use more of your money!" He laughed a booming laugh.

That was all I needed to hear.

As with the entirety of the evening, I didn't have any particular intention of joining the card game, and yet, as it happened, I found myself being dealt in.

Much to my mother's chagrin, I was not new to cards and gambling—nor to drinking, for that matter. I had done all of those things often enough to do them well and all at the same time—I was a good multitasker. That night, however, I had a mission: recover the money the Swede had taken from my fellow settlers and put it back in the hands of hard-working farmers—farmers like me. It just seemed the right thing to do. Frank kept up a steady supply of beer and I went to work.

Gory details aside, I truly had not cheated the man—I hadn't needed to. The Swede was easy to "read". He pulled on his beard when he was uncertain, he grinned without control when he felt he had a winning hand, and he sighed when he picked up an unfavourable card. I knew exactly when to press my luck, bluff, or fold.

And yet, as easy as the Swede was to read, I never saw his fist coming from across the table....

The cool night air roused my stuporous brain as I stepped out of the bar, looked up at the stars, and took a breath of the bracing air to clear my head. It was a long walk home and the drinks I'd had over the course of the day were coming back to bite me, muffling my thoughts and making my head buzz. I pulled my jacket close against the chill in the air and started my lengthy trek home.

By the time I walked onto the farmyard, I was tired, cold, and may have been just a little unsteady on my feet. I found my bed in the dark, not wanting to light a lamp and risk waking my brother who was sleeping across the room. I dropped onto my bed without taking off my boots.

I was out as I fell.

June 15, 1913

June 15, 1913

John proposed to me today. It was the worst day of my life.

I shan't write about it. I do not need to describe it for memory's sake because I am certain I will never forget this torturous day.

My life is ruined!

Prodigious rot! The words of a young, incapable, and very weak-willed girl if ever there were any. I am embarrassed to read what I once was.

If I had known anything about the world and the path which I would have to take through it, I would never have had the audacity to write such self-involved melodrama. Nor, for that matter, would I have lent much credence to the perceived devastation of the day's happenings. While that episode did go on to chart a very determined and somewhat exacting course for me, it merited no such title and the events of that day would ultimately resolve into a mere vexing complication—a festering splinter that could not be retrieved.

No, I did not wish to marry John and yet, I had agreed to it, bowing to the will of both our fathers in exchange for a small bid to see what I was made of. It would prove to be their undoing.

John had stood before me, flanked by both of our fathers, and asked for my hand in marriage as had been planned some time prior. Words spoken in a tone of one selling an old mare and asking if the prospective purchaser wished to buy the horse or not? There was no talk of love nor was there a ring in the offering to symbolize it because love was not at the heart of the matter.

Practicality, not love, was the currency of the plan put forward by John's father and mine.

Our farm had seen a disastrous beginning. Papa had moved Mum and a then one-year-old daughter from England to Canada in pursuit of the government's advertised free land. Papa had been an excellent business man in England, dealing in farm equipment and felt he would surely be able to make a viable business out of a farm in a country where there was nothing but land to supply product without limit. Unfortunately, that was not the entirety of the farming business as my father soon discovered. He would never have "proved up" on his land in time to collect the title had it not been for the help of Abe, a very experienced farmer. My father simply didn't have the understanding, experience, or frankly the stamina to do the work required.

Abe, however, had all of those things in spades. He had brought his own wife and young son over from the Ukraine based on the same promise of free land. I was certain that, given his vast farming experience, Abe would surely have done well in establishing his own farm. Sadly, his wife had become ill shortly after their arrival in Canada. Abe could not possibly look after his sick wife and their small son while trying to clear enough field to prove up on a parcel of land. He had been forced, instead, to seek work as a farm hand and my father had eagerly hired him on. It was a most suitable arrangement at the time, with Abe helping Papa with the farm and Mum helping Abe's wife and looking after both the toddlers in the bargain. Abe's wife had later passed away, but by that time, Abe had become settled in his new life. His young son was just entering his teen years and Abe saw fit to have him join in the farm work to teach him the trade.

Things came to a boil, however, when I overheard Papa talking to Abe about the future of the farm and the security of Abe and John should something happen to Papa. After all, Abe had said, he had as much invested in the farm as my father did. That was when talk turned to a union between John and me and that was when I determined I would not become chattel to be auctioned off along with the farm. So I formed my own plan: I would become a Nurse with my own income and buy out John's part of the farm.

Making certain my father did not hear of it, I applied to and was accepted into the College of Nursing in the spring of 1913. I was very proud as the school had been established only recently and they were quite selective in their applicants. There was just one difficulty: I needed the signature of my father on the enrollment form—witnessed by the minister who had recommended me for the program. There was no way around it. I would have to ask Papa's permission to go to Nursing school.

There was, of course, the anticipated heated debate when I approached my father. I told him about my acceptance into the Nursing program one evening after supper as he sat behind the weighty wooden desk in his study, going over the accounting books.

"You *what*?!" Papa had sputtered. In the light of the oil lamp, he looked down at the enrollment form I had set before him. His dark eyes lifted to mine. He pinned me with a look that was not unlike the expression someone might wear if they were to catch a thief as he is carrying away all of one's prized possessions.

I winced and took a half-step back.

"I want to be a Nurse with my own money and a career," I put forward, my voice trembling slightly as I tried to reason with the unreasonable.

"Nursing?! Absolutely not! That is a business just shy of—of *acting*!" Papa barked, his face red. "My daughter will never fall into that—that…*'profession'*," Papa spat. "Besides, you are not cut out for the rigors of physical labour nor do you have the capacity to order about unruly patients."

"Nursing is not what it used to be," I objected, feeling the heat begin in my cheeks. "It is becoming a very acceptable profession with decent education and training. This program is in an actual hospital school with practice overseen in the attached hospital. You cannot support me forever and being able to earn my own way will keep me from being a burden on you."

"You would never be a burden on us—the farm title is in your name. Everything will go to you after I die."

"Everything except the half Abe wants set aside for John," I said in my best *I-know-what-you're-not-telling-me* tone. "I overheard you talking."

Papa's mouth pressed into a line and he let out a slow, loud breath like the steam of a train.

"You still don't need to worry about your security. Abe and I have negotiated what I feel to be a rather equitable arrangement for all concerned."

"And just what would that be?" I asked.

"You will marry John and secure your future. In exchange, John will own half the farm—something he deserves after all the years he and Abe have helped work the land. Everyone will get what they ought."

"Everyone but me!" I objected. "I don't want to marry John!"

"And why not? You will have no better offers. You've turned down practically every boy in town!" Papa said. I turned away briefly, recalling a particular afternoon when one of the boys had, within the time of our very first conversation, indicated he could certainly see himself marrying me. Ridiculous. How on earth would he know that after exactly eighty-seven minutes of fractured conversation on our front porch? I recalled that, in recounting the episode to Mum, I had voiced my opinion of the local boys quite strongly, calling them "hicks" or "low-brows" or something of that ilk.

"Please, Papa, not John. I can't extract more than monosyllabic words from him and he hardly ever goes to church! And surely you cannot approve of his frequenting the poolhall! I've seen him come home in the middle of the night drunk and barely able to walk! We've all seen him the next day—slow-witted and lazy, unable to move about let alone do a lick of actual work. Abe covers for him all the time, but I know perfectly well he gambles all of Abe's wages away! That's why they haven't gotten their own farm by now. All that and he's mean too!"

"Now what makes you say that?"

"I've seen him whip the horses and once he kicked one of the dogs. I wouldn't know what to do with myself if he came home in such a state and behaved like that in my house."

"Now Abbi," Papa said in a tone he used when he was working very hard to be patient with me and explain things in a way I might understand. "I know you're the anxious sort and not inclined to look at things rationally. Sharing the farm with Abe and John is the only fair and reasonable thing to do after all the years they've worked it with us. The only way to ensure your security here is for you to marry John and stay on the farm with him—and that is exactly what you will do." His tone lowered at the end and I felt a chill sweep over me.

"But, Papa, if I have my own income, perhaps I can buy out John's share of the farm. I can give the money directly to Abe or even purchase land and give it to them so John can't gamble it away. Although," I said, considering, "John could likely find a way to gamble off his father's farm given his penchant for hard living...Regardless, I wouldn't have to marry John."

Papa shook his head and cast me his patented *my-poor-misguided-daughter* look. "And who would help you run the farm?" Papa asked, setting his hands on his desk top, fingers laced. I hated that. It always signaled Papa was about to end the argument by giving me a pat on my head and sending me off to find mother and a cookie.

"I could run the farm myself," I had insisted, but the tremor in my voice betrayed my lack of confidence.

"You need a man to do the work of farming," Papa replied in an *I-know-you-know-this-as-well-as-I-do* tone.

I made a face and looked down. It wasn't true. I had not been idle in my years growing up on the farm. I had listened while I served the men coffee at the dinner table. I had watched and learned, gaining an understanding of the complexities that went into a good crop versus the mistakes that went into a bad crop. I could probably do tolerably well at managing a farm. What I couldn't do, however, was lift an eighty-pound bag of seed or toss about bales of hay…

"Look," Papa began in a *please-do-try-to-be-reasonable* tone. "You don't need to worry about John. John will settle down after he's married. A man changes when he has a wife and children and a farm of his own to run. You will see."

"You cannot promise me that."

"Perhaps not, but what I can promise you is that you will not be going into Nursing," Papa replied, pushing the enrollment form back across the desk toward me. He sat back in his great leather desk chair, laying his hands on the armrests and studied me. He never blinked.

Nor did I.

I looked at the paper on the desk but all I could see was John's lecherous grin when I had passed him in the yard that morning, his eyes roving up and down me. I thought he might at any moment lick his lips like a cat stalking a mouse. The image drove me to desperation. I felt the heat rise up into my chest and then into my face. Papa blanched and it inspired only just enough confidence in me to continue on. My insides trembling, I leaned on the desk with one hand and slid the paper back in front of my father with the other.

"And I can promise you," I began, forcing my voice louder as I went on, "that if you do not sign this, I will become a scullery maid or a nanny or, or, *anything* in order to support myself, move out on my own, and leave John with the entirety of the farm. I would rather do without it than marry John." It was a most audacious bluff and unlike anything I had ever done before. My knees were quivering like the string of a bow after the launch of the arrow. I couldn't breathe as I waited for Papa's response.

"Unacceptable," Papa blurted. "I won't have you throw away a farm I've worked so hard for! You wouldn't do that!"

I said nothing. I straightened, folding my arms, and locked icy glares with Papa. It took some doing to keep from squirming under his glare. He looked down at the paper in front of him then up at me, his expression changing as he thought. He looked at me as though he had just roped the calf he had been chasing down. An uncomfortable, rather prickly sensation chased around in my gut. I forced myself to stand still.

"I'll offer you another deal," my father said, his jaw set tight. "I do not believe you possess the fortitude or perseverance to withstand such labours. I will sign this enrollment form and you will go get this Nursing nonsense out of your head. I doubt you will last the first term. When you have failed—and fail you will—you will come back to marry John without so much as a question or complaint. By then, John will have grown up a little and settled down, you will have learned a valuable lesson regarding the limits of your abilities and where exactly it is that you belong—and everyone will be back here at the end of all things, nicely content and the farm in hand."

I considered the deal.

"The offer won't get any better from here," Papa said, his tone dropping.

"And what if I complete the course?"

"IF you manage to survive the training, you are free to proceed with your career until the age of twenty-one. At that time, you will return to the farm and marry John."

"And if I can earn enough money to buy out John's half of the farm before I turn twenty-one??"

"Well, that's something you can discuss with John, although I doubt he will take the offer—it's the farming income he wants. Besides, I think that scenario is highly unlikely. Do we have a bargain?"

"We do," I said with a sigh.

Papa cast me an apologetic frown. "You do see the sense to it, Abbi, don't you? If you marry John, you will have a good life on your own land—something I've worked so hard to give you. That must appeal to some part of you."

"I understand that is how it looks to you."

Papa signed the enrollment papers and I signed the agreement to marry John and share the farm with him on my return.

Yes, practicality dictated a union between John and me to guarantee my support and the continuation of the farm as a single entity. In return, I was allowed to go to Nursing school. Thus, John's marriage proposal was simply the first half of an agreement which would later be finalized. The second part of the agreement was outlined in a document stipulating that John would own half of the farm once the two of us were married. It was signed by all concerned parties, the drafting of a cage to which I was consigned.

I did not then fully comprehend John's thoughts on the matter. Indeed, we had barely exchanged a few sentences outside of talk about farm issues or polite talk following the church service on the rare occasions he attended. However, I would much later go on to learn John's view in a very clear and tangible way.

July 2, 1915

War Diary

Private Henry Ryzak

July 2, 1915

Volume 1

Diary Text: 8 Pages

[July 2, 1915]

I was jolted awake the next morning by a solid dousing of ice cold well-water. I sucked in a sharp breath as I shot to my feet. I swayed once then jerked myself upright. I instantly regretted the quick movement—my head felt as though it might explode. I ducked my head into my hands trying to hold it together and sank down onto my bed with a groan.

"Get up!" my father bellowed.

I dropped my hands and squinted up at him, peering through the stabbing pain behind my eyes. I got to my feet again, but a lot more slowly than before. My father stood before me, empty washbasin in one hand and his other hand on one hip. I looked down at the floor. I had been in that spot before and I knew what was coming.

"It is six a.m.," my father announced loudly, "and well past time for you to be doing something useful with your day. You may choose to stay out drinking all night, but that does not mean I must choose to let you off your responsibilities."

He waited, but I waited longer. I wouldn't give him the satisfaction of a stuttering answer—I was freezing from the dousing. Besides, what was I supposed to say to that? "You're right"? "I'm sorry"? I had no idea what he wanted from me. I just stood there, trying not to shiver. I clenched my teeth to keep them from rattling.

"As you seem to have nothing to say for yourself, you can get out to the yard and finish chopping that cord of wood."

"Yes, sir." I replied tightly, refusing to meet his gaze.

My father leaned in toward me. "Any more trouble from you today and you will learn the meaning of *hard labour*. Do I make myself clear?" my father asked in a low tone that sounded more like he was pronouncing someone dead.

"Yes, sir." I replied as evenly as I could. I still hadn't looked up at him.

My father turned and headed out of my room. "I want the wood done by noon," he called back.

I sighed and sat back down on the edge of my bed.

How was it that I could topple a man half again my size but I couldn't stand up to my father?

I changed into a dry shirt, mopped my face with the one I had taken off, and hung it on the headboard to dry. I flipped the quilt over the footboard and hoped my bed would dry by evening.

I headed down the stairs and into the kitchen, not bothering to stop in the washroom to wash up for the day—that had been done for me—and the washbasin was apparently empty.

My mother stood by the kitchen sink, pumping water over a stack of dishes and into the steaming water in which they soaked. I went over and scooped several handfuls of water into my mouth from the pump spout. I splashed some hot water from the sink on my face for good measure.

My mother stood aside and waited for me to be done. When I straightened, she studied me for a moment then touched her fingers to my cheek.

"What happened?" she asked, frowning.

"Nothing, Mother," I said, taking her hand from my face. "Here," I said, smiling as I pulled a handful of bills from my pocket. I held them out to her.

She looked down at the bunched up money then back up at me, her eyes narrowing. "Where did you get that?"

"It'll help pay off the loan father had to take out for the plow."

"It would, yes, but you didn't answer my question. Henry, you know I won't take gambling money." She pushed the bills back at me.

"I won it fair and square. It's yours now." I shoved the money toward her again. When she didn't take it, I took her hand and dropped the money into it, closing her fist around the bills.

She walked over to the table and slapped the money down hard, pulling her hand away as if it burned her. "No, I don't want anything to do with gambling. The money doesn't belong to you—you didn't earn it. I won't take it."

I sighed. "Mother, please, I'm only trying to help," I objected. "It's all I can do now with the railway shut down."

My mother's face softened and she sighed. "Henry, go chop the wood like your father asked."

I shook my head and started for the door.

"Wait," my mother called. I turned to see what she wanted. "You'll need breakfast."

She moved to the counter where she took out a loaf of bread from the breadbox. She cut a thick slice and spread bacon drippings on it. She pulled a plate of ham from the wooden icebox and laid a slice on the bread. She folded the whole lot up and handed it to me.

"Thanks," I said with a grin.

She rolled her eyes and shook her head. "Off with you now before your father comes to see why you're not at your chores." I took a large bite of the sandwich and headed out the back door.

The sun was high overhead and the chill had already left the early morning air. It would be a long, hot day.

I retrieved the axe from the barn and went to work on the wood pile. Of course, bending over to chop the wood served only to increase the pressure in my head. Every time my axe connected with a log, a rather painful jolt shot from the front of my head straight through to the back of it. Within thirty minutes I was sick to my stomach with a pounding headache—just as my father had intended. Every time I had a hangover he set me to a chore that would best ensure I felt the full brunt of my poor choices.

I felt it to be sure, but I still chopped the wood.

I wasn't stupid. I aimed properly and swung hard. The fewer times I laid my axe to the wood, the fewer times my head would take the jarring of it. It helped, but I still felt it enough times to make my father's punishment hit home—

likely not enough to "teach me a lesson" or to keep me from drinking in the future, but still, I got his message loud and clear.

I was just starting on the last three logs when I saw Will walking across the yard from where he had been working on the tractor with father and heading my way.

"Here," he said, handing me a jug of water, "You look like you need this."

"Thanks."

I took the water gratefully, trading him for my axe. He turned to the logs and set in to chopping the rest of the wood while I downed the cool water. I sat on the woodpile and let the throbbing in my head ease.

"Another late night, huh?" Will asked between swings of the axe.

"Yeah," I said. "And another good night at the tables. I won some cash for the tractor."

"Why do you keep doing that? You know they'll never take the money." Will swung the axe again, splitting another log cleanly.

"I left it with Mother—she can do with it as she pleases, but as far as I'm concerned, I contributed. I did my part."

"You know, Father wouldn't give you so much grief all the time if you just put all that effort into helping with the farm instead of carousing." Will cast me a pointed glance as he retrieved another log.

"I don't have a problem with doing work around here since I've been laid off, but we all know I don't belong here. It's obvious Father prefers working with you and doesn't want me in the way. He's training you to take over this place, not me."

"We could work it together," Will said. "There's enough land and I'm happy to share it."

"I don't think Father sees it that way," I said, letting a meaningful tone steep my words. "I'm just the useless younger brother."

"Wouldn't be his decision once I have the farm," Will said.

I shook my head. "I'm pretty sure he'd find a way to disrupt that plan. Besides, I wouldn't put you in that situation. I'll find a job somewhere else just as soon as things pick up. Then I'll get out of everyone's way."

"Where will you find work?"

"Haven't you heard? 'War is good for the economy' the papers are saying. Things will shake up soon with the war started."

Will threw the last piece of wood on the pile then stood, frowning at me.

"So…" I said, letting my words take on a teasing tone, "how was the *dance*?" I raised one eyebrow at him.

Will blushed. He actually blushed! He smiled then and looked away.

"That good, huh?" I asked. "What's her name?"

"Alice," Will said and just saying the name made his smile widen. "They just moved here from Ontario. She's amazing."

"Well," I chuckled, "at least mother's efforts were not entirely wasted."

We laughed then Will turned serious.

"Henry?"

"Yes?"

"Have you thought about enlisting?"

I scoffed in reply. "No. Bad odds. That's a wager even *I* wouldn't place. Why would anyone want to do such a stupid thing as purposefully going to get himself killed?"

"Do you think it's that bad?" Will asked.

"I think it's worse."

"But the papers say it's going alright and will be over soon."

"I'm pretty sure we only know the half of it. I've heard there are sensors going through all the mail that comes home and taking out what they don't want the soldiers telling people."

"They just take out the information about the battles though, right? You know, so the enemy doesn't get wind of things—don't they?"

I shrugged. "That's not what I heard…"

Will drew in a deep breath and one side of his mouth turned down.

"You're not thinking about enlisting are you?" I asked.

"I don't know—maybe. There was a lot of talk at the dance. The army was turning men away before but now they're starting to recruit again in Winnipeg. I'm thinking this might be my last chance to enlist before the whole thing's over."

"Doesn't it seem at all suspicious to you that they are recruiting again after Ypres didn't turn out so well? I heard a lot of men died in that battle. Naturally, they'll be needing more men to fill the ranks now. I'm not convinced the war will be over as quickly as people say."

"Maybe not, but folks at the dance were talking. Kinda had me feeling like a coward if I don't enlist—like I'm not supporting our country. And what about the men who already died? We can't let them die for nothing. Least, that's what most of the older men were saying last night."

"Let them say what they want—at least you're not dead in some field overseas."

"Yeah, I guess."

"Look, no slight to you, but you wouldn't last a minute on a battle field. You've never even taken a punch let alone landed one on someone else." He cast me a look that verified my assumption "Right," I continued, "and the only gun you've picked up was the BB gun we used to kill gophers—you don't even like using Father's rifle on them." It was true and something that rankled me—I'd had to rid the fields of the vermin by myself. A BB gun didn't kill the things.

"They train you before they ship you over," Will objected.

"Not that much, they don't. Do you really think you can learn everything you need to know to stay alive in a war with only a few months of training? Hardly!"

"I know, but Henry, maybe it's the right thing to do."

"Well here's another 'right thing to do' for you to consider: aside from likely getting yourself killed, this goes badly for *me* if you enlist. Father would be angry if you left—especially now, just before seeding—and guess who would have to deal with that? Me. I'd receive the full brunt of his fury. Every day that you were gone, he'd resent me more."

"You don't think he'd get to know you a bit better? Maybe work things out better between the two of you? Maybe even cut you in on the farm?"

I laughed. "I would lay down good money that he would hate me more every day you were gone—just because I'm not you. And heaven only knows what he'd think of me if you got yourself killed over there and I was still here. Besides, what do you think your leaving would do to Mother?"

Will looked squarely at me then. "Right," he said. Then: "Forget it. Let's go in, it's probably lunch time."

"Will," I cautioned, "please don't do anything stupid."

Will only looked at me, saying nothing, then turned and walked toward the house. I followed in his wake as we entered the house: Will acting as my own living shield.

September 6, 1913

September 6, 1913

At last I am here! I have arrived at Nursing school. It is quite the tumult in the students' dormitory these initial days. Everyone is bustling about, trying to find their rooms, bring in their things, introduce themselves, and generally get the 'lay of the land'. I have never before been in the company of so many girls of my age. It is very exciting—in a rather terrifying sort of way. The head Matron is overseeing the influx of students. She is a most stern looking creature and walks about with a frown permanently fixed on her face. She has not yelled, but has set one or two students to rights straight away with a firm command. One girl was complaining she was feeling faint and her heart was all aflutter due to the constant buzzing about her. The other was crying because she had forgotten her nightgown at home. It seems, however, neither panic nor poor organization will be tolerated as the Matron sternly set aside such minor complaints with orders for the girls to control themselves or consider returning home immediately. I think I should faint dead away if ever Matron barked at me that way. We will see how things work out...

December 22, 1913

We are getting into the thick of things now. First term classes are done and exams will be written tomorrow. We are on the wards until exams then have four days off over Christmas. Esther has been given permission for an extra half-day on either side to travel home for the break. Ward routine has become, well, routine in some ways. At least we are learning the schedule of the day: get patients up, give them their medications, help them wash and dress as they are able. Then it is time for dressing changes and cuppings and other procedures or exercises to be done. Lunch arrives to break up the day and is followed by a rest in the afternoon. That gives staff a chance to wash laundry, stock supplies, make up bandages, clean and disinfect equipment, etc. Then supper arrives and all the patients are helped to eat and given medications again. Evenings are spent preparing patients for bed and settling them in for the night with warm milk and massages. I'm ever so grateful we aren't assigned to night shifts. I expect there wouldn't be much by way of learning during that time what with everyone sleeping. Am so very much looking forward to some time at home.

I did go home that Christmas but it was not as much of a break as I would have liked. We had John and his father to Christmas dinner as we had done every year since I could remember.

Sadly, my time at home was ruined by John's vulgarity. I had gone out for a walk the day before I was to return to classes, feeling rather ill over the thought of having to leave my family once again. I was simply wandering about the farmyard, trying to screw up my courage for the return trip, and decided to warm myself in the barn for a spell.

I found one of the horses in a stall and went to give her some oats. As I was petting the horse, John came in carrying an empty bucket (heaven forbid he should carry anything with more weight to it). He looked at me and grinned, watching me like a common thief watching a lady's handbag. I nodded to him, gathered up my skirts, and started out of the barn. As I passed him, John dropped the bucket and stepped in front of me. He moved in very close and I backed up a step or two. John kept walking and I found myself caught between John and one of the stalls.

"So you're back?" John asked, his mouth twisted into a corruption of a smile. "You quit school then?"

"I'm only back for a few days over the holiday," I replied with a shake of my head. "I'll be returning tomorrow."

"Too bad," John replied thickly, fingering a strand of my hair. "I'm lookin' forward to getting better 'quainted now that we're engaged…" He put his hands on either side of me, leaning against the stable door.

John's fetid breath fell heavily across my face, burdened with alcohol and cigarette smoke and suffocating me like a wet blanket. I turned my head to the side so I could take a breath.

"You've been drinking," I said pushing futilely against his chest. He didn't budge.

John reached up to stroke my cheek with a rough finger. "Just a little," he said, his crooked and yellowed teeth sneaking out from between stretched lips.

My heart was beating at a hummingbird pace, with John about to pounce. I was having difficulty pulling in a full breath when we heard footfalls outside the barn. John very slowly straightened and took a step back.

"We can finish our *talk* later," he said. His face settled into an unreadable expression. He turned a walked away casting me one backward glance. I took a breath then, listening to the echo of John's chuckle as he left the barn.

At least one thing came of the episode: it made my return to school the next day ever so much easier. In fact, so anxious was I about leaving again, my encounter with John might have been the only thing that could have sent me back.

July 28, 1914

I haven't much time to write. Matron is keeping us simply buzzing today with patients just out of the theatre. So many dressings to change and repositioning of heavy patients! In addition to their many needs for care it would seem each one of them is intent on drinking the river dry with their constant requests for water every time we pass them! But enough of the daily chaff. I need to put in that England has declared war against those German bullies! England is bent on putting them in their place which means us colonials will be asked to step up alongside our Monarch. Everyone went out to the streets and cheered and waved flags when the announcement came down.

I did not cheer. I was breathless with astonishment. To think such a thing is truly happening and then to watch as people rejoice in its occurrence. Absurd! I do not think war is something to be cheered. The masses rave only because they are certain we will win. But I have to wonder at what cost? It is rather frightening not knowing what is in store for our country or our men. What will the ransom of freedom cost us?

In July of 1914, Germany invaded Belgium, intent on reaching the borders of France. The small and underpowered country of Belgium quickly invoked the Treaty of London, an agreement with Britain signed in 1839, and called upon Britain to defend them from the Germans.

Britain was intent on keeping its promise and immediately stepped up to help the underdog in the battle. A great deal of ink was spilled in the next weeks and months rationalizing why we must go to war, but I felt the answer was ever so much simpler than all the politicians had said about it. It boiled down to standing up to a bully when one sees him trouncing a smaller child on the playground and that, it would seem, was exactly what England meant to do. Really, how could one argue the point?

I thought about that: having someone step in to face the bully when one cannot possibly defeat him on one's own. What must that feel like to have someone swoop in and come to one's rescue? Certainly, it would be thrilling to see such a hero in action and turn from victim to victor in a single moment. I recalled the scene with John in the barn and thought I very much would have liked someone to rescue me in that way and even more, would have been quite pleased to have had John set straight.

Happily, the war was somewhat slow to reach our part of the country, landlocked as we were in the middle of the Canadian prairies—a thing for which I was grateful no matter how necessary the job was to take on. It took some time to put together the process of recruiting men, to say nothing of building the training camps for the soldiers. Then there was the question of just how to get the soldiers over to England. As a result, my classes went on as usual. Our days were far too full of nursing duties and studies to be much involved with a war in the offing far across the ocean.

October 21, 1914

I am beginning to feel the drudgery of my fourth term at school. The studying is endless and it seems I will never learn all I need know. Fortunately, my grades have been spared my ignorance as I seem to be able to sit an exam well. However, grades do not much help on the ward. There is the daily toil on the units with scarce time to think! One simply drops into bed at the end of the day, wanting nothing save a few moments to breathe. I have had the occasional thought that perhaps I might have made a mistake in taking on these studies, but then I recall John and his proposal and am glad to be here.

For as much as I used to balk at the idea, I am also very grateful at this point that Papa runs a farm. They are saying farmers will not be allowed to enlist because they are needed to keep up the food supply for the country but mostly for the soldiers. Yes, I am very thankful Papa will be staying at home and not entering such a nasty business. I do wonder if we nurses shall be called upon to help. I have not yet made up my mind whether I hope we are or whether I hope very much we are not.

February 24, 1915

We are so very close to being done! The Matron is more severe with us than ever. I secretly wonder if she is worried that, upon our graduation, we will be turned out on unsuspecting patients without knowing all we ought to know and that our sorry performance will reflect badly on her. She has been so rigorous in our training, however, I can hardly imagine that happening.

We were given a rare half-day the other day. I went to the shops for a time and simply looked at all the lovely things I might afford once I have my own money. Some of the other girls have mentioned that the army is providing good pay if one is able to be approved for enlisting. It seems there are a great many Sisters volunteering to go over. I am *wondering if it might be a good place to begin, having guaranteed work if one enlists. Certainly one would gain most valuable skills in the war! And if there were steady income—well what on earth would be wrong with that? Further, I would be far removed from John... Well, I will think about enlisting when I am done school.*

I did consider my options while in the final months of my training. There were some jobs to be had in the local hospitals and perhaps a physician might take on a nurse to assist him, but nothing compared to the guaranteed work and income of the war. Nor were any jobs able to provide the training and building of skills as one could obtain in the war. There was one other reason I was considering enlisting: it seemed the right thing to do. There was a job to be done and I felt strongly someone—myself if necessary—had best get on and do it. Also, I did feel it may be my personal responsibility to enlist for I had one thing many of the other nurses did not: British citizenship. The army, having thousands more applicants than were needed, had set exacting standards for their recruits. The nurse was expected to be physically fit, of high moral character, and was required to be a British citizen—which I was, having been born in England just before my father brought us over to Canada. Not every nurse could lay claim to that and so, not many could actually apply to enlist. I wondered if it didn't fall to me then to step up to represent the country in which I had been raised by helping the country which in which I had been born.

June 1, 1915

I have returned home complete with my Nursing diploma! We had a lovely ceremony for our graduation. Mum and Papa came up to watch me walk across the stage and collect my parchment. We were each presented with a small, white bible specially made for Nurses. (I have tucked mine up very carefully and put it amongst my uniforms where it will not be disturbed.) Papa was cautious with his congratulations. From the look on his face I expect he is greatly disappointed I did not fail and come running home with my tail between my legs. I am very pleased to have disappointed him!

It was most difficult saying goodbye to Esther, however, but we have promised faithfully to write to one another no less than once each month. I shall do my best to keep to that arrangement.

June 10, 1915

Not two weeks home and I have decided most definitively to enlist! I pressed Mum to write to Uncle Jasper in Halifax and make the necessary connections for me. As the pastor in one of the churches there, Uncle Jasper knows the ins and outs of things and can connect anyone to anything. He knew precisely of whom to inquire about recruitment. He said in his last letter that had spoken to a person of some rank in the military and had been directed to the person recruiting medical staff. He wrote that he had given such a report of me as to make me blush. That, along with the letter of recommendation from Matron at the school and a list of my final grades which I had forwarded, convinced the recruiter to assure me a placement with the No. 7 Stationary Hospital upon my arrival. Training begins in October so I will have just enough time to help get in the garden before I go.

It is daunting to be certain, going off to war, but I cannot bear to remain here with John. I must be away from him and will not return until I am able to purchase my land back from him. Anything is better than remaining here and succumbing to my pre-determined fate without a fight! I shall go off to fight my own personal war while supporting our country in the larger one.

Aside from all of this, there are very few nursing jobs nearby—I've asked at all the hospitals. It seems it is enlist or get married...

It was true: I intended to put up the fiercest resistance possible to the scheme concocted by my father and nothing—not war itself—would deter me. In fact, I felt the war rather paralleled my personal state of affairs: instead of the Kaiser, I faced John and where the Kaiser would take over entire countries, destroying them in his wake, John would take over my farm and destroy my life.

News reports from England expounded the virtues of the war saying it would "do everyone good" and "brace everyone up" like a good stint of hard labour. Perhaps it was naivety to sell a war as tonic for the fatigued and bored. I rather thought then, as I do now, that while there was certainly overdone optimism about the war and its impact on countries and people, the messages were likely a very well-played sales pitch. Like shop keepers, the papers pulled out a good lot of "stick up for the little guy" spirit and put it on display, surprising their customers who had no idea such an item was present and thought surely they must have some if it was so rare. The fact that its romantic ideas were well past date of expiration in a war growing increasingly fierce did not enter into their well-intentioned thoughts in the least, leaving the patron quite undisturbed and savouring this most diverting pep up. [29]

It concerned me not one wit. I would go no matter the promises nor the risks; no matter the profits nor the losses of investing in such notions. I had little concern for the war, I had only concern for my own battle that raged.

It was John's own doing that had made up my mind.

Upon the moment I resumed my chores around the farm, John haunted my every step. He had once pulled me behind the barn, burning my wrist with his tight grip. He had laughed a hyena laugh when I had struggled to get away and had pressed me against the barn. I pushed at him but he only pinned my wrists to the barn and leaned full against me and slobbered on my neck. I felt the bars of my cage close in against me. I was about to call out when the bark of the dog heralded the coming of a wagon out front and John straightened away from me. He gripped my chin roughly and leaned his face down to mine.

John shook his head. "Not yet. Soon though, I think," he bit out roughly. He grinned like a mobster grabbing cash from a bank teller and walked away.

From that time on, I was careful to stay within sight of Papa when I was out in the yard. My departure to the war—regardless of the enemy awaiting me there—could not come soon enough.

War Diary

Private Henry Ryzak

July 12, 1915

Volume 1

Diary Text: 13 Pages

[July 12, 1915]

I was working in the yard, using a pricking iron to make stitching holes in the leather strap of a harness when I heard my mother's sharp gasp issue from the house, followed by her horrified "NO!".

I dropped the hammer and iron onto my workbench and ran for the house. I rushed through the porch and found my mother standing in the kitchen, sobbing into her hands.

"Mother! What is it? What's happened?"

She looked up at me with tears running down her cheeks and pointed an accusatory finger at a note that lay on the kitchen table. The note glared up at me and, for some reason, I hesitated before picking it up. I forced my hand to the task and read the following:

Dear Mother and Father,

*I am going by boat to Winnipeg to enlist.
I hear they are forming a battalion there.
I know this will be difficult for you and
I'm sorry for that, but this is something I
feel I have to do. You can count on
Henry's help while I'm gone.*

Will

I closed my eyes and felt something squeeze in my chest—a great fist holding my heart fast. *The idiot!* He wouldn't last three minutes on a battlefield—all he knew was farming! He couldn't fight and he couldn't hold a gun— or even a knife! He'd be dead within a week—and my mother likely knew all of that.

My father stepped through the back door just then. "What's going on?" he barked. "And why aren't *you* getting that harness fixed?" he asked, levelling a glare at me.

I handed him the note then stepped back a couple of steps. My father had a long reach when he was angry. I watched him carefully as he read Will's note.

My father's face paled visibly, turning his dark tan a sickly grey colour. He looked up at my mother and they only stared at one another for several seconds.

Then he rounded on me.

"This is all your doing, isn't it?!" my father roared.

It took me a couple of seconds to process his words.

"Of course not! I told him *not* to do it!" I said. "I told him it was a bad idea!"

"Perhaps that's what you said, but you knew about this and didn't do a single thing to stop him! He probably thinks he's going to be a tough guy like you—probably thinks that going off to war will make him a man!"

"Well, maybe it will," I replied hotly.

My father took a step closer to me and leaned in. I was very grateful, as I had been on many previous occasions in my life, that I was taller than my father—even if it didn't feel like it at that moment. I forced myself to stand my ground.

"Only if he doesn't get himself killed!" My father's words had that quiet tone he sometimes used, making me more afraid of him than if he had bellowed.

My mother burst out into a fresh wave of sobs. My father turned and pulled her to him. Unfortunately, his anger didn't dissipate as I thought it would, holding my mother's shaking body. He wasn't done yet. He studied me with a baleful expression, looking over my mother's head.

"You're thinking that it should have been me," I said for him, just to have the satisfaction of saying it first. "You think I should have been the one to enlist."

"At least you would have done something useful with your life instead of drinking and gambling your time away. Maybe if you had enlisted, your brother wouldn't have felt he had to."

And there it was. One firm pull of the lever and the floor of the gallows fell out from under me—a quick drop to suffocating pain.

I drew in several steadying breaths as my father and I simply regarded one another. I nodded in understanding. He looked away then, holding my mother tightly, her face buried in his shoulder.

I turned and headed up the stairs for my room.

I grabbed my satchel and stuffed a few items of clothing into it along with my watch, a comb, my razor, and a few handkerchiefs. I stopped briefly to grab a bar of soap and a cake of shaving soap from the washroom and dropped those into my bag too. Then I went back downstairs.

I walked into the kitchen where my mother and father were still talking in muted tones, my father trying to stem my mother's flow of tears with empty reassurances. I ignored them and went to the cupboard behind the table. I pulled out the brown ceramic sugar jar where mother hid the gambling proceeds I gave her and took it out—all of it— every last cent I'd given her since I had returned home. I bunched the bills into a wad and jammed it into my pocket.

"Just what are you doing?" demanded my father.

I glanced at him but said nothing. I went through the kitchen to the porch and pulled my coat from its hook.

Then I turned to my father.

"I'm going to find your son and send him back to you."

"No, Henry!" my mother cried. "You can't go too!"

"*Someone* has to go after Will and keep him out of trouble," I said to her. I turned to my father, "and since I'm the one who apparently ought to have gone in the first place, I'm perfect for the job."

"No! Please, Henry, don't go," my mother begged. "Your father doesn't mean it!"

"Let him go," my father said quietly. "If he can send Will home alive at least he will have done us some service."

I felt the jerk of the noose again and pulled in several difficult breaths, staring at my father. He raised his chin in challenge. It was tempting, but I didn't hit him.

I turned and walked out of the house, out of the yard, and out of my life.

. . .

I started down the road into town, my satchel feeling heavy across my shoulders. I had no particular goal—nowhere to head *to*, just a vague cloud of anger and resentment driving me *away* from the farm. I heard the sound of horse hooves clopping along the dirt road and turned to see one of the neighboring farmers driving toward me in his wagon. He pulled to a stop when he reached me.

"G'day, neighbor," the man announced cheerily.

I knew him, of course: Joah MacCleod. He lived a couple of homesteads over along with his wife and two children.

"Hello!" I said. "You wouldn't happen to be heading into town, would you?" I asked.

"I am indeed. Hop in."

I climbed into the seat beside Joah and made small talk with the man on our way into town, dodging questions about what my business there might be.

We arrived in town a short time later and I stepped off the wagon, thanking Joah for the ride.

I walked up Railroad Street, heading straight to the CPR station. I counted my bills along the way, wondering if I had enough money for a ticket to Winnipeg. It would be cheaper to get there by the riverboat that brought people and goods up river from Selkirk, but the train would be faster. I intended to beat my brother to the recruitment office and send him home before it was too late.

It turned out I had a lot more money than I thought—I let out a low laugh when I realized just how much—the tally recently increased significantly by the large Swede at the bar. It seemed Mother had done the right thing with all the money I'd given her after all.

I laid a few bills down at the ticket booth and purchased a one-way ticket to Winnipeg.

. . .

The train ground to a halt at the Winnipeg station with great gusts of billowing, sooty steam and the screeching of metal on metal. Clouds of dust bloomed up from under the train, blocking out the windows. We stopped with a lurch that either set people back in their seats or propelled them forward, depending on which direction they were facing.

I stood the moment the pitching of the train stopped, grabbed my bag from the overhead compartment, and exited the train. I stepped out onto the wooden platform that ran the length of the station and went directly into the ticket office, my boots clunking out a determined rhythm. Once inside the relative cool of the building, I glanced around, in need of information. I didn't have to look far.

A large poster hung on the wall just inside the station:

Fall in Grenadiers

Our 78th Battalion now holding the line in France Needs Reinforcements.

Early departure for training in England.

Apply at Grenadier Headquarters: Cor. Of Main and York

I stopped briefly at the ticket booth to ask for directions to Main and York, then hurried out the door.

I found the headquarters without much difficulty—it wasn't far from the station. I was hurrying down the wooden sidewalk when the door of the headquarters building opened right in front of me, forcing me to a quick halt.

Will stepped out onto the sidewalk, intent on several papers he held in his hand.

I felt a rock drop into the pit of my stomach.

I'm too late.

Will looked up just then and paused. He took a step back when he saw me and straightened. He winced then.

"I've already signed up," he said cautiously, uncertainty painting his features.

I sighed heavily and lowered my head, running my hand through my hair. I nodded then and looked up at him. There was only one thing I could do.

"Wait here. Do not move until I get back," I said sternly, jabbing my finger sharply into his chest.

"What are you going to do?" he asked warily. "Henry, they won't let me back out now—" he warned, but stopped when he saw the look I cast him.

I jerked the door of the recruiting station open, hesitating only long enough to draw in a breath before I forced my feet forward.

The man behind the desk looked up at me as I entered.

"Here to sign up?" he asked. His tone was stern but underneath there was an eagerness that made me uneasy.

"Yes," I replied, "but only if I'm in the same unit as my brother." I jerked my chin in the direction of the door as though that would tell the man who my brother was.

The man glanced at the door then looked me up and down. He raised his chin and narrowed his eyes as he considered a moment.

"Can't make any guarantees, but we'll do the best we can."

"And what exactly does that mean?" I asked.

"You can likely stay together until you get to England. After that, you might have to do some *negotiating* if you're wanting to stay in the same unit."

There was nothing for it: I could do my best to fulfill my promise to my parents or I could give up now, having barely tried. Besides, what were negotiations if not a round at the card table?

"Well," I said with a firm nod, "I'm good at *negotiating*."

"Very good. Let us begin."

The man gestured to the chair in front of his desk and I sat, setting my bag on the floor. He asked a goodly number of questions as he scribbled the answers on the form in front of him: Name? Address? Birthday? Next of kin? Occupation? Religion? Are you willing to be vaccinated? Any military training? Are you wanting to be part of the Canadian Overseas Expeditionary Force? Sign here please.

"Go into the next room and strip down to your drawers. The doctor will examine you."

The examination was perfunctory at best, shoddy at worst: weight measured, lungs checked for less time than it took to draw a full breath in and out, heart listened to only long enough to ensure it was beating, teeth inspected. A few demonstrations of physical movements, papers shoved into my hand, and I was dressed and out the door. The papers felt heavy in my hand and I stared down at them curiously as I exited the building.

I stepped out onto the sidewalk, my entire life changed within minutes.

Will stood, before me. He glanced down at my papers and then up at me.

"Why'd you do that?" he asked.

"It's a rather long story," I replied.

Will drew a deep breath.

"The man said to wait at the station for the next train to camp. We'd best get going," I said, moving past Will and down the sidewalk. Will fell in beside me.

We arrived back at the station and checked in with the ticket master. He informed us the train to Sewell camp—or Camp Hughes as it was recently renamed—would be arriving in another hour. Will and I went out and took a seat on the bench in front of the building, grateful for the shade in which it sat.

Will leaned forward, elbows on knees and turned to look at me.

"Henry, why'd you sign up?" Will asked, this time as if daring me to answer the question.

I looked away down the rail line, wishing the train would pull up and spare me from answering, but luck was not with me that day—it had, in some capricious turn of spite, chosen that particular day to desert me. I decided it was true: luck was fickle. I wondered if she would be back any time soon.

"Mother was upset, Father was angry, I promised I'd send you home safe."

Will was silent for a time.

"I'm pretty sure that's not the whole story," he replied. "Father blamed you, didn't he? Did he make you do this?"

"No. I simply made my choice before things got too ugly," was all I said.

Will nodded and heaved a sigh. He studied the wooden planks of the porch for a time.

"I'm sorry, Henry. I never meant for you to enlist too."

"It doesn't matter," I replied with more assertion than I felt, "I have nowhere else to be."

"Don't say that," Will said, his face carved with a frown. "There's always a place for you at home."

"Is there?" I asked, casting Will a sharp look. I turned away again, releasing him from my misplaced anger. I shook my head. "Like I said: I don't belong there."

"Well, you will when it's mine!"

I turned to look at him then. It was the strongest conviction Will had ever demonstrated.

"Thanks, brother," I said, nodding. Will nodded in agreement: a pact between brothers. Maybe having that was better than having luck.

. . .

Will and I waited for the train that would take us to the training camp. Over the hour that it took for the train to arrive, several more men showed up, all carrying enlistment papers.

The first to arrive was a smaller man with thin dark hair slicked to one side, the part so severe it looked as though it had been carved with a knife. He carried a satchel that weighed heavily on his shoulder and had a square look to it as though it was filled with books rather than personal items. He scuttled across the walkway in crab-like steps, dragged down by the satchel and making his was toward the bench on which Will and I sat. His eyes darted up and down the train track a couple of times before lighting on me.

He glanced at Will, then at me, ducking his head in a perfunctory greeting.

"Hello?" He said as though it were a question. "Are you awaiting transport to Camp Hughes?" he asked with a hint of English accent.

"Yup," Will answered. "We just enlisted."

"Excellent! I'm in the right place. I have just enlisted as well," the man said. He extended his hand first to Will, then to me. "Allow me to introduce myself. My name is Richard Ransley—Dick to those who know me."

"I'm Will and this is my brother Henry," Will said with a jerk of his thumb in my direction.

"Pleased to meet you."

Will slid closer to me on the bench, making room for Ransley.

"Have a seat," Will said. "Train should be here soon."

Ransley sat on the far side of Will and glanced up and down the rail line again. He let his bag drop to the platform where it landed with a heavy thud.

Definitely books.

Ransley's gaze darted around the station and down the tracks again before he turned back to Will.

"I understand we are to complete our training at the camp near Carberry," Ransley said in a tone that suggested he might be offering us a piece of pie rather than a scrap of used information.

"That's what they told us," Will replied politely.

"I hear there has been quite a bit of development at that particular camp in anticipation of training and mobilizing more men."

"Yup," Will replied. "Guess Ypres didn't go so well. Seems like we'll have more of a fight than we thought."

"Appropriate deduction," Ransley said.

"If you don't mind me asking," Will began, "where are you from? Sounds like you're not from around here."

"I live with my parents on their homestead near Selkirk. I came over with them from England a number of years ago to help them settle their land. And yourselves?"

"Our parents came over from Sheffield just after I was born," Will replied. "They got their settlement near Selkirk and proved up a while ago. We're helping them to run the farm."

Ransley nodded in understanding.

The conversation was interrupted by the approach of lazy footsteps pounding along the wooden platform. The three of us turned to watch as a lanky youth ambled toward us. He was dressed in simple pants and shirt, each of which might have had their own colour at one time, but neither now gave any hint as to what those colours might have been. The lad wore a jacket that was too large for his coatrack frame, his suspenders peeked out from under the jacket, highlighting the fact that the pants hung loose about his waist. He carried nothing with him save the obligatory papers.

The youth stopped in front of us, looking down the line for a moment before turning to us. He scanned each of our faces then directed his question to me.

"This where I catch the train to army camp?" He flashed his papers at me.

"Yes," I replied. "It should be here shortly."

The youth ducked his head once in my direction as he stuffed his papers into his jacket pocket then moved to the far end of the platform. He sat down on the wooden planks, his back to us and his feet hanging over the end of the porch.

The train arrived a short time later, carrying with it a cloud of dust, and adding to the already cloying heat of the afternoon. The conductor stepped off the train, emerging from a burst of steam as though the man had spewed forth from the train along with the cloud that wafted down the platform along with him.

"This way, boys," he called and stood aside as he gestured to the door of the train. "Let me see your papers."

I stood and led Will over to the man, handing him our forms. Ransley appeared to have a bit of a dispute with his bag which insisted on remaining where it sat. He won the skirmish but not without some difficulty, and fell in behind us. The youth at the end of the platform stood and watched as the conductor checked our enlistment records. The boy pulled his papers out and looked down at them, his brow creased. He glanced between the conductor and his documents several times before taking a few slow steps forward. He grasped the pages in a white-knuckled grip.

I boarded the train and slung my bag up onto the baggage shelf then dropped into a seat next to the window. Will took a seat beside me even though the entire passenger car was empty. Ransley chose a seat opposite ours.

I watched out the window as the boy walked up to the conductor and hesitated, staring at the man for several seconds before handing him the fistful of scrunched credentials. The lad stood motionless and bit his lip as the conductor looked over the forms.

"You boarding for training camp?" the conductor asked, his voice only just rising above the hiss of the train engine.

The boy nodded.

The conductor studied the boy through narrowed eyes and looked over the notes once more. He glanced skeptically at the youth, then waved the boy's papers at him and ushered him onto the train. The boy grabbed his pages and hurried on board. He moved well past us and took up residence on the rear-most seat of the train car.

I watched out the window as the conductor turned and waved to a man on the porch of the train's engine. The engineer ducked back inside the train and a moment later the train jerked ahead. It hesitated, then lunged again and slowly began crawling forward. There was a shout behind us and we all turned to look out the window.

A man was running down the platform. He was engulfed by a cloud of steam, but I could still make out a large hand as he waved his enlistment credentials in the air.

"Stop! Wait!" the man shouted.

The train did not slow, but then, it was barely moving. The conductor leaned out the front door of the train and waved the man in. The man jumped on board, landing with a heavy thud, then stood in the aisle with his back to us as the conductor checked his papers, great breaths heaving the man's wide shoulders. The conductor handed the man his papers and the man saluted the conductor with them. The man turned then and glanced at the faces in the seats. He stopped at mine and his face split into a solemn smile.

The giant Swede sat down in the seat in front of me.

He turned around, grinned at me, and said, "So, we meet again, Homesteader's Son." His grin broadened into a shrewd smile.

July 13, 1915

War Diary

Private Henry Ryzak

July 13, 1915

Volume 1

Diary Text: 21 Pages

[July 13, 1915-October 28, 1915]

The train pulled to a stop at a station just past Carberry. The conductor waved us off the car with, "Take care, gentlemen" and a nod to each of us. I was the first of our group off the train with Will close on my heels. I assumed the others fell in behind us, but I didn't turn to check.

I led Will along the front of the station and stepped off the end of the platform. The camp sprawled across the field behind the station. There were numerous white marquee-style tents in rows off to one side. To the other side were several wooden buildings with officers moving in and out of them. Off in the distance, I could just make out water tanks on tall legs. I stood, assessing the scene.

"Where do we go?" Ransley asked.

I turned to glance at him—I'd forgotten about him. His eyes darted around, barely lighting on any one scene for long.

"Command center would be my guess," I replied. I saw an officer enter one of the wooden buildings and headed toward it. Again, the others fell in behind me. We entered the building and I glanced around.

"Yes?" barked an older man behind a desk. He looked up at us as if daring me to speak. I didn't miss the way a fine tremor seized his hand.

"We're new recruits, just arrived," I said, meeting his glare. "Where do we go."

"There was no one to meet you at the train?" he growled.

"No," I answered. I arched an eyebrow at Shaky. "Should there have been?" If his men weren't where they were supposed to be, that was certainly no fault of mine.

"That's "No, Sir" to you from now on," Shaky commanded.

I paused and we measured one another for a moment. "Yes, Sir," I replied dutifully.

The man nodded once. "Private!" Shaky snapped at a soldier who happened to be passing by.

"Yes, Sir?" the private squeaked.

"Take these men to the quartermaster and get them in uniform."

"Yes, Sir!"

The private looked squarely at me then led our group out of the building.

We were marched down the main thoroughfare of the camp, rows of tents stretching out on one side and more wooden buildings lining the other. There were a number of buildings still under construction.

We were handed over to the quartermaster, a rough bear of a man who spoke only in one-syllable words. He led us through several buildings, doling out uniforms, kit, and bedding to each of us in turn. When finished, the Bear led us back outside and proceeded toward a row of tents. We marched down one of the outermost rows and toward the more distant tents.

"Those two," the Bear growled, gesturing loosely to a couple of tents on our right. He turned and lumbered away.

An older man sat on a three-legged folding canvas stool outside one of the indicated tents, leaning against a sturdy tent pole with feet stretched out before him. He studied each member of our group as he took a long draw on his pipe. His gaze settled on me.

"Welcome," the man said with a nod. "I've got one of the bunks in here, but there's room for three more." The man jerked his thumb at the tent behind him. "There's a feller in that one, but lots of room left," he said, indicating the tent closer to where we stood.

I considered a moment, then headed into the tent where the older man was lodged. The man looked old enough to know a thing or two and I thought his tent might be the better one if he had chosen to take it instead of any other. "Come on, Will," I said, slipping through the tent flap. Will followed me inside and we each dropped our supplies on one of the bunks.

The tent was a simple canvas structure, but did have a wooden floor, so that was something at least. There was only a small cook stove at the far end of the tent. Large enough for heating water but not big enough to give much heat were it to be needed.

I turned, intent on talking to the man outside and ran directly into a wall. At least, it could have been a wall. It was, in actuality, the Swede. He grinned down at me and I looked way up at him, my heart beginning to beat just a little faster. I took a breath.

"Are we going to have a problem?" I asked cautiously.

The Swede's grin widened into a smile. "No, no problem," he said. "You gave me money to get my lumber sold and I sell it. This was good for you to do. I owe you favour. I am with you to repay favour."

"Really?" I asked in a low tone, watching for any "tell" that would indicate he was lying. He only stared me in the eye with that foolish grin fixed firmly in place.

"*Ja*, I say it is so," the Swede insisted. "And also, you beat me in fight—this is surprising me. You are good fighter. Good to keep close to you. *Ja.*"

"All right…" I replied. "I don't remember your name." If this man was about to kill me, I'd prefer to know who was doing the killing—that and Will would catch his name to track him down later.

"Tove Lundgren," he replied with a nod, confirming it. He held out his very large hand.

I hesitated, studying him a moment. It could be a trap…but I could generally manage traps. I took a breath, ready for anything, and shook the man's hand. My hand was completely engulfed by the man's fist and he likely could have broken my wrist had he chosen to. To my relief, he only shook my hand with a smile on his face. I couldn't help replying in kind.

I shook my head slightly and squeezed past the wall of a man. I stepped out of the tent and turned to the older gentleman sitting outside.

I offered him my hand. "I'm Henry Ryzak," I said. "This is my brother, Will, and that's Tove Lundgren."

"Galt," the man said, shaking my hand then reaching rather uncertainly to shake Lundgren's hand. He then reached for Will's. "Augen Galt."

"Any idea what we're to do now?" I asked as Ransley and the Kid fell in beside us.

"Well," Galt drawled, "Hard to know for sure. Things aren't settled just yet and the battalion's still forming up. No consistent Command either, so there's no orders comin' down."

"I expected things to be more organized," I said.

Galt shook his head. "Naw—it's always like this starting out. I was in the Boer War and saw the same thing every time a new battalion was being formed. Top brass never knows what's going on in the ranks. Only thing for sure today is that the mess bell will sound soon. Ration delivery is spotty just now," Galt said. "Likely wise to get your uniforms on and be ready for mess in thirty minutes. First men there get food—the rest might not. Best to line up early. I can show you where it is if you're ready on time, but I'll not be waitin' on ya to do it."

We glanced at one another then hurried to get changed—Will, Lundgren and I slipping into our tent, Ransley and the youth heading to the neighbouring one. It took me a few tries to get the puttees on and even then, they didn't feel very secure.

"What are these?" Lundgren asked, dangling the strips of broadcloth in the air.

"Puttees," I replied.

"What are they for?"

"You wrap them around your legs to protect them," I answered. I showed him mine.

Lundgren took several attempts and a couple of curses to get his on, but he finally all got them on in some semblance of order.

We went outside to find Galt still sitting on his stool. Ransley stepped out of his tent followed by the Kid and another man just before Galt led the way to the mess tent. Along the way I learned the new man's name was Gerald Stewart. He was a farmer and had a young family back home. He had left his parents in England in order to get free Canadian land some years ago. He now felt it his duty to enlist in support of Britain.

I could smell wood smoke and stewing meat, and my mouth started watering. Galt led us to a queue that was just beginning to form and we stood, waiting. A loud bell clanged and soldiers came rushing over, crowding and jostling into a line behind us.

The cook began spooning watery stew into the men's tins as we moved through the line, collecting our rations along with a slice of bread so dense and unyielding it could easily have been mistaken for a brick.

We relied on Galt to keep us on track for the first few days of training. He showed us how to put on our puttees so they would stay, how to pack our kit so everything would fit, where to find the wells toward the east of the camp, and where to shower and shave. He toured us around camp, showing us the mechanical building, the stables, the supply building, paymaster's office, and the camp hospital that was just being built. There was a strip of non-military buildings on the outskirts of the camp set up by tradesmen. There was a bank, a barber shop, a milk depot, a photography studio, a couple of restaurants, and even a movie theatre with another being built.

Drills began a couple of days after our arrival. They were poor attempts at orderly conduct, with new men being added to our numbers daily so that half our compliment was always unfamiliar with the exercises. We took up training on everything from kit packing and saluting to grenade launching and riflery. There was a lot of marching and much time was spent on the firing range. There were work parties to build new buildings and dig new trench lines for battle practice. We learned the daily routines of life in the trenches and how to mount an assault by "going over the top" of the trench. There were many hours of physical conditioning and some bayonet training thrown in for good measure. Each night we went to bed sore and tired with never enough food to calm our grumbling stomachs. Each morning we fell in for count, trying our best to form neat, orderly rows. That is, *most* of us tried.

There were a number of men among the new soldiers who were not interested in learning army ways. They fell into line seemingly at their leisure and ambled about on marches, entirely unconcerned with the command sergeant's squawking. They gave half-hearted salutes if and when they felt like it and obeyed orders in a desultory fashion—if at all. I was sorely tempted to join their lot, but I knew I would have to commit to this life if I was to succeed in keeping Will alive long enough to send him home.

Slater, however, was unabashedly one of those men. He had taken the fourth bunk in with Ransley, Stewart, and the Kid (whose name I still did not know). I didn't care that Slater didn't take command seriously—the haphazard training rankled me too at times, seeming almost like "busy work" to keep us recruits occupied while we waited to be moved to the front.

No, it wasn't Slater's slack approach to authority that bothered me—it was his loner attitude that made me leery of him. He groused about everyone, never lent a hand, and was disruptive, doing his own things in his own time. The man was simply not a team player. Men like Slater did as they pleased—and what pleased them was to do what benefitted them. They were wild cards in any situation and could not be counted on. Men like that posed a risk to everyone around them, and I was keeping my eye on him. I knew he'd go down at some point, and I was intent on keeping my distance so he wouldn't drag me down with him when he fell. Besides, some small and insecure part of me recognized him—just as though I had seen his face in the mirror when I looked into it. He was a mean reflection of myself and the thought crawled under my skin and wormed its way into the pit of my stomach. I didn't want anything to do with the man.

The men in our tent and Ransley's were made into a squad under Staff Sergeant MacDonald. He was reasonable enough, but strict. He butted heads with Slater on more than one occasion and I made sure Will and I kept our heads down whenever that happened.

Captain Dowell headed Company D to which our squad was assigned. He was less reasonable. Fortunately, his attention focused on the rowdier units, leaving ours mostly to MacDonald's management—unless Slater required an attitude correction and that generally brought all of us to the Captain's attention.

Training was severe—likely to weed out those who would not keep up on the battle field. A few men were drummed out within the first several weeks. I could manage all right, thanks to my father's tutelage—I supposed he had taught me some valuable lessons about perseverance and stamina after all, although I credited him for his unknowing help grudgingly. Will kept up on the marches reasonably well, despite the 60-pound kit every soldier was expected to carry. He was exhausted by the end of some of the marches, however. Galt made out as though a 3-hour march under a heavy load didn't even count with him. On arriving back at camp, he would simply stow his pack, take out his pipe, and sit down to write a letter home—nothing to it. Lundgren was also fine with the marches—the pack barely comprised any additional weight for him. Ransley took to it surprisingly well considering his wiry frame and I wondered if lugging all his books around before enlisting had built him up.

The Kid (as I had come to call him) was another matter.

I noticed the boy struggling one day about half-way through a morning's march. It was raining with a fine, cool drizzle wetting the ground into a slippery clay and making the uphill climb over mud and wet grass almost impossible. After the first slip and slide down the hill, I had learned to dig my toes into the firmer ground under the slime and made it to the top of the hill, my boots heavy with caked on mud. Will followed me up the hill just a few steps behind me. I saw the Kid then and watched as he slid back down the hill with every step he took, straining to keep his feet under him. One step forward and a long slide back—every time. Desperate, he reached down, trying to claw his way through the mud, grasping at the tall grass. This did not help his cause—the grass was wet and slippery too.

Will came up and stood beside me, both of us intent on the boy's struggle.

"Maybe we should give him a hand," Will commented as the Kid took another back-sliding step, losing more ground than he had gained.

"Maybe he should figure it out," I replied. "Looks like a fair fight."

"C'mon, he's just a kid."

"A kid who decided to join the army. Best he's drummed out now than get killed his first day in the trenches." Honestly, I would have felt better had the Kid been sent home. He looked much too young to be there. "Besides, he'd ask for help if he wanted it," I reasoned.

"I doubt it," Will said. "He doesn't talk to anyone much. I did hear him talking to Galt a couple of days ago—Galt was telling him about the Boer War."

"Do we even know the Kid's name?"

"Nope."

I watched the boy struggle for another moment before deciding I couldn't stand it anymore.

"He's going to make us late for mess," I griped.

The rule was, you couldn't line up until your entire squad was present. If we didn't have the Kid with us, we couldn't line up; if we couldn't line up, we ran the risk of not getting food. I sighed heavily then walked back down the hill, digging my heels in hard. When I was within reach of the boy, I stretched out my hand. The boy straightened, looked at my hand, then turned a cold expression on me.

"I don't need your help," he said stonily. That's what he said, but I didn't miss his red-rimmed eyes and his trembling lower lip.

"Looks to me like you need *someone's* help," I answered. "Might as well be me."

The boy only gave me a sullen glare and clenched his jaw. His lip stopped trembling.

"Fine," I said, dropping my hand, "but you've got no right to make all of us miss rations. You're getting up the hill under your own steam or I'll have Lundgren carry you up, like it or no. Dig your toes in with each step until you've got a good footing on the dry dirt underneath—don't just slide around on top of the mud." I turned and started back up the hill, demonstrating how to dig in the toe of my boot. I reached the top again and turned, expecting to find the kid still at the bottom of the hill, but to my surprise, he was only a half-dozen steps behind me—still using his hands to claw his way up, but at least he was moving more forward than back. He reached the top of the hill, gave me a reluctant, but resolute nod, and marched off, the weight of his pack pressing down on him and bending him low.

Will clapped me on the back and grinned at me before marching back toward camp. I shook my head at him. I hoped desperately that helping the Kid wouldn't become a habit—I didn't need another person to look after on the battlefield—but I had the sinking feeling that I had just picked up a stray cat.

We got back to camp and hurried to swap our packs for our mess tins then went to line up for food. We only just beat the dinner bell and the ensuing crowd.

Will kept up with physical training, being accustomed to hard labour on the farm, but his gunmanship was another story. His grenade aim was worse. This did not escape the notice of Captain Dowell as he was inspecting our unit one day on the firing range. I was some ways down the firing line from where Will stood, but I could hear the conversation as it bounced along the flat prairie grass.

"Private Ryzak!" the Captain barked, moving to stand behind Will. Will and I both turned at the sound of our name, but the Captain was focused on Will.

"At what, exactly, are you aiming?"

Will cast him a confused look, glancing at the targets place at the far end of the field. "The target, sir?"

"I find that difficult to believe, considering you've not hit it once. You will have the Hun bearing down on you out in the field, boy! If you can't hit them, you will die and others will die with you! Do you want to die out there?!"

"No, Sir!"

"Then hit the target!"

Will turned and took shaky aim under the stare of the Captain. He missed, of course.

"Again!" bellowed the Captain.

Will fired and missed again, just grazing the side of the target.

"Pathetic," the Captain said. "You'll remain on this firing range until you can show the Sergeant a target with ten hits. Sergeant MacDonald!" the Captain called out. MacDonald appeared out of nowhere.

"Yes, Sir?" he asked.

"There are a number of soldiers on this range who are grossly incompetent with their weapons."

"Sorry, Sir," the Sergeant replied. "Some of them haven't handled a rifle before."

"Well the Germans will like that just fine, I'm sure! This soldier is to practice shooting until he can hit that target. He will not leave until he can show you his target with ten centre hits. You will supervise him for however long that takes. There are several others as well. Follow me and I will point them out."

MacDonald cast Will an irritated glance. "Yes, Sir," he replied to the Captain.

Will and the others remained on the firing range under MacDonald's scrutiny while the rest of us moved back to camp. They stayed there through mess and into the evening. It made me feel slightly nauseated, thinking of Will standing there without the skills to get himself out of the situation—and having missed rations. I hated the feeling. I couldn't just wait around, wondering how he was doing, so I wandered over to the bar in the merchant row, hoping to take my mind off Will and hoping even more, that he would be back in our tent by the time I returned.

I hadn't been in the bar at camp before. I stepped into the plain wooden building and found the atmosphere agreeable. There were lanterns on the walls casting a warm, yellow light. A couple of squares had been cut into opposite side walls and were propped open to let in the warm summer breeze just as it started to cool for the evening. There were a few small tables scattered about, some occupied, others not. The bartender looked up at me expectantly. I dropped a coin onto the bar and ordered a beer. It wasn't as cold as I would have liked, but it would do. I sat nursing my drink and trying not to be impatient with Will.

"Hey, Soldier. Need some company?" whispered a sultry voice. I could feel a warm breath on my ear.

I slowly turned, knowing what I would find. A skinny brunette in a low-cut dress that hung loose about her hips laid a hand on my shoulder and leaned an elbow on the bar. Her pose provided a spectacular glimpse of things that should have remained concealed—which was likely her sole purpose in the arrangement.

"No thanks," I said, shrugging my shoulder out from under her hand and turning back to my drink. I certainly had my faults and vices, but women like her were not one of them.

Will and I had had a sister once. She hadn't lived a full year before dying of diphtheria. Whenever I saw a "working woman" all I could think was: what if she were my sister? Surely she was *someone's* sister or daughter? The thought sickened me to the point of obscuring all other thoughts.

The girl pouted and cast me the sort of glance that fell just shy of a five-year-old sticking out her tongue. She moved off to a table of older soldiers to try her luck with them. They gave her a warmer greeting than I had given her.

I consumed a couple more beer then decided enough time had passed. Surely Will could have hit the target ten times by now…then again, maybe not. I made my way back to the tent to see if he was there.

He wasn't.

I turned to Galt. "Will's not back?" I huffed in disbelief.

"Haven't seen him," Galt replied, watching me through narrowed eyes.

I grabbed my rifle from under my bunk.

"Where are you going with that?" Galt asked sitting up from where he lounged on his bunk and planting his booted feet firmly on the floor. Lundgren's eyes flashed to Galt then up to meet mine. "You've been drinking," Galt cautioned, "Guns and drink don't get on well together—particularly in a crowded camp."

I briefly wondered how he knew I had been drinking, but didn't pursue the thought. I had other things to attend to.

"I'm getting Will off the firing range," I said, and exited the tent with my rifle in hand.

I stole back to the range, keeping out of sight of MacDonald and moved quietly into a copse of brush about five hundred yards to the rear and side of the range. MacDonald was pacing sullenly behind the four men still working at hitting their targets. Shots rang out one after another. I could see Will standing, his shoulders stooped and his rifle looking heavy in his hands. He was studying the ground and shaking his head ruefully as he opened and closed his hand a couple of times. I looked down the field to Will's target—he had managed to hit it a few times, at least. Will raised the gun, sighting along the barrel.

Just a little help is all he needs.

I raised my rifle and took aim. I squeezed off a round and saw the target jump. Will's head popped up and he grinned to himself. He raised his rifle again and I did the same. I shot again and saw the target move again. Will's shoulders straightened a little.

I stayed, hitting Will's target for him for another four rounds to tally the ten hits Will needed.

"Sergeant," Will called out.

MacDonald moved over to Will and looked down the field at his target. MacDonald nodded and waved Will off. Will turned to leave, a weary hitch in his step.

I hurried back to the tent, stowing my rifle before Will got back. Galt and Lundgren watched my every move. I quickly dropped down onto my bunk, closing my eyes just as Will came in.

"Took you long enough," I said, sitting up as Will fell onto his bunk, dropping his gun on the floor beside him.

"Shut up," Will replied, closing his eyes.

I grinned. "I saved some rations for you," I said. I pulled out my mess tin from under my bunk and held it out to him.

Will looked over at me and quickly sat up, grabbing the tin of bread and meat from my hand. He began wolfing down the meal. "Thanks," he replied around a large mouthful of bread.

I gave him a nod. "Tomorrow I'll take you down to the range and practice with you."

Will cast me a frown and nodded reluctantly.

"So…" Galt began uncertainly, "…no one died, then?"

I gave an intentional chuckle. "None of the men out there could have shot anyone had they tried." I cast Galt a warning look.

Gault cast me a *well-all-right-then* sort of shrug and nodded. He said nothing further.

I dropped back onto my bunk and was out until the next day.

I was awakened by Will shaking me roughly. "Henry! Get up! Time to fall in."

I opened my eyes and groaned. I quickly shut my eyes against the bright and glaring sunlight, seeming to intensify like a beam of sun through a magnifying glass as it diffused through the ivory canvas of the tent. I threw my elbow across my eyes to block out the light.

"Henry! Everyone is falling in already—get moving!"

"What about breakfast?" I groaned.

"You slept through it. Get up. I'll meet you out there."

I took a deep breath, feeling a familiar dull ache building at the back of my head. I rolled into a sitting position and grabbed the water jug on the cook stove. I chugged several large swallows then poured some water over my head and swiped some of it over my face as it fell to the floor. I got dressed and went out to the parade field, noting the ranks already lined up and filled. I quietly made my way to my spot.

"Ryzak!" MacDonald shouted the moment I stepped into place.

"Yes, Sir!" I replied, the sound of my own voice splitting my head in two. I winced.

"Nice of you to join us," MacDonald barked for everyone to hear. He came to stand uncomfortably close to me. He tugged my crooked collar into place and yanked on my shirt front to straighten it, sending another tooth-jarring jolt through my head. "Having a little difficulty with roll call today?"

"A little, Sir."

MacDonald winced and turned his face away. "Yes, I can smell why that might be. After parade you will meet me at my command tent. I have a job for you."

"Yes, Sir," I replied, feeling the full weight of the implications his words carried settle on my shoulders.

I figured there must be some secret manual of discipline given to all heads of state, work force, and family which outlined the sort of punishment to be meted out for every type of rule infraction. I had to assume MacDonald and my father ascribed to its regulations religiously for MacDonald immediately assigned me to a work detail digging trench lines for battle practice. My only thought was to find the author of said manual and slaughter him in his sleep.

"That should help clear your head," MacDonald added satisfactorily as I lowered myself into the trench line with my shovel.

I dug in the nauseatingly hot sun for the next six hours. I would like to say I learned my lesson and never touched another drink again, having gained insight into the evil repercussions associated with it, but that would have been a lie.

...

The summer months moved apace and during that time, we learned to lay barbed wire, live in the trenches, shoot, and even how to care for ourselves. Word around camp was that it took four men and three women working at home to support each soldier. However, that evaluation fell short of the actual work of the thing. Let's face it, up to that point every one of us had a woman to rely on to do our mending, cooking, and washing, whether it was a mother, a wife, a sister, or a grandmother. In camp, on our own for the first time, we had to learn all of those skills and then some—it was incredible to me how much time and effort was required to simply mend a torn shirt, let alone keep oneself fed, groomed, and supplied in clean clothes!

What was truly infuriating, however, was that such seemingly trivial tasks were foreign to me and made me feel like a school kid in need of proper tutelage. I hadn't even considered these tasks before, reasoning that they must be entirely simple and, therefore, easy. Now I was needing Lundgren's help to sew on my buttons. Maddening!

We were to discover there was another aspect of our care which we had previously assigned to the women in our lives: health care. At home, any personal illness or injury had been brought to the immediate attention of Mother who would quickly and deftly put a person to rights again. Not in camp. We struggled through colds and flus as best we could. Ransley was reasonably proficient at doling out tea for a head cold or even showing us how to steam stuffy noses, but when it came to outright injuries, we were lost. This became very apparent early on and in the face of one particular training injury.

We were on the firing range when it happened.

"Will," I mocked, "Something's wrong: you're actually hitting the target!"

Will turned and gave me a sardonic grin. "If we keep up the practice," he replied, "I'll soon best you."

"I think not," I replied and adeptly put a bullet in the centre of his target from where I stood.

We faced off against our own targets, firing quickly and trying to see who would get the better score. It was only practice for us now. Will had been able to pass the rifle requirements after his second try. Still, I would have felt better had he been a crack shot.

A ways off to my left, the Sergeant was badgering some poor soul from another unit about the slow pace of his firing. We were aiming to match the firing speed of the English troops: fifteen rounds per minute. At that particular moment, the soldier was trying to explain why our goal was impossible:

"Yes, Sir, but the problem is, the Brits have the Lee-Enfield rifle over there while our poor lot has got the Ross. Bad deal, that. The Ross is fine and good for hunting and anything you needs to shoot far off and steady like, but it ain't gonna shoot fast, Sir. It's a precisely engineered tool and just too persnickety over the fit of the casings, you see. When we shoot fast, the barrel gets hot and the bullets don't fit the way they should—the beast jams every time!" the man groused.

"It's a poor workman who blames his tool," MacDonald replied coolly.

The soldier gave him a hard look and took up his rifle again, sighting down the barrel. "Fine, I'll just shows you if you don't believe me."

The man began firing at a rapid rate, ejecting the casings and firing again as quickly as he could. On the fourth or fifth shot, the gun jammed. The soldier pulled back the bolt, to eject the round. The hot casing flew back into the man's eye. The soldier dropped his rifle, his hands flying up to his face as he screamed. He sank to his knees holding his face and yelling for help.

The Sergeant merely stood, his mouth opened slightly, watching the man like one would watch a horse running amuck in the barracks.

Galt, however, moved quickly to grab his water bottle. He ran over to the man, dousing the soldier's face with water and yelling for the medic. They came with a clean, wet cloth and covered the soldier's face with it while leading him away. Galt told me later the man's eye had been charred and they would likely have to take it out—he'd seen the injury before. My lesson was learned however: don't eject a cartridge and sight your gun at the same time. I also learned that none of us had any idea on how to deal with injuries.

By the end of the summer, we felt we had a handle on army life and were getting a little anxious to be doing something more than drills and training. Slater in particular was becoming impatient to get to the "real war" as he put it and to "do what he came to do".

We were in the trenches one morning when, just before dawn, the call went out to "stand to". Everyone roused themselves quickly, picked up their rifles, and took watch over the edge of the trench in anticipation of a mock attack—everyone except Slater. He lounged against the trench wall, still dozing. The Sergeant came around the corner just then and nearly tripped over Slater's booted feet.

"Private Slater!" MacDonald barked, "You were ordered to stand to! Get up!"

Slater looked up at the Sergeant and slowly stood, but didn't pick up his rifle and didn't move to the trench wall.

"You will salute when an officer addresses you!" MacDonald commanded.

Slater tilted his head, watching MacDonald for a second or two. "I signed up to fight, not salute," Slater replied.

"Is that so?" MacDonald asked, leaning over the slightly shorter Slater. They glared at each other for a moment. "Then I guess you will do neither. Guard!" MacDonald called.

The guard appeared over the edge of the trench and looked down at our group. "Yes, Sir?"

"Take this soldier and his unit to the end of the trench. As their unit does not have all men standing to and they are not ready for an attack, we will have them do something more useful: they can extend this trench another six feet! No rations until the job is completed!"

Our unit erupted in cries of "Slater!", "No!", "Not fair!", and "Fool!".

The Sergeant stepped back and pointed to the end of the trench. We moved off, each of us casting Slater dark looks over our shoulders while the guard escorted us along the top of the trench.

The October sun was cooling into fall, but the day was still uncomfortably warm as we dug. Slater laughed, trying to convince us he'd gotten the better of the Sergeant since he never had saluted nor stood to. The guard soon tired of the heat and of Slater's rhetoric and went to find some shade in which to sit. Slater's diatribe continued for much of the morning until morning moved on into afternoon without rations and turned Slater's guffaws into complaints of being hungry.

"Come on, men!" he yelled. "We've already missed noon mess. We could have had this done by now! We'll be out here all day at this rate and we'll all starve to death too. Hurry up, the lot of yous!" He gave Stewart who was digging next to him a hard shove, sending Stewart stumbling backward as he tripped over his own shovel.

I looked over at Stewart then turned to Slater. I should have left it alone—but I didn't. Instead, I turned, resting my shovel on the dirt. I planted my feet, and glared at Slater. Lundgren and Galt looked over at me and stopped their digging to watch, shovels gripped firmly. Lundgren grinned in a way that almost didn't look like a grin.

"Well maybe you should have just followed orders," said. "If you had, we wouldn't be stuck in this mess in the first place!"

"Well maybe you think we have to do whatever they tell us, just like you listened to your mamma, huh?"

"You're in the army man! That's how this game is played. If you don't like it, then why did you join?!"

Slater dropped his shovel and came to stand in front of me. He leaned in, his face directly in front of mine and much too close. I could smell the heat of sweat and anger coming off him.

"I signed up to kill some Hun!" he spat, "not take orders from schoolboys just out of knickers!"

"Well you aren't doing either at the moment. All you're doing is causing everyone problems! You need to learn to follow orders or you'll get us all killed!"

"Oh, really," Slater asked, "and who's gonna teach me to mind orders? You?!"

"I'm thinking some German will teach you that lesson rather quickly once we get to the front and we'll all be safer without you," I countered.

As was so often the case, Slater didn't stop to think. His right fist shot out, heading straight for my jaw. Slater had set down his shovel, but I had kept mine tightly in hand. I hefted it in both hands, deflecting the punch. Slater's forearm smacked into the hard wood of the handle and he cried out, grabbing his arm with his other hand and holding it close.

I knew that, once begun, a fight with a bully like Slater would have to be finished, and convincingly so, or else one would face retribution later on. I held my shovel cross-wise in both hands and shoved Slater hard. He stumbled backward, but didn't fall.

Rage darkened his expression, and he lunged forward, hands outstretched to take hold of my shovel. I let him take hold of the handle with both hands, and pulled his weight toward me while planting my booted foot in his mid-section. He doubled over and wrapped both his arms across his middle. I brought up the blade of the shovel, catching him squarely on his jaw as he pitched forward. His head snapped to the side and he fell hard, still clutching at his gut.

I lowered my shovel to the ground, keeping a firm grasp of it as I took a steadying breath and watched Slater closely. After a moment he opened his eyes and rested up on his elbow, his other hand moving to rub his jaw. He only glowered up at me.

When I was certain Slater wouldn't be coming at me again, I turned to the others. "Anyone have a problem with this?" I asked, looking at the others in turn.

My question was met with replies of "Nope" "Should've been done sooner" and "Only that I didn't do it myself" (which came from Galt) as they all returned to their digging.

I resumed my work and, after another couple of minutes, Slater got up and started digging along with us. He said nothing further and kept his eyes on his work.

The weather turned cooler and in late October we entrained for our winter barracks at the old agricultural college in Winnipeg. It felt good to be moving on.

October 19, 1915

October 19, 1915

I left home immediately after Thanksgiving, content with having secured the garden produce in boiled and gleaming jars in the pantry. I arrived in Halifax where Uncle Jasper helped me to enlist. The process was so simple as to be discomfiting. One expects, perhaps, some measure of fanfare to accompany the end of their former life and the beginning of what may very well prove to be a great sacrifice, but the experience was, instead, quite anticlimactic.

The woman at the recruiting station sat, dwarfed behind her high-handed wooden desk, as she filled out a solitary form neatly laid out on the desktop between us: the "Officer's Declaration Paper". Evidently, we Nursing Sisters are to be made Lieutenants straight off with an Officer's pay of $4.10 per day! After answering a few questions (name, next of kin, religion, will I agree to be vaccinated, where have I served, and the like), the Medical Officer looked me over, signed the Certificate of Medical Examination declaring me fit for duty, and off I went: a Lieutenant in the Canadian Overseas Expeditionary Corps!

I will be serving in the No. 7 Stationary Hospital under the charge of Matron Hubley, but first, six weeks of military training. Uncle says I look quite sharp in my uniform. It is a double-breasted navy dress with red cuffs that match the lining of the navy wool cape. It makes one feel very grown up indeed! I wish Mum could see it. Uncle Jasper had me sit for a portrait which he will send to her. The working uniform is nice as well, although not so fancy. It is a light blue serge with simple white cuffs and collar and apron. I must say it is a sturdy thing and I expect it shall wear like iron!

I shall be staying with Uncle Jasper until training begins. My first order of business will be touring all of Halifax! Uncle Jasper has promised to take me to as many local landmarks as time permits before my training begins.

While Saskatchewan had not yet fully realized the war, Halifax was abuzz with it. There were soldiers and soon-to-be soldiers everywhere one looked. There were marching drills and convoys of supplies in the streets, flowing in a long khaki stream. Ships sailed in and out of the harbor almost as numerous as the waves themselves.

A bungle of red tape, Matron had informed us with a snort, had been amassed by hidebound officials in the Military Office and caused a week's delay in beginning our training. All was sorted in the end, however, and training began at the end of October. (I rather suspected Matron's flinty glare and an attitude just as cutting had much to do with getting through such red tape.) We were drilled and marched and lectured, learning military exercises like saluting and falling in. One Medical Officer who was helping to set up the hospitals oversees spoke to us, giving us a vague and somewhat diluted description of what we might expect over the next several months. As it would turn out, he was so entirely incorrect as to make a politician blush. When I thought on the lecturer later, I doubted very much he had ever been over to England and was likely simply regurgitating information sent him by his superiors.

Training moved on apace and the six weeks fairly flew by!

December 30, 1915

Well, it is time! We have had our turkeys and our Christmas puddings and tomorrow we will set off for England to join the war effort. I am happy to be away. The thought of home and John unsettles me and I marvel every now and again that Papa would ever give away his farm and his daughter to a man who is rather lacking in intellect and makes no effort whatever to conceal the fact! I am anxious to begin earning money and learning how to look out for myself—two things I will very much need on my return home, for I have every intention of getting out of the contract with John! Yes, frightfully good to finally be on my way.

On December 31, 1915, our unit was marched to the Halifax train station where we entrained for St. John's harbor. We were billeted at a local hotel and on January 1st, 1916 we found ourselves on the pier enduring an interminable wait—something to which we should very soon not only learn to expect, but to depend upon in what we would dub "army time". We practiced our smiles of calm forbearance on one another as we loitered on the dock, not knowing how much we would come to rely on such adroit self-deception.

Our ship, the *H.M.S. Metagama*, finally arrived in port. I stood back a moment, looking high above to the smoke stacks of the great ship. One of the latest in the Canadian Pacific North Atlantic fleet as we were told, the ship loomed above the dock, taller than any building I had hitherto seen. To say it was impressive would be to call the Taj Mahal "adequate". There was quite suddenly much scurrying about as medical supplies, baggage, and personnel were loaded for the ten-day voyage. I saw the others already half-way up the gangplank and jumped to, hurrying to catch up.

I found the journey over endless water a terrifyingly fascinating experience—something akin to watching a house burn down: one simply could not draw one's eyes away no matter the distress of the thing. The ship, having set off on its maiden voyage only the past March, had the best of cabins set aside for us, although I was later told they were third-class accommodations. I could not conceive what first class might have offered that our cabins had not already afforded us! For many of the others, however, the journey drew forth from its afflicted passengers a decisive "never again!", intoned as an expletive. (How they thought they were to return home was quite beyond my imagination.) I did chuckle, however, at one of the Volunteer Aides who repeatedly quoted the only singularly comforting bible verse she could think of: "there shall be no more sea".[29]

January 10, 1916

We have made it to England safe and sound. I have dropped Mum a speedily dashed-off card telling her so. We are settling in, but it is difficult to get one's bearings as there is nothing familiar nor any routine from which to draw guidance. For now, we are simply trying to learn the layout of the camp and the hospital building, find the mess hall, and determine where to bathe and rest. It is a work in progress, shall we say.

To the great relief of our unit, we arrived safely on England's shores, docking at Plymouth. From there, we entrained for the Shornecliffe Military Hospital, arriving the same day. Once at Shorncliffe, we were marched to the hospital and the building in which we were assigned our rooms. Carrying all of our belongings in heavy duffels and totes, we marched along, through a maelstrom of soldiers, horses, motor vehicles, and army units marching and running and training with bayonets. We wove among the supply wagons, the soldier's tents, and the cook houses. We walked with the orderlies who were delivering supplies to the hospital, riding in the wake of their group as they sailed among the inhabitants of the training camp.

At one point, a Scottish orderly was walking alongside several of us Nursing Sisters and engaged us in polite chat. One of the Sisters asked him what had made him enlist. With a profound and unassuming honesty that bordered on poetic simplicity, the man said, "Acht, Sister, I thocht it was tim. Yon Kaiser is steppin' ower far. Ee's well out o' 'is bounds."[29]

We were led to our rooms in the building just beside the hospital where we were unceremoniously deposited along with our baggage but without further instruction. However, it is not in the nature of a proper Nursing Sister to await directions when none are forthcoming. We are rather much better at giving them and, in that one setting, I felt I had some measure of command over the situation. After all, we were women of action if nothing, or we would not have gotten to that point.

We quickly divided ourselves into small groups and each group volunteered to find some bit of information to bring back to the others: where the mess hall was located and the times of the meals; where the Medical Officer was and what orders did we have at present; and, most importantly: where were the waterclosets and where might we get a bath. We dispersed and returned quite quickly (again, as Nurses were wont to do, moving about at all times at double speed and Heaven help any person in the way), having secured all the sought-for information.

We determined we all had time for a brief wash before supper. We were given no orders other than to settle ourselves in. We would be taking over the administration of the hospital once the current unit in charged received their orders to move out. We would soon learn, once again, that patience was a virtue, particularly when waiting on the "higher ups" to make decisions and relay such plans to the lowly foot-soldiers. We spent the next several weeks being oriented to the hospital and slowly being incorporated into their staffing schedules.

February 5, 1916

We took charge of the Moore Barracks hospital today with hand-off completed yesterday at end of day shift. The departing unit had today to pack and ready themselves for their travel to France where they will provide support at "the front" (as some of the VAs call it).

I find myself amidst a curious array of Nursing Sisters, having been compiled into a unit while at Shorncliffe. A more disparate lot I cannot imagine. I feel this variance of temperaments will lead either to the sharing of strengths in strong solidarity, or a fractiousness resulting in such enmity as to turn the war envious. Time will tell. As for myself, I am finding the playing out of the thing far too intriguing for me to align with any one faction or person in particular (although there are a few from whom I have already chosen to distance myself for prudence's sake).

There was a particular passion in our work in the following days, each member of our unit wanting to "outshine" the previous unit by showing our handiwork at its best. There were curious displays of this zeal such as giving every stock cupboard a thorough cleaning or determined but polite skirmishes over who required the mop first in order to clean their ward. I would not say tensions were high, but rather, patience with one another was certainly put to the test during that period of time. This was the first trial of our little "melting pot" of personalities and provided no end of fascinating drama.

My roommate was Gwendolyn Barnette. She was pretty in a sensible sort of way and a truly clever girl. Gwen, as we dubbed her—largely due to the fact that whenever we gave her instructions, she would set off to work practically before we could finish saying her name—was from a wealthy family. She would blanch for a second or two when faced with an unpleasant task. One would then see her face turn to marble as she commenced with the work set down before her. At first, I did not understand her choice of entering nursing much less leaving her home to enlist. When I asked her, she had simply said, "Well, you see, it didn't seem right not to." Later, after a number of late-night cocoas, I discovered the more likely reason for her curious choice. Gwen told me she had been jilted at the altar—why ever for was anyone's guess. What man would desert a clever, pretty, wealthy girl? Never the less, that was the tale and Gwen had subsequently run away to nursing school. Over the coming months, Gwen would often come to question her decision, but never once did she say outright, "I ought not to have done this."

There were several other respectable Sisters within our group.

Rose Garvie was a woman of some vintage with a quick but somewhat heavy tongue. She had trained in an English teaching hospital before Canada had ever established any nursing schools, and one would have thought the Devil himself had seen to her education. She moved about the ward, attending to her work (and to that of others) as though the fires of hell were licking at her heels. There was no sign of fear in her. No, Rose was sheer determination.

Rose had married after several years of nursing and had been forced to quit her profession. She and her husband had then moved to Canada where they took on the predatory Canadian prairie, living in a soddie and eking out a rough existent from her soil. Rose's husband had died one bitterly cold prairie day before they could prove up on their section of land and Rose had returned to nursing in order to support herself. When she had the opportunity to enlist, she had not hesitated. She jumped at the chance to return home to aide her country. Rose often said she was looking forward to retiring to the country to live with her sister when "that nasty man is finally given his comeuppance."

Mary Middleton, bless her, was a force to be reckoned with to be certain. She had an unfortunate build rather reminiscent of a tree trunk, her movements slow but unerringly steady like that of a grindstone pulled by a mule. I was convinced that, should a mountain fall directly upon her, Mary would have every chance of simply standing up, mountain and all, and carrying it off to deposit it elsewhere.

Vickie Hanes was a sweet young thing. She was not a Nursing Sister, but rather a VA. Unlike the other VAs whose jealousy of our rank and pay turned their hearts sour toward nurses, Vickie followed us everywhere, jumping in to help with our work and mending socks and sheets alongside us while we drank tea on our afternoons off. She was small and plain-looking and an owl of a thing she was: she watched all and spoke seldom. When she did speak, however, her words carried a weight to them like the rolling of a boulder down a mountainside and one knew instantly to stop what they were doing and pay heed. She explained that, were she to be fortunate enough to return home after the war, she fully intended to become a Nurse and wished to gain as much experience as possible while the opportunity presented itself.

There were several other much less respectable members of our unit with whom I spent as little time as possible.

Lena Ashwell was a foolish young thing who was too pretty for her own good. She was not very clever and wore lace stockings under her uniform whenever she could get away with it. It remained an enigma to me for some time how she had been accepted into any nursing school let alone how she had managed to complete the course. Rose finally shed light on the mystery. Rose told us the girl was from a well-known and wealthy family who had indulged the girl far too much. When the girl developed a taste for men's affections and her parents realized how badly they had muddled the girl's discipline, her father had shipped her off to the local nursing school—along with a very handsome donation to the school—in order to quarter her more firmly among women and less in the way of gentlemen. In the end, this endeavor created a fantastically self-important child, but produced very little application to her assigned duties.

Lastly there were Charlotte Lathan and Katherine Hutchinson. Two of the silliest girls I had ever had the misfortune to meet, their chance pairing only serving to exponentially intensify their collective foolishness. At times, I was quite convinced they had not yet realized they were at war, but rather fancied themselves on a sight-seeing tour of the English countryside.

April 23, 1916

Today was Easter Sunday—my first Easter not spent with Mum and Papa. We had church parade before our shift. It was a pleasant little service Padre put on for us in the mess hall. It was rather poorly attended I thought. A shame that. Even if one did not ascribe to religion, the singing of hymns braces one up so.

We will be serving ham and boiled potatoes to the patients tonight. Some of the sisters have collected their own money to purchase fruit for the patients to serve with the meal. Word has gotten round and they can speak of little else. There was talk of an egg hunt or perhaps an egg and spoon race, but Matron would not let us join in. "It isn't dignified!" she had espoused with her snoot in the air. In the end, there is no one to put it on and so it will not be happening.

May 29, 1916

I believe I have underestimated war or perhaps overestimated my fortitude. We are still in camp and yet I find myself rather stricken with fear at what is to come, having gotten my initial acquaintance with the wounds suffered by our men. The life of a soldier is not safe simply because he is yet in training. Whoever thought it was a good idea to quarter large groups of untrained men together then give eager boys live grenades and loaded rifles was much worse than a fool. The hospital is full of the sick from living in close quarters and the injured from training exercises gone wrong. Beyond that, someone must address the rifles these men are made to use. Today alone we have had one man lose part of his face to a bullet from a jammed rifle and another burn the palms of both hands from his over-heated barrel. Disgraceful to send our men into battle with faulty weaponry!

I remember the first time I saw Henry, although it would take a second meeting for me to attach his face to the memory of the moment. Strangely, that ever-so-brief but manifest point in time passed me by as a half-attended thought only to solidify over the coming days and months into a singularly solid rise in the line of time—a fulcrum on which my life had tipped into another direction. My path turned on a seemingly inauspicious minute of which I did not realize the import until much later.

I had been assigned to the rehabilitation ward that week, a ward which housed the injured men who would not be going to war after all. The patients inhabiting the ward had been injured in training to such an extent as to make them "unfit" for soldiering. They were to be rehabilitated enough to be discharged and sent back home.

It was a somewhat busy shift as there had been a grenade accident in one of the trenches and the surgical ward had received more than its share of cases that day. In order to clear recovery beds for the new post-surgical patients, there were several heavier patients who had, in my opinion, been transferred from the surgical ward too early and still required quite a bit of care.

I was attending to one such man, unaware of Henry's presence—unaware of his existence. The man had lost the lower part of his left arm when the grenade had not been thrown far enough. He had been blown down by the blast and a large rock had landed on his arm, pinning it beneath the boulder and crushing it beyond saving. The surgeon had a difficult time closing the wound after the amputation given the mangled mush with which he was left to work. The patient's wound oozed persistently and his bandages were in constant need of changing. Every dressing change caused him nightmarish pain as the dry gauze, hardened with secretions and blood, stuck to the wound. Their removal pulled at the healing skin and tore at freshly exposed nerves. Much to his credit, the man seldom cried out, but one could hear him choking back the pain, hidden under a low moan.

I had thought to soak the dressing before removing it, hoping to loose it from the wound and lessen the irritation of the area as I took off the crusted bandages. I was rewrapping the stump with clean gauze when the man moaned. It was a low, somehow far-off sound that caught in my own throat as it was leaving his.

"I'm so sorry," I said. It was a reflex to apologize and I knew the words would not help the man. I continued anyway, likely for my own comfort more than for his. "I know this hurts."

The soldier grimaced and nodded in silent agony as he clutched his injured arm with his good hand, trying to wring the pain from it.

I stood and settled the man back onto his pillows, watching as his eyes squeezed shut less tightly and his jaw slack just a little. I wasn't satisfied. I took the bottle of morphia from the bedside stand and measured out several drams of the caustic potion. I perched on the edge of the cot and spooned the concoction into the man's mouth. I hated having to resort to it. To my mind, it was a miracle drug somehow sent by Satan. While the elixir freed a man from his pain, it also, at the very same moment, chained him to its powerful demands, exacting a heavy toll in exchange for the temporary relief it gave.

I breathed in a small measure of satisfaction when the man closed his eyes and let his full weight settle into his pillows. I set down the phial and took up a cloth from the basin beside his bed. I wrung it out and wiped the perspiration from his brow, watching as his brow relaxed and his breathing slowed.

I dropped the cloth back into the basin and studied the man for a moment or two—sometimes a patient's breathing slowed too much after the morphia took full effect. The man settled into a fragmented sleep, but his breathing remained even. I stood and drew in a slow breath—in sympathy perhaps. I pulled the man's blanket up over his good arm and shoulder, careful not to cover the injured arm lest the weight of the blanket grate on the nerves.

I turned, the vague idea of other tasks waiting making me move without conscious will, my body in motion but my mind still lost in the man's pain. It spun out wonderings of how the man's life had been so radically changed within one very short hour and thoughts of how one never saw those portentous and life altering moments until they were upon one and how, even in the midst of the moment, the significance of the events would not be truly felt until much later and how it was all so very much beyond anyone's control.

With that gut-paralyzing notion, I realized that, for the seconds or minutes in which my thoughts had scurried about unchecked, harrying one another, my eyes had—of their own accord it seemed—fallen in with those of a soldier seated nearby. And I understood suddenly that, for those splintered moments I had, in fact, been staring into the soldier's brilliantly cerulean eyes, drifting on the ocean contained therein—and I didn't care. I stood as I was, wrapped in his gaze, unwilling to break off the connection that was the only thing grounding me to reality amidst the barrage of surreal understandings. Ever so slowly, my reality came back into focus, guided by the soldier's clear-sky eyes.

A Sister nearby barked out a sharp command: "Ryzak!". The soldier and I both straightened and the moment was shattered like a china cup dropping to a barn floor. We turned away from one another and back to our own stories.

As I said, one seldom recognizes those most peculiarly significant moments while they are in them.

May 12, 1916

War Diary

Private Henry Ryzak

May 12, 1916–June 4, 1916

Volume 2

Diary Text: 16 Pages

[May 12, 1916]

In mid-May we entrained for Halifax to begin our journey to Britain. There we were incorporated into the British forces and given more training before entering the fighting in France.

[May 20th, 1916]

Will and I, along with the others in our unit, boarded the *SS Empress of Britain* as members of the Winnipeg Grenadiers, 78th Battalion, 4th Canadian Division. The voyage overseas was surreal for a couple of prairie boys like us. The endless ocean we could manage—what was that compared to endless fields and boundless prairie sky? It was the tight confines of life on board a boat that made us feel like cattle in a chute. Men, jammed together, practically on top of one another night and day, was simply too much. The jostling was ceaseless and the rocking of the boat endless, constantly propelling us into one another. Within the confines of our billets, the air hung close with the dank smells of vomit and unwashed bodies. One was never alone. Not for one moment.

Even the smallest noise echoed in the bunk room, ricocheting off the metal walls and rising up over the roar of the ocean that pressed in on us just on the other side of the ship's walls. There was no quiet—not the kind Will and I were accustomed to, having been raised in the middle of the still, hushed prairies with only the whisper of the breeze in the wheat.

With so many people and so much noise pressing in on me, it felt as though not even my own thoughts were private.

Will and I spent as much time above-board as we could manage, including during the long nights of fitful sleep the others endured. At my suggestion, Will and I volunteered for extra night watch duties and sought our rest during the days when most of the men were topside, giving us a more peaceful sleep for the most part. This system worked in our favour in other ways as well. We had full access to any leftover rations throughout the night. Also, the cooks rose early to bake bread and prepare breakfast. Will and I made certain to check on the kitchen staff when we smelled the aroma of baking rolls. Often the cooks and bakers would have some for us to sample. Will and I would wander off to find a place where we could enjoy our pre-breakfast rations in as much peace as the ocean's roar would afford us.

[May 29, 1916]

It was just over a week's journey before making port in Southampton, England where we were finally able to disembark. I, for one, was grateful that part of the journey was over and I could feel solid, unmoving ground beneath my feet again.

We were told to collect our kit and gather on the dock. A few of the soldiers were ordered to return to the boat to scrub the floors below decks. I was grateful Will and I had done extra night patrols or we might have gotten that assignment. The deck was a horrid mess of urine and vomit by the time we made port and I had no desire to clean it up. The rest of us waited on the docks while the poor souls assigned to the chore went back on board. When they were finished the loathsome task, they trudged down the gangplank looking white and shaky. A few of them immediately emptied their stomachs when they reached the docks.[1]

Orders were called out to form ranks and we marched to a nearby train station. Here out unit boarded a train headed for Shorncliffe training camp. We arrived at camp and were directed to our barracks. We were again billeted in tents, although these had a stove set at the back of each one. The beds were simple boards set on blocks to keep them about ten inches up off the floor. Will and I claimed the bunks to one side of a tent. Ransley and Stewart stepped into the tent, looking a little uncertain and set their kit and rifles on the bunks opposite mine and Will's.

"Galt told us to bunk with you two," Ransley said. "He's bunking with the others in the next tent."

"Oh?" I asked.

"Said he wanted to keep an eye on Slater," Stewart answered. "Said you'd had your turn and he was looking to have his."

I chuckled to myself and nodded.

We found the mess tent and got our food. There were some tables lined up in a field next to the mess tent and we walked over to them to eat our lunch. I could see Galt scoping out the other soldiers at the tables as we approached with our mess tins of greasy meat and dry biscuits.

"Over here," Galt said to me, and led us to one of the tables where a few older soldiers sat.

Galt began talking to the others while we ate. I quickly understood his seating choice had been intentional—he had sat with men who looked as though they knew the lay of the land at this camp and he was plying them for information: how long had they been there; had they been given any leave during their training; how were their barracks; where was a good source of water; where could a man get a decent shave; was there anywhere to buy food nearby? The other soldiers answered his questions and volunteered additional details such as the location of the nearest drinking establishment. Galt seemed uninterested in this particular piece of information, turning instead to questions concerning the command and movement of units. I, however, made a mental note of the afore-mentioned instructions, tucking them away for later reference. We were told the command was loose and shoddy—no one knew who was in charge or what their orders were exactly. Evidently, it was all quite chaotic. Galt nodded gravely at this last bit of news.

We returned to our tents following lunch and were told by a passing guard to present to the hospital tent for inoculations. We told him we did not know where the hospital was, and he pointed in the direction from which we had just come.

I took a deep breath, thinking this whole affair really might have been better organized, and headed off in the indicated direction with the others following me. After asking for directions a second time, we found the hospital building. Staff there seemed surprised at our arrival and we had to explain our orders. These instructions were generally met with a frown and some exclamation regarding inconvenience. Eventually the Nursing Sister in charge that afternoon took us onto one of the wards and had us wait along one end of the room. She gathered her equipment and sat us down one at a time to give each of us a needle.

I looked around the ward while I waited for the Sister to call me. Men lay in cots lined up on either side of the long narrow room with another row down the centre. They had various assortments of bandages about their arms, heads, and legs. One or two of the men were missing a limb.

A man nearby groaned and I looked over to see a nurse wrapping the stump of his arm in a strip of bandage.

"I'm so sorry," she said quietly. "I know this hurts."

The soldier simply clenched his jaw and nodded.

The Nurse finished dressing the stump and eased the man back onto his pillow. She reached for a small bottle sitting on the bedside table and poured a spoonful of medicine from it, holding the spoon out for the soldier to take. He took it and lay back, closing his eyes, seeming almost to melt into the pillow as his body went limp. The Sister set aside the spoon. She reached into a near-by basin and wrung out a cloth. Gently and slowly, she wiped the man's brow several times. She dropped the cloth back into the basin and sat on the edge of the soldier's cot, simply watching him, her brow creased. She stood, let out a slow, deep breath, then pulled the man's thin blanket up over his shoulders. She turned to leave and, in that moment, our eyes met.

I suddenly, and rather definitively, found myself trapped in her smoky-glass eyes, staring helplessly as if watching a faltering candle trying to fight back the surrounding darkness even as its light ebbed. The candle's light seemingly guttered in the wake of a malicious breeze. It threatened to go out entirely, but managed to rekindle itself, the woman's eyes lightening to a transparent chestnut as she straightened and drew back her shoulders. Throughout all of this, she regarded me silently with unseeing eyes.

"Private Ryzak!"

I jumped guiltily, although I had no idea why.

The Sister in charge glared at me as she pointed to the chair in front of her. I moved to the chair, sat directly, and rolled up my shirt sleeve. I looked back to where the other Nurse had been, but she was nowhere to be seen—a dream lost to the morning's light.

I jerked my chin toward the man I had been watching. "What happened to him, Sister?" I asked the Nurse as she drew a solution from a phial and into a glass syringe. "We aren't anywhere near the fighting. How did he get injured?"

The nurse straightened beside me, needle held aloft. She considered me with a stern countenance. "That's Lieutenant to you—all nurses have the rank of Lieutenant and outrank you. Remember that!"

That caught me off-guard, but I nodded quickly and added, "Yes, Ma'am."

"And as for what's happened to him…" she glanced back over her shoulder at the man in the cot, "that's his story to tell, not mine," she said firmly. "But I will say this: the Germans at the front aren't the only thing that will kill you in this war. Keep your guns clean and firing aright."

I looked up at her. She nodded twice, bent over, stabbed me in the arm with the needle, then sent me on my way.

It was then that I realized my thinking was faulty. I had assumed that, being well away from the front lines, Will and I were safe for the time being. Evidently, I was much mistaken, considering the number of the soldiers presently occupying beds in the infirmary of the training camp—even mere training for the war was hazardous!

How on earth am I going to keep Will safe through all of this?

The thought of the insurmountable odds facing me on my self-appointed mission, and the mere possibility of failure with all of its implications made me want to get a drink—just to calm the jittering in my stomach. I couldn't fail—I simply couldn't. How would I ever face Father again if I were to fail? I walked back to the barracks, running through those thoughts and others like it, and wondering how on earth I could possibly succeed. I came up with no solution to my problem and by the time we reached our tents, I was quite agitated and felt a few drinks would go down rather nicely—just to slow my racing thoughts.

I did not happen to wind up at the canteen—at least not just at that moment.

A runner was waiting for us when we returned to our tents.

"Your unit has been granted six days' leave," the soldier announced.

"We just got here," Galt objected. "How can we be given leave already?"

"They're waiting for more platoons to arrive so they can form enough companies for a battalion. Command says you're to have your leave while they're waiting."

We all exchanged glances.

"Well, then, I'm off to Oxford," Ransley announced enthusiastically, a broad smile capturing his face. He headed for his tent.

"Good idea!" Will said, elbowing me in the side.

I turned a questioning look on him, frowning.

"Let's go to London!" Will suggested. "We likely won't get another chance to see the sights."

"I suppose…" I hedged.

"Great—get your gear," Will directed. He hurried into our tent.

I turned to Galt, not quite certain what to make of this turn of events.

"Fool army!" Galt replied, shaking his head. "One hand doesn't ever know what the other hand is doing. Just take it as it comes, son. That's really all you can do." He clapped me on the shoulder and started off for his tent.

"Where are you heading?" I called after him.

"Got family in Brighton that I haven't seen in a dog's age. Should be nice down by the beach just now. I'll have me a visit home."

I nodded then turned to look at the others.

"I come with you," Lundgren said. It wasn't a question.

"Me, too," added Stewart.

I shrugged. "Why not?"

They nodded and hurried to their tents.

"You louts do as you please," Slater said. "I hear there's plenty of hospitality nearby. Shouldn't have to go far to find what I need." He walked away.

That left me looking at the Kid.

"You coming with us?" I asked.

The Kid considered me a moment. "Guess so," he replied uncertainly. "Least ways as far as it suits me. If I don't like where we're goin', I can get back on my own." He left to go get his things.

Happy to have you join us.

I shook my head and went to gather what I would be taking with me.

An hour later I found myself on the back of a wagon, bumping along a rough road in a generally north-westerly direction, jostling with the others as we made our way to London. We reached the city and found a couple of rooms at the local YMCA. We got some advice from the people there and toured around London over the next few days, taking in the famous bridge, a couple of the cathedrals, and seeing Big Ben. Will purchased post cards and sent some home to our parents—I believe he snuck in one to Alice too—thinking to reassure folks back home that we were doing well. Lundgren said little, simply taking in the sights and grinning the entire time. The Kid must have liked what he saw as he remained with our unit for the entirety of the trip.

There was a social and dance put on by the Y on our last night in town. Stewart and I attended reluctantly at the insistence of the others. The others talked to the girls there and did some dancing. Stewart and I watched from our table, sampling the local brew.

The Kid seemed to enjoy the attention he received from several of the girls. He was a good dancer and seemed charming enough when he smiled. I wondered at their interest in him given his young age, but then, there were likely few men around these days and perhaps the women could not be choosey.

Will tried to get me to dance with one of the girls, but I declined. I looked at the girl briefly, and couldn't help comparing her insubstantial blue eyes to those of the nurse I had seen at the hospital. I couldn't shake the image of the faltering light illuminating the unending depths of the Sister's eyes making a vexing mystery of what lay hidden beyond the light. After that, the blue-eyed girl seemed somehow lessened—an opaque form seen through a dusty window. I didn't think I could tolerate her conversation, not even for the brief duration of a dance. I declined and the girl left with a slightly petulant tilt to her mouth.

[June 4, 1916]

We were to return to camp the next day. Our problems began, however, when we woke up rather late in the day, having stayed at the social much too long into the night and having had several more drinks than we ought. Stewart gave my shoulder a rough shove just after noon, crying, "Henry!

Henry! Wake up. We have to get back to camp by 1700 hours!"

I peered up at him through bleary eyes, even the dim light of our room was sharp enough to stab through my head. "So what's the problem?" I muttered, trying to roll away from him and get back to sleep. I wasn't exactly hung over, but my entire body felt a lot heavier than it usually did.

Stewart pulled my shoulder. "It's already 12:30 and everyone is still asleep!"

That woke me up in double time. It had taken us most of a day just to get there on the trudging cart and then on foot through town. We would never make it back by 17:00 the same way we'd come.

"Wake the others," I said, sitting up, suddenly very much awake. "Have them collect their things and meet me downstairs."

I had no idea what I was planning to do to get us back to camp. I briefly wondered why this was my problem to solve, but certainly, it had to be solved. My mother had always told me, "If you see a job that needs doing—it's yours to do. If you don't, you're making someone else do your work." I supposed that applied here—besides, I couldn't let Will get in trouble. I was fairly certain Father would deem that my fault for being a bad influence if he were to find out.

I collected my things and went downstairs. I explained our difficulty to the man at the desk. He suggested inquiring at the local hospital. The ambulances from the camps were often in town picking up supplies and perhaps, he'd said, we might find one heading back this afternoon. He gave me directions and, after gathering the others, we hurried over to the hospital.

We located a couple of ambulances parked beside the hospital. Sure enough, one of them was heading back to camp with their supplies after they were done loading the van. The driver indicated he was not supposed to transport passengers, but a few of my gambling dollars convinced him this would be a good time to make an exception to that rule. The driver took the money and told us to come back in a few hours.

We spent the time finding some food then returned to the hospital.

"I'll have to let you out just before camp," the driver cautioned as he let the others into the back of the ambulance. "Can't have you be seen getting out of the vehicle."

"That's fine," I agreed.

"You won't all fit back here," the driver said, closing up the back of the ambulance before I could get in. "You'll have to ride up front with me."

I went around to the front, climbed onto the seat, and we drove off through town.

Just before the buildings became smaller and the streets turned to roads, I saw a slight figure standing on the sidewalk. The woman was looking around anxiously and I wondered at her concern. She glanced up and down the street before turning a hopeful gaze on our vehicle. Disappointment quickly settled on her features when she saw the ambulance. She frowned at the van as we passed. I only just had time to make out her features through the open door of the ambulance.

"Stop!" I called out to the driver.

He immediately stepped on the brakes. I worried briefly about the others in the back of the ambulance when I heard a thud, a few sharp cries and one expletive, but I didn't have time to deal with that. I was already out of my seat before we had completely stopped.

"Wait here," I called back to the driver as I hopped out of the ambulance and onto the road. The driver frowned at me. "I'll only be a minute."

"Make it a short minute!" he shouted after me. "I have a delivery to make!" I heard him slide back the small window between the driver's seat and the box of the ambulance, and heard Lundgren bellowing questions.

I walked back several paces to where the woman stood on the curb, still watching up the street as though she would demand it to produce what she needed.

She turned at the sound of my approach, a wary look in her shadowed-forest eyes.

"Hello," I said, stopping a couple of paces away, lest I frighten her. "I'm Private Ryzak." I saw her features relax, but only slightly. She continued to watch me like a cat watching a fox. "I recognize you from the hospital," I added for good measure. It was true—she was the nurse I had seen helping the man with the dressing—the girl with the smoky brown eyes.

The woman took a deep breath and set her shoulders back.

"Yes, I'm a Nursing Sister there," she replied. "Do I know you?"

"No," I replied with a shake of my head. "I simply saw you once, that's all. You seem troubled. Can I help you?"

The woman's head tilted and her brow creased. "What makes you ask such a question?" she asked in a *just-what-are-you-doing?* tone.

I choked back a laugh. It was only too obvious. "You were watching the street and pacing. You appeared distressed."

"I was to meet my group, but they haven't arrived," she said with a frown.

"Might I be of assistance?" I asked again.

She hesitated, looking between me and the ambulance behind me. She looked up the street again before turning back to me. "I am not certain…I'm waiting for my ride back to the hospital—I am on duty tonight. However, my party has not come to collect me and it is getting late. I will be in a great deal of trouble if I fail to show for my shift. Regardless, I'm not certain you can help me with any of this—I have no escort."

"Happily, you are wrong," I said. She looked at me as though I had just said her hat was ugly. I hurried to explain.

"I believe I can help. My group is heading back to camp. We have convinced the ambulance driver to give us a lift as he is bringing supplies back to the hospital there. You can come along with us if you'd like. The driver will be with us and there you have your escort."

She looked back at the ambulance then turned to me, nodding quickly. "It is as needs must. I will accept your offer, thank you."

I smiled and gestured to the ambulance. I helped her into the seat I had just vacated and stood on the side step of the vehicle, holding on to the windscreen support to keep from flying off as we drove. The driver took off with a solid lurch, casting me a frown in the process. I tightened my grip and barely managed to keep from falling off the trundling vehicle.

The woman studied me as we drove, then examined the seat on which she sat.

"Wait," she called up to me, "this is a rather long drive. You can't simply give me your seat and stand the entire way!"

"And yet I did—and I can." I couldn't help grinning just a little as she continued to frown up at me, consternation etching a line in her brow.

"No, please, I cannot allow you to do that," she pleaded. She slid up tight against the driver, patting the seat beside her. "I do not take up much space," she said matter-of-factly. It was true—she didn't. "There's plenty of room for you to sit down."

I weighed my options: impress her by standing all the way back to camp or sit cozily beside her for the duration of the ride. It was a difficult choice but her insistent "Please, do sit down" tipped me in favour of sitting.

It was warm enough, but with the passing wind through the open cab of the ambulance, I could feel her arms were cold against my own and felt a shiver run through her. The woman wore only a light summer dress with short sleeves— flattering, certainly, but not meant for warmth. I immediately pulled my jacket from my pack and held it out to her.

She hesitated briefly but took the proffered jacket and slipped it on, pulling it around her in the front. We were sitting so close together that I felt her take a deep breath. She turned to me.

"Thank you for your help," she said, looking at me like she was trying to make out a set of instructions. "Even though it *is* against rules." One corner of her mouth turned down.

"You mean the ambulance ride?"

"Well, yes, that too, but as an officer, I'm not supposed to fraternize with enlisted men."

"Really?"

She nodded. "Truly," she insisted.

"Huh. Terrible rule if you ask me. Well, no one will know—the driver is dropping our lot off outside of camp. We'll walk in the rest of the way so he doesn't get into trouble, and you can go along with the driver straight to the hospital."

I felt her take another breath. "Yes, I suppose that should work," she replied. She said it like she had lost an argument.

"We haven't been properly introduced," I said, studying her profile. "I'm Henry Ryzak," I told her, extending a hand to her. She stiffened and looked down at my hand, but didn't shake it. She looked back up at me instead.

"I'm not supposed to tell you my name," she said, turning to look at the road ahead as she pulled my jacket about her. I dropped my hand onto my knee.

"We have a ways to camp," I said. "You might as well break as many rules as you care to in that time."

She turned to look at me as though I had just suggested she lift a mule. She turned away, blinked several times, then looked back at me. "I'm Lieutenant Grieves, Nursing Sister," she said finally.

"Nice to meet you, Lieutenant Grieves," I replied, offering her my hand again. She looked at it then took it briefly. Her hand shake was firmer than I would have expected given her small size and, for some reason, that thought made me smile. "I'd press you for your first name, but I'm fairly certain that is most definitely beyond your limits of propriety."

"It certainly is," she replied coolly, refusing to meet my gaze.

I smiled and turned my attention to our surroundings. I glanced at her on occasion, taking in her long, wavy hair and her deep chestnut eyes. Every once in a while the sunlight would find a sable coil of her hair, bringing to life a burst of coppery sparks. Other times, a ray of sun would catch her eyes at just the right angle, illuminating them briefly and turning them a burnt umber but never quite illuminating the secrets that lay just beyond the light. I was fascinated. She squirmed under my scrutiny, but still, I watched.

Just before we reached camp, the ambulance driver pulled over and let me and the others off. Lieutenant Grieves remained in the front seat. I stood, watching as the ambulance set off with her, grinning to myself. They had just pulled forward when, suddenly, the ambulance jerked to a halt. The Lieutenant's face appeared around the side of the vehicle. She held my jacket out the side of the ambulance and waved it at me.

"Private! You forgot your jacket!"

I walked up to take my jacket and I looked her full on. "Oh, I hadn't *forgotten* it," I replied. "I fully intended to collect it later."

She drew in a sharp breath and I watched in delight as a warm pink infused her cheeks. She blinked up at me several times just before she ducked back into the ambulance, pressing herself into the seat and staring straight ahead.

I stepped aside and watched the ambulance drive away, somewhat disappointed I no longer had an excuse to seek her out later, but truly savouring her reaction. I pulled on the jacket and stopped in my tracks as I was surrounded by the smell of roses. I pulled in a great breath, reveling in the scent. I was still thinking about the charming picture of her blush when the others caught up to me. There were questioning looks cast my way.

I sobered. "Hurry up, you lot," I commanded. "I don't intend to miss rations." I set off at a brisk pace and the others fell in behind me.

June 5, 1916

June 5, 1916

Well, I've certainly learned my lesson! I shall never again go to town with Latham and Hutchinson! They left me stranded, without a thought to my need to return to the hospital. If it weren't for that Private whom I saw the other day, I should never have returned in time for my shift. What would the Matron have done to me had I absented myself from my shift without notice?! I shudder to think on it.

I was ever so grateful for the Private's assistance. He likely saved me from two weeks of scrubbing floors like a char-woman and a good tongue-lashing to boot! He was frightfully cheeky though, flirting terribly. I suspect he often gets away with that sort of behaviour given those remarkable blue eyes and that handsome face of his, but what is that to me? I am engaged after all. Besides, the faint redness to his eyes made me suspicious that he had been drinking—John's eyes are like that after a night on the town. Never, not ever, will I entertain the attentions of a man who drinks! I can still recall the smell of liquor on John as he menaced me in the barn. The thought of it makes me cringe. And yet, the Private was good about helping me, I will credit him with that much honour at least.

Hutchinson, Latham, and I had been granted a half-day off the previous day for shift turn-around before we took on the night shift for a week. As was their wont, Hutchinson and Lathan had plans to drive to town for tea at the invitation of two officers from camp. The officers were to pick them up at noon and drive them to town in the officers' motor car. I asked them if they might have time to purchase thread for me so that I could continue working on some lace I was making. I thought it would make my night shifts so much more tolerable if I had something to do during the long, still hours of early mornings.

"Oh, simply come with us and you can pick your colours yourself!" Hutchinson said with a laugh, and Latham quickly added, "Oh, yes! Teddy and Bernard will not mind at all—they are such good sports about everything!"

I ought to have taken the lack of formality as a warning, but I so wanted to work on my lace to ease my nights. After a small bit more cajoling, I agreed to ride with them to town.

Once in town, they dropped me off at the dry goods store while they went off to tea. The plan was to meet out front of the dry goods store at three o'clock that afternoon and return to camp with them. That would allow a couple hours' rest before starting our shift.

I spent a marvelous afternoon, picking out several lovely colours of thread and splurged on a new hook simply for the elegance of its design—a decadent thing to do to be certain. I also purchased a tin of biscuits to keep in my room and share with Barnette when in need of a bit of tea. I walked about the town and found a tea house where I lunched on eggs, bacon, biscuits, and tea. It was only two o'clock when I had finished. The waitress was kind enough to direct me to a store where I found socks and a nightgown.

I was waiting in front of the dry goods store promptly at three o'clock, but there was no sign of my ride anywhere. Nor was there any sign of the party at three-twenty, nor at three-thirty, nor even at three-fifty. By Four o'clock I was becoming quite anxious to be back, knowing my night shift would begin at seven that evening. The day was growing tiring and I had no idea how I would make it through the night's work without rest!

I paced and watched the street but there was frustratingly little movement. I heard a vehicle and looked up, fervently praying it was the Officers' car, but I quickly realized it was only an ambulance and it passed by. I went back to my pacing, wondering what on earth I would do and trying to devise a plan to get myself back to camp.

In my anxious state, I did not hear the ambulance stop a short way down the road, nor was I aware of the man approaching until he was very nearly upon me. The sound of booted feet walking quickly toward me broke through my fretful thoughts and I turned to see a tall, solid soldier hurrying toward me up the walkway.

The man stopped a short distance away—a gesture comforting to me in my agitated state—like having my own personal moat.

"Hello," the man said, taking off his hat and holding it in both hands as he spoke. "I'm Private Ryzak. I recognize you from the hospital."

I was fully aware of who the man was and how we were acquainted for I could never have forgotten the eyes in which I had become thoroughly lost. I wasn't quite certain which was more unnerving at that moment: my tardiness or the presence of Private Ryzak with his sapphire blue eyes fixed squarely upon me. I straightened my shoulders and took a steadying breath.

"Yes," I replied, pretending I didn't remember him. "I'm a Nursing Sister there. Do I know you?" I asked, drawing the man's attention to our glaring lack of formal introduction—no one from my circle had vouched for this man nor given him permission to address me.

"No," Ryzak began, most unapologetic for his impertinence. "I simply saw you once, that's all." I might have become somewhat piqued at his audacity, but I hadn't the time to become truly offended as he continued with: "You seem troubled. Can I help you?"

It felt as though the ground beneath my feet had tilted of a sudden. I didn't know to which I should respond, so I replied with a question instead.

"What makes you ask such a question?"

Ryzak gestured up the street with his hat. "You were watching the street and pacing. You appeared troubled."

"I was to meet my group, but they have not arrived," I said simply.

"Might I be of assistance?" Ryzak asked.

I glanced at the ambulance then scanned the street—still no sign of my ride.

"I am not certain…" I hedged, wondering now if the man might be willing to give me a lift back to the hospital—he seemed headed in that direction. It would be rather untoward, however, accepting a ride from a man I did not know. "I'm waiting for my ride back to the hospital—I am on duty tonight. However, my party has not come to collect me and it is getting late. I will be in a great deal of trouble if I fail to show for my shift. Regardless, I'm not certain you can help me with any of this—I have no escort."

"Happily, you are wrong," Ryzak said, his blue eyes shining.

Had he just told me I was *wrong*? The cheek! I most definitely was not *wrong*.

"I believe I can help," he clarified. "My group is heading back to camp. We have convinced the ambulance driver to give us a lift as he is bringing supplies back to the hospital there. You can come along with us if you'd like. The driver will be with us and there you have your escort."

It was quite a dilemma, accepting a ride with men whom I did not know, but then, I could not fail to show for my night shift. After a moment of considering my options, the hard place seemed less problematic than the rock.

"It is as needs must. I will accept your offer, thank you."

Private Ryzak smiled the sort of smile one might see on a boy who has just been told he can keep the stray puppy he has dragged home. He swept his hat in the direction of the ambulance and waited for me to precede him. He offered me his hand at the open door of the vehicle, holding me steady as I hoisted my skirts while navigating the very small step into the cab of the ambulance. Private Ryzak stepped onto the side of the ambulance and took hold of the windscreen as the driver set off. I waited for Ryzak to sit down, but he only remained perched outside of the door while we trundled along the bumpy road. I realized then he had likely given up his seat for me and a stab of guilt pricked at the pit of my stomach.

"Wait," I called against the noise of the wind in the open cab, "this is a rather long drive. You can't simply give me your seat and stand the entire way!"

"And yet I did—and I can," Ryzak replied, grinning like my father always did when he had told a very bad joke and was waiting for Mum and me to laugh. We always did laugh, but not always at the joke.

"No, please, I cannot allow you to do that." I slid closer to the driver, and gave the seat beside me a pat indicating for Ryzak to sit. "I do not take up much space," I commanded. "There's plenty of room for you to sit down."

Ryzak only studied me with a look not unlike the look I saw on my mother's face when she had to choose between two fine materials for her next dress.

"Please, do sit down," I insisted. I wasn't about to have him cause us delay by falling off the silly little step on which he was very precariously perched. I gave a sigh of relief when the man dropped onto the seat beside me.

It was only when I felt the compelling warmth emanating from Ryzak that I realized how cool the air was as it blew through the open cab. I shivered and my arms turned to gooseflesh. Before I understood what he was doing, Private Ryzak had pulled his jacket out from the haversack that sat between his feet and was holding the jacket out to me. There was no point in refusing the offer. I quickly settled the jacket around my shoulders, breathing in the calming warmth.

"Thank you for your help," I said, looking at Ryzak and trying to figure out how it was that he had twice known what it was I had needed. "Even though it *is* against rules," I chastised. It seems this man had me breaking all sorts of rules today.

"You mean the ambulance ride?"

"Well, yes, that too, but as an officer, I'm not supposed to fraternize with enlisted men."

"Really?"

"Truly," I said.

"Huh," he replied with a scoff. "Terrible rule if you ask me. Well, no one will know—the driver is dropping our lot off outside of camp. We'll walk in the rest of the way so he doesn't get into trouble and you can go along with the driver straight to the hospital."

"Yes, I suppose that should work," I said. It was a perfectly good way to avoid any difficulties, yet somehow it seemed unsatisfactory to have the others not accompany us all the way—it was their ride after all.

"We haven't been properly introduced," Ryzak said, watching me like a dog watching a stick that is about to be thrown. "I'm Henry Ryzak," he continued, offering me his hand.

Did he truly not understand the situation?

"I'm not supposed to tell you my name," I said, turning to study the road and making a show of pulling Ryzak's jacket closer about me to cover my hands. Ryzak's hand fell to his knee and I again felt a prick of conscience. I stared straight ahead.

"We have a ways to camp," Ryzak went on and I could feel the full weight of his eyes on my face. "You might as well break as many rules as you care to in that time."

The nerve of the man! What sort of person would simply go around breaking whatever rules might be inconvenient?!

I made the mistake of looking full into his eyes and saw a green hue in them where a ray of sun caught them at an angle. I quickly turned away. It was the expression in his blue-green eyes that undid my resolve. In that briefest of contacts, all I could see in my mind was Ryzak's dark blue eyes as he hoisted his rifle and stepped up over the edge of the trench, off to battle. I wondered then, if breaking the rules might not sometimes be the proper thing to do when one is at war. After all, the man merely wanted to know my name. In any other time, that would be the courteous thing to offer, having accepted his help.

"I'm Lieutenant Grieves, Nursing Sister," I said, refusing to become trapped in the snare of his sky-blue eyes again.

"Nice to meet you, Lieutenant Grieves," Ryzak answered, once again extending his hand to me. This time I pulled my hand out from under his jacket and shook his hand briefly, feeling the warmth and roughness of it. The way his large hand engulfed mine left me with an odd sensation in my chest, as though I had felt the tang of it before or quite possibly was to feel again—which I could not have said. I took a breath and pulled my hand back under the jacket.

"I'd press you for your first name," Ryzak said, "but I'm fairly certain that is most definitely beyond your limits of propriety."

"It certainly is," I replied, keeping my eyes front.

We rode in silence for a time, but I could feel Ryzak glance at me frequently. I squeezed down into his jacket as far as I was able and stared out the windscreen. The camp soon came into view and the driver pulled to the side of the road to let the men out.

We had no sooner set off again than I realized I was still scrunched tightly under the Private's jacket.

"Stop!" I said to the driver. He frowned at me, but had no choice but to stop the ambulance—I was a Lieutenant after all. I leaned out the side of the open door, waving the jacket.

"Private! You forgot your jacket!" I called.

Private Ryzak walked toward me at an infuriatingly leisurely pace and took his jacket. He looked at me, locking eyes.

"Oh, I hadn't *forgotten* it," he said with a crooked grin. "I fully intended to fetch it later."

Understanding dropped on me like a bomb and I sucked in a breath at the impudence of his plan. I felt the heat rise in my cheeks and quickly pressed myself back into the seat of the ambulance, breaking free of his cerulean eyes. I felt my cheeks heat full to overflowing and devoutly hoped he could not see it. I believe he must have, however, because I heard his low throaty chuckle as we pulled away.

June 16, 1916

War Diary

Private Henry Ryzak

June 16, 1916-August 11, 1916

Volume 2

Diary Text: 28 Pages

[June 16-August 11, 1916]

Our adventure behind us, we returned to camp with its training, and work details. The drills were similar to those at our previous camp, but we were under British command at Shorncliffe. While our unit remained under Staff Sergeant MacDonald in England, our Lieutenant from Sewell camp had remained behind to train new recruits rather than accompanying us to England. Instead, we had been placed under Lieutenant Hastings upon our arrival at Shorncliffe camp. He was a small, scholarly looking specimen—even smaller than Ransley. The Lieutenant was the type to make up for his deficit of height and strength by wielding his power of rank and bullying anyone who served under him. His insecurities and meanness made for a volatile combination.

During one of our field training exercises, the Lieutenant decided we should build our strength by hauling wagon loads of munitions up a hill then bring them back down again. Not an easy task and one made even more difficult by the still-wet grass that day, the area having received some rain over night. Sergeant MacDonald voiced his objections to the exercise, citing safety concerns surrounding wagons, wet slopes, and ammunition, but the Sergeant's objections only served to harden Hastings' resolve.

"It's those very conditions they'll be facing at the front, man! And they shall have to move those very munitions too. Of course they need to be capable!"

As we walked over to the field, I spoke quietly to Lundgren.

"Lundgren," I said as I came up beside the giant of a man. "Do me a favour? Pair up with the Kid will you? I don't think he'll do well on this."

"*Ja*," Lundgren said simply. "You are right. It is good you look out for him."

"Uh, uh," I replied with a firm shake of my head. "I'm not looking out for him. I just don't want the entire unit paying for his mistakes. Best he doesn't make any."

Lundgren considered me a moment, grunted slightly, and said. "All right. As you say."

When we got to the hill, Lundgren immediately pulled the Kid over to a wagon—literally, pulled him, no conversation or discussion involved. They filled the wagon with munitions then Lundgren took the lead and hauled the wagon up the hill while the Kid pushed as best he could. It would be obvious to anyone watching who was doing the heavy lifting in that operation—I just hoped Hastings wouldn't bother making an inspection at the wrong time.

I told Will to help Stewart while I teamed up with Ransley. Galt and Slater made up the last team, Galt keeping Slater on task by challenging him to a friendly competition to see who could pull the wagon the farthest. I was fairly certain Galt lost that challenge intentionally, allowing Slater to pull the wagon most of the way and saving himself the effort.

We were making out all right until the Kid slipped on the wet grass. Lundgren didn't even notice. He simply continued up the hill with the wagon in tow, oblivious to the fact that he had lost the Kid. After that, there was no hiding the fact that the Kid was contributing nothing to the effort of their team. As a mean streak of fortune would have it, Hastings chose that very moment to make an appearance, riding over on his horse to check on us.

Hastings pulled the Kid aside and tore a strip off him, berating him for his ineffectual efforts and calling him names to shame him in front of everyone. He demanded the boy pull the wagon up on his own the next trip. Lundgren brought the wagon down the hill reluctantly. He and the Kid loaded it up, but I could see that Lundgren was trying to load only the lighter ammo boxes. When the wagon was full, the Kid cast Hastings a sharp look then took the handle. He struggled up the hill a short distance, straining under a load that was likely many times the weight of the Kid himself. Then, inevitably, the Kid slipped under the heavier weight of the wagon. The wagon wrenched from his grip and barreled down the hillside, gathering speed as it rolled, unchecked, past a dumbfounded Hastings and straight into the remaining stack of munition boxes.

"Cover!!" Galt yelled. I raced over to Will, tackling him and taking him down with me. Everyone else dropped to the ground, covering their heads with their hands or ducked behind shelter if any was nearby. I only just saw Hastings racing away on his horse before there was a tremendous thundering and a blinding flash. Dirt, fragments of boxes and exploding shells rose up high in the air then rained down on the area at the bottom of the hill. Fortunately, most of us were higher up on the hillside, but the drivers of the truck lay on the ground near the toppled munitions truck, neither of them moving.

We all raced down the hill, reaching the drivers just as they began to stir. They had seen what was about to happen and had, fortunately, taken cover behind the truck. However, the blast was sufficient to send the truck into the air and tumble it well over top of the men, leaving them exposed to the still-flying shrapnel. The truck now lay on its side a short distance away. Fortune, it would seem, had not been so mean as to allow the truck to land on the men. The men had received only a number of lacerations from the falling debris and shrapnel and lay stunned on the ground. We called over some medics who took them to the hospital for treatment.

I could see the Lieutenant and Sergeant MacDonald having words, but couldn't make out what they were saying over the ringing in my ears. I went over to where the Kid sat on the hillside, staring down at the destruction below. His lip trembling and his eyes red.

"You all right?" I asked, reaching out my hand to help him up.

He said nothing and didn't reach for my hand. He only glanced up at me then looked away, staring straight ahead and working hard not to cry.

We saw MacDonald coming toward us and the Kid stood up fast. MacDonald said nothing for a moment as he studied the boy and heaved a sigh. "Hastings is going over to check on those drivers then he wants to see you at the command tent. Says for you to go wait there."

The boy only nodded and trudged off.

The Kid didn't return to our tents. He wasn't at supper and missed out on rations. That worried me—I didn't trust the Kid not to mess up more nor did I trust Hastings, worried he would do something even more harebrained than he'd already done. It had been a stupid situation to begin with and I just couldn't see things getting any better from that point on.

At the mess tent, I asked the others if they knew what had happened to the Kid, but none of them had heard anything. That didn't sit well with me. We returned to our tents, but I couldn't sit there for long.

"I'm getting a drink," I said to Will.

"You sure that's a good idea?" he asked cautiously.

"I don't have an answer for that," I replied as I left the tent.

I went over to the bar on the main strip and had a few beers. It was horrid stuff—English swill—but it dulled the panic I was feeling whenever I thought of the Kid and what might be happening to him. I finished my fourth drink and headed outside, intent on seeing if the Kid was back in his tent.

I saw straight off that the Kid was certainly not to be found in his tent.

Hastings had the Kid dead centre on the main strip. The boy was straining against a rope attached to a wooden sledge, the sledge loaded with two barrels of water, each of which was nearly the size of the Kid himself. Hastings was standing at the side of the road, yelling at the boy to pull harder and regaling everyone with the story about the wagon.

To his credit, the Kid was trying with all his might to pull that sledge. It would jerk forward a few inches every now and then, but I could see he wouldn't be getting far any time soon.

Hastings began yelling at the Kid: useless; stray mongrel; never amount to anything; he should never have been allowed to enlist—all the things bullies yell at people smaller and weaker than themselves. The Kid just kept trying to pull that stupid sledge until he stopped suddenly and dropped to his knees.

Then Hastings got mad. He went over to his horse and took his horse whip out from under the saddle. I saw him walking intently over to the Kid. I froze for a what felt like a full minute, my mind refusing to acknowledge what Hastings was about to do.

Surely no one would be that cruel?!

And yet, Hastings was.

I saw Hastings raise the whip and watched as he brought it down hard on the boy's back several times. The boy tried to stand, but only managed to raise himself to one knee. Hastings struck him again, roaring at him to get up and pull.

Hastings raised the whip once again.

I tore down the street.

I don't know how I reached Hastings before the next strike of the whip, but I did.

I caught Hasting's arm just as the crop was coming down on the Kid again. I wrenched Hasting's wrist back over his head and pushed him hard. He staggered a couple of steps but regained his footing without falling. He rounded on me, whip held high. I heard it crack and only had time to put up my arm to fend off the strike. I felt the whip cut into my forearm, it's short lash wrapping around my arm and biting into it, tearing flesh and refusing to let go. It stung like the blazes and I saw the blood dripping off my elbow.

I jerked my arm back and the attached whip came forward, pulling a surprised Hastings toward me. I launched my opposite shoulder into his gut and drove him back until he fell to the ground. I stepped to one side, yanking the clinging whip from my arm. I had the whip raised and would not have hesitated to follow through on the strike, but my wrist was suddenly caught in a vise and would not move.

I looked up and saw Lundgren beside me, my arm held fast in his unyielding grip.

"You will be shot if you do this," he said simply.

I stared at him for several moments. I wasn't deciding, exactly, more like trying to calm the white-hot rage that burned in my gut—a rage that, far from spent, still wanted more than anything to whip Hastings as he had whipped the Kid. After several good breaths, my head cleared and I could think again. I nodded and Lundgren let go of my arm, taking a step back. I turned, handing him the whip and hurried over to where the Kid knelt in the dirt on his hands and knees. Lundgren folded his arms, Hastings' whip firmly in his hand. He towered over Hastings with the look of a cat waiting for one final move of a mouse. Hastings got up slowly, keeping a cautious eye on Lundgren.

I knelt down beside the Kid and helped him up. The back of his shirt was torn and blood seeped through the edges of the ripped cloth, already starting to crust along the edges. The boy hadn't the strength to stand, so I hefted him to his feet and pulled his arm around my shoulders. I started walking toward the hospital. Behind us, Hastings shouted for the guards.

The guards stopped us in our tracks. The Kid and I were marched to the Captain's tent, Hastings walking a judicious length behind us. Lundgren followed at a distance, still carrying Hastings' whip.

Hastings entered Captain Drewe's tent and emerged several moments later, calling us inside along with the guards. Lundgren followed us in, uninvited—and unhindered. It seemed none of the guards wanted to take on the large man carrying the whip.

Captain Drewe glanced up from his seat behind his desk and paused, looking between me and the Kid who was sagging off my shoulders. Drewe's stern frown turned into a puzzled one, and he looked between the two of us as though he were in the midst of a carnival hustle and trying to sort which cup hid the marble. The Kid had caught his breath and pushed away from me, swaying slightly as he tried to stand on his own. The Captain looked at the blood dripping from my wrist and at the boy's pale face as the Kid took a sidestep in an attempt to keep his balance. Drewe turned a hard look on Hastings.

"What's going on here?" the Captain asked roughly.

"As I explained," Hastings began, "I was having the boy do some extra training to discipline him for the wagon incident this afternoon when Private Ryzak attacked me. I'm charging him with assaulting an officer."

"Is this true, Ryzak?" the Captain asked.

"Yes, Sir, I suppose it is," I replied.

"I'm surprised, Ryzak. I was told you had your issues, but were generally all right as a soldier. Why did you attack the Lieutenant?"

"He was whipping the boy in the middle of the strip for something that wasn't the Kid's fault," I answered. I put a hand on the Kid's shoulder and turned him around for the Captain to see the bloody, torn shirt and the cuts underneath. Lundgren stepped forward, holding out Hastings' whip in his clenched fist as proof. Lundgren handed the whip to the Captain then turned to me and pulled my cut arm up for more evidence. I pulled my arm down again, but not before the Captain had considered it with a frown.

The Captain sobered and turned a hard-set expression on Hastings.

"I want to talk to these men alone," the Captain ordered, coming around his desk and standing in front of Hastings, hands on hips.

Hastings hesitated, but the guards moved to stand on either side of the Captain and ushered Hastings out of the tent.

"Now," the Captain said, turning back to the Kid and me, "tell me exactly what happened."

I told him the whole story—how we all warned Hastings the hill training exercise was foolhardy and how the results were due to Hastings ill-advised orders all around. I told him of the sledge and the whip. I told him how I had made it stop. The Kid stood silent throughout the story, watching me through narrowed eyes.

"Is this true?" the Captain asked, turning a *don't-you-dare-lie-to-me* look on the Kid.

The Kid's gaze darted to the Captain. "Every word of it, Sir," he said solemnly.

"And you?" the Captain asked, turning a hard look on Lundgren.

"*Ja*, just what he says."

"I see," the Captain replied. He leaned back on his desk, crossing his arms and staring down at the wooden floor of the tent. "I don't want to court martial you for assaulting an officer," Drewe said, "but I can't just let this go either—you can't go around fighting with officers or everyone would think they could do the same, just cause or no." He studied the ground for a moment longer then moved around to the back of his desk and called the others back in.

"I'm charging these two with being Drunk and Disorderly and sentencing them to seven days hard labour and half rations on Fox Farm."[1]

"But, but, Captain, Sir," sputtered Hastings. "he assaulted an officer."

"You and I will discuss that in a moment," the Captain replied. "Soldier," Drewe called to one of the guards, "take these two to their temporary barracks and then see if you can get someone to come down from the hospital to dress their wounds."

"Yes, Sir," the soldier replied.

"You," Drewe said to the other soldier, "will stay on guard outside this tent and await Lieutenant Hastings."

"Yes, Sir," the other guard replied.

We exited the tent, leaving Hastings and Drewe inside.

The guard escorted the Kid and me to the area known as Fox Farm and Lundgren returned to his tent. Fox Farm was a row of tents on the far side of the camp where military prisoners were sent for disciplinary action, generally consisting of work details. The guard showed us to one of the tents where we each dropped down onto a cot. That is, I dropped onto my cot while the Kid lowered himself down very carefully.

"Wait here," the guard said. "I'll get someone from the hospital."

The guard returned a short while later.

"Get up you two!" the guard ordered. "Both of you come with me, I'm taking you to the hospital—they're too busy to send someone."

The Kid and I moaned in unison as we both heaved ourselves up off our cots. My head spun a few times when I stood up and I noticed the Kid moved forward with shaky steps, holding his stomach and breathing hard.

"You gonna make it, Kid?" I asked.

He only looked at me then turned away again, heading out of the tent. I shook my head and followed him.

Our slow, disjointed pace eventually got us to the hospital and down a corridor. The guard pointed to a bench. "Wait there," he said and walked away.

I sat down, holding my arm close. It was bloodied and the shirt sleeve was mostly torn away. It still pulsed with a nauseating rhythm that, coupled with the drinks I'd had, brought me near to vomiting. The Kid sat forward on the bench, leaning his elbows on his knees and being careful not to let his back come into contact with the wall behind us.

The guard appeared in front of me as if out of nowhere. "This way," he ordered, and led me into a treatment room. He gestured to the examination table and I slid up onto it. My head was starting to pound and I let it drop forward, closing my eyes and trying to still my spinning head as I sat, waiting.

I heard someone enter the room and looked up to see a Sister carrying in a tray. She had her back to me as she set the tray on a nearby table, opening the draping and preparing her instruments. Her blue dress was covered with a crisp, comfortingly white apron. Her hair was caught up in a twist and secured neatly under her nurses' cap. She turned to me.

"You?!" Lieutenant Grieves asked in a tone one might use when bitten by a snake. I didn't care for the implication of that. "*You* are the 'Drunk and Disorderly' I am to tend?" She looked at me as if I had offered her a bouquet of roses and instead handed her a handful of briar. I had seen that look many times before on the face of my mother. I closed my eyes and tried to control my rolling stomach.

A silence fell and I eventually looked up at Grieves' face. She took a deep breath, straightened her shoulders, and stepped forward, taking my lacerated arm in her hands. She glanced up at me briefly then turned and picked up scissors. She cut off the lower part of my tattered sleeve and looked over the wound. She frowned and got a basin of warm water from the sink across the room. Returning to my side, she set the basin on the table next to me and began to wash the long, deep cut that went most of the way around my forearm. It hurt like anything and my beer-muddled brain was not so steadfast as to tolerate it. I tried to jerk my arm away, but the Lieutenant held it fast, continuing to douse it with hot, prickling water. The water in the basin turned pink then crimson, but her surprisingly obstinate grip held my arm firmly in place.

"That really stings, you know," I growled, clenching my teeth. Her hand held firm against my straining muscles like a ship's anchor weighing down a boat in high seas, and I wondered at both her strength and at her tenacity—I was much larger than her after all.

"Serves you right," she replied, not looking up at me. She set aside the basin and caught my arm in a clean towel, rubbing it dry—none too carefully, I might add.

"Drunk and brawling in the street. Shame on you."

She turned and moved to a cupboard, collecting a bandage.

"I'm not certain you fully understand the situation," I said with just a touch of indignation in my tone.

She came back and started wrapping my arm with the cloth—tightly. Even as frustrated as I was at that moment, some part of my mind still recognized the fragrance that hovered about her—the same rose scent I had smelled on my jacket after she had worn it. Her hands were warm and soft, too, and somehow the way she held my arm eased the sting of it and the knots in my stomach unwound. She still hadn't looked up at me, intent on her work. She jerked the bandage tight, sending a searing heat up my arm. She tore the strip down its length a ways and wrapped one end around my arm. She brought the ends together and tied them securely, giving the ties one final, excruciating, tug.

"*Ouch!*" I yanked my arm free then, despite her grip. "You don't understand. This wasn't my fault."

"Oh ho!" she scoffed. "Every D&D says the very same thing. Oh, I see things clearly enough: a drunkard is taking up my time needlessly when there are *sick* and *injured* men I should be tending to." She looked up at me then, the light in her eyes searing and hot, turning them the colour of autumn leaves lit by a fiery sun. She arched one brow and met my gaze full on as if daring me to challenge her opinion.

Anything I might have said at that point would have sounded like excuses to her ears and, besides that, she wasn't entirely wrong.

"Right," I replied when I could no longer bear the heat from her gaze as it burned into my own, "I suppose that *is* what you see." I looked away, blinking several times to douse the flames.

There was another silence and I heard her take a breath.

"I'm finished here," she said quietly. I quickly looked up at her. "You can go. Come back tomorrow and have someone check on that wound—can't have it getting infected." I wondered if it were fatigue or disappointment that made her speak as though she were taking leave of a wearying social affair.

I slid off the table. I paused there to steady myself then gathered up what strength I had and walked out of the room, leaving Lieutenant Grieves behind, the expression on her face and the flickering shadows in her eyes when she looked at me clawing at my stomach.

The guard told me to return to my tent while he waited for the Kid to be tended to. I made my way back to Fox farm as quickly as my uncoordinated steps would allow. I dropped onto my cot again and was out almost before I could pull off my boots.

[June 18, 1916]

The light slowly diffused into the tent through the sun-drenched canvas, relentlessly pursuing me in my dreams until catching me and flinging me into an unwelcome awakening. I opened my eyes and lay still for several minutes as I wrestled with my nightmares until they relinquished their hold and gave the reins over to reality. I rolled my head to the side and saw the Kid lying face down on the cot opposite mine, his head and one arm hanging over the side of the cot, his bandaged back safely away from all surfaces. He squirmed further onto his cot with a moan. I raised myself just enough to see the Kid's eyes open, then let my weighty head drop back onto my cot with no small amount of relief. I heard the Kid's breath catch sharply.

"You all right?" I asked, keeping my head where it was. It felt as though it would burst like an over-inflated balloon if I moved it too quickly. There was a pause.

"I've had worse," the boy replied hoarsely.

"Really? Worse than a whipping?" I asked. My arm was throbbing in time with my head and my stomach felt like it was on a cargo ship in a hurricane. "That's a pretty bold statement to live up to. What's your story, Kid?"

Silence.

"C'mon Kid," I coaxed, "enough of the attitude. We're gonna be in this war together for a long time—maybe the rest of our short, miserable lives—you can give me something to go on. How old are you, anyway?"

"Eighteen," the boy said a little too quickly.

I laughed. "I doubt that very much. More like 14?"

"15!" the Kid cried indignantly.

"That's better. What do I call you? I can't keep calling you 'Kid' all the time."

"You can call me Tommy."

"Like they call all us Canucks?" I asked, "Might just as well call you 'Kid'."

"No, really, that's my name: Tommy Colbert—as far as the army knows, anyway."

"Hmmm…and what is it to the people who actually know who you are?"

"Tommaso Corelli," the Kid answered quietly and grudgingly.

"OK, now we're getting somewhere. So where are you from? Why'd you sign up?"

Silence again.

"C'mon *Tommy*," I said firmly, "I've done you a few good turns now. I deserve something out of this."

Tommy heaved a sigh. "I grew up on the streets. Got into some trouble with the local law. Thought I might as well join the army before I got caught and thrown in jail."

"I'm not sure your plan was very well thought out. Didn't anyone try to stop you? Where are your parents? Couldn't they have helped you?"

Colbert snorted. "They wouldn't have been of much help. They weren't ever married. My father came over from Italy to settle a homestead. He didn't get that far at first— he met my mother, Trinette Edgard, when he landed in Montreal. She was a hotel maid at the *Montréal's Hôtel de Ville*—still is as far as I know. When my father found out my mother was going to have me, he high-tailed it out west."

"But that still leaves you with your mother. Why didn't she stop you from enlisting?"

"Haven't seen my mother in years. She couldn't keep me *and* her job and she couldn't keep me *without* her job. Tried to leave me with her brother and his wife, but he just wanted to hire me out for money. Thought if I had to work, I'd be doing it for myself. I got a job shoveling coal for the local station only, after a while, there weren't no work. I stole some stuff to keep going—clothes, food and such like. Didn't take long before the sheriff was after me. Thought I'd be better off here."

"Bold move. That why you changed your name— because it's Italian?"

"Yeah. Didn't figure that would go over very good with the army, what with Italy maybe fighting alongside the Germans."

"Nope, I expect not. Well, your secret's safe with me." I replied. My head was starting to spin from all the talking.

The tent flap drew back and a guard stepped in. He looked at Colbert and me and said, "All right, you've slept long enough—get washed up and get some food in you— doctor's orders."

I was inexplicably starving despite the somersaults my stomach was doing and was happy to do what I was told— doctor's orders or no. I heaved myself up off my bed and went over to Tommy's cot. I helped him up, wincing on his behalf when his breath caught with every movement. Blood had soaked through his bandages and hardened them into boards. They were likely adding to the Kid's pain more than anything else they might have been doing.

The guard handed us each a new shirt and directed us to some wash basins outside the tent. When we returned, there were two large trays of food set on a table outside the tent. I had to look twice at the trays to make sure they were real. They were loaded with toast, eggs, biscuits, sausages, and fried potatoes, along with a glass of milk and a cup of steaming tea.

"Enjoy your breakfast, gents," the guard said with a grin as he gestured to the trays.

Colbert and I cast each other a confused look.

Turning back to the guard, I asked, "I hate to look a gift-horse in the mouth, but is this some sort of joke? Who's setting us up? We're supposed to be on half rations for the duration."

"Doctor's orders," the guard replied. "Said you couldn't heal up without 'proper nutrition' and 'adequate rest'."

Colbert and I looked at each other for the briefest of seconds before sitting down at the table and diving into the best breakfast the army had ever served us.

I expected to be worked hard for the remainder of the day—more ascribing to the rule book regarding punishment of those who drink, but we were set to light duties only, helping to prepare lunch then clean up the mess tent and wash some dishes, pots, and pans. Tommy handled it as well as could be expected and I did my best to make up for what he couldn't manage. After lunch mess was cleaned up, we were brought back to the hospital to have our dressings changed.

I sat on the examination table, stripped from the waist up and shivering slightly. It was a stupid reaction, really. I wasn't cold, I was nervous, or perhaps admitting to being outright scared would have been more truthful. I was anxiously hoping Lieutenant Grieves would step through the door while at the same time, I was very much afraid of that very thing. I wanted to see her again—to explain things to her and try to convince her I wasn't the wretch she took me for, but I was terrified she would not believe anything I said no matter how much I tried to convince her. I wasn't certain I could bear it if she looked at me with disappointment painted across her lovely face again.

I was put out of my misery when a nurse I had never seen before entered the room with a dressing tray.

"I'm Lieutenant Bryant," the husky nurse informed me.

"Yes, Ma'am," I replied.

Of course I wanted to ask where Lieutenant Grieves was and why she hadn't come to change my bandages, but I thought that might get her into trouble—fraternizing and all that. The next thing I knew, the question was out of my mouth: "Is Lieutenant Grieves not on duty today?"

The nurse looked down her nose at me for a moment, one eyebrow raised. "Now why would you be needing to know that?"

I shook my head. "I just wanted to talk to her about yesterday. It's not important."

The Sister waved her dressing scissors at me.

"You caused a lot of bother for the night staff yesterday…" She frowned at me and cast me a look like my mother had when I was four and she had caught me chasing the chickens around the yard, pretending they were cattle to be rounded up.

"Apologies, Ma'am. I hadn't meant to."

The Nurse began cutting off my bandage.

"Oh, yes," she continued. "taking up all Lieutenant Grieves' time all night what with getting those orders signed. She chased those poor officers all 'round the 'ospital and camp, she did."

"I don't understand. Orders for what?"

"You needing 'proper diet' and 'rest'. Bah! A strong man like you don't need coddlin', says I. But Grieves can be relentless when she has a mind to be. Insisted on the orders getting signed and over to your Captain before her shift ended."

The Nurse brought over a basin of warm water and a cloth. She laid my arm across the basin and washed it down. The cut still looked red and angry, but it had stopped bleeding.

"And the Captain followed them..." I said under my breath.

"Did he now?" the nurse replied. "Lucky you, says I."

"Why would that be so important to either of them?" I asked, looking up at the Sister. She had dried my arm and was wrapping a new bandage around it.

"Wouldn't know nuffin 'bout that. Now myself, I wouldn't have been bothered." She tied off the gauze and stepped back. "All right now, the cut is looking fine. Take off the wraps tomorrow then make sure you keep it good and clean for the next week. Come back if it pains you or starts to smell bad."

Colbert and I were given full rations for the remainder of our sentence. While not quite the feast we had enjoyed the first day at Fox Farm, it was entirely adequate. Our work was light and remained that way for the duration of our punishment. Our "sentence" included a rest break in the middle of each day.

[June 20, 1916]

I was relaxing on my cot a few days later when Will stepped into the tent. I sat up and Will looked me over several times, grinning like a bandit.

"You always have all the odds figured, don't you?" he said. "Leave it to you to break all the rules and still come out ahead." Will sat down across from me on Colbert's cot, still grinning and shaking his head.

"Yeah—looks like I caught a few lucky breaks. I don't understand what's going on, though."

Will's brows shot up. "You haven't heard?"

"Heard what?"

"You've become a local hero!"

"What?!" I responded. "I was informed—by more than one person I might add—that I am an irresponsible drunk, not worthy of tending to, and one who should be court marshalled. How does that make me a hero?"

"Whoever told you that was dead wrong. Every soldier here wants to thank you—including the Captain."

"What for?"

"Hastings had his stripes removed for what he did to the boy. Captain demoted him to Private and assigned him to another platoon. Scuttlebutt has it the men in the unit he was assigned to taught him his place right quick. I think he's still in hospital. Lieutenant Eylon has taken over command of our platoon—most level-headed man I've seen so far and seems to know a thing or two about commanding soldiers—Canadian ones at that. All the men say you did everyone a good turn."

I only stared at Will for a few moments. "So *that's* why they're going so easy on us?"

"Sure," Will said with a nod of his head. "Captain's glad you stood up for the boy and grateful you gave him a reason to demote Hastings. Said he had never liked him very much and that there would have been trouble from the men if Hastings had been allowed to continue. The Captain would have had to answer for that."

I ran my hand through my hair. "Well, that's good, I guess…"

"*You guess?*" asked Will in disbelief. "That's the best thing that could have happened. What more could you ask for?"

"Well…" I looked at Will then turned away. "Lieutenant Grieves didn't think so highly of me last time I saw her."

"So why didn't you just tell her what happened?"

"I don't know. I started to, but I suppose I didn't think she'd believe me." I looked up at Will then. "Do you think maybe she's heard by now? She did get orders signed for extra rations and rest…maybe she heard the story and figured out I wasn't so bad?"

Will's face fell and he shook his head. "Sorry, Henry. Her unit was transferred to France the morning after you saw her. She would have left when her night shift ended the next morning. The whole story didn't get around for a couple days after it happened. She made sure you got extra rations? Maybe she just felt she owed you for the ride back to camp."

"That's why she insisted the orders be processed before the end of her shift…she knew she was leaving."

She left believing I was an irresponsible drunk!

But then—she was right. Would I have stepped in to help the Kid if my anger hadn't been fueled by copious amounts of alcohol?

It felt like a noose tightened around my throat and I couldn't draw a breath.

My next thought stopped all others: *my father was right about me.*

My eyes began to burn and my vision blurred, and all I could do was nod.

June 18, 1916

We have handed off the Shornecliffe hospital and are sailing for France to take over a hospital there. I am presently sitting on the deck of the City of Benares as I write this. It is almost dark and I ought to be below decks, but I needed air. I feel most nauseated. My state is not due to the rocking of the ship (I find that rather comforting although most do not). Rather, it is my own idiotic assumptions and subsequent mistake that is bearing down on me. I have made the most grievous error concerning Private Ryzak and have treated him cruelly exactly when I ought to have extended him a large measure of respect for aiding another at great risk to himself. What must he think of me? Treating a hero as rubbish beneath my boot? Oh it grieves me so to think! I must surely have lost his regard by attacking him most maliciously when he had acted so valorously, but I had no understanding of the situation— a fact of which he tried to apprise me. I did what I could to make up for wronging him, but I very much doubt he will know of my feeble attempt to make amends. I am afraid that, if ever we meet again, he will look upon me with contempt (if he even considers me at all) and he would have every right to do so.

It was a hurried night shift. We were to hand off the Shorncliffe hospital the next morning and everything was to be in place and ready for the next hospital staff by 0800 hours on the 18th. Preparing a hospital for hand-over was a tall order in and of itself, but added to that was a heavy workload. Many of the wards were filled with freshly injured from a work detail accident. The previous day, a group of soldiers in training thought to have a lark by first drinking copious amounts of alcohol then claiming to be "too ill" to fall in for drills. An unthinking Captain had other feelings about the matter. He commanded the men to a work detail moving heavy munitions needing to be hauled to the ships for transport to the front.

Drunken men and explosives do not mix well. As two of the men worked to lift one of the very heavy crates, it became unsteady and toppled. That alone may not have done much damage aside from a squashed toe. Unfortunately, the toppling of the crate caused the other man to stumble back, tripping over a crate containing stick explosives. The cigarette he held between his teeth fell between the slats of said crate, sparking the wooden case and catching fire.

Well, I needn't explain what happened next.

Suffice it to say, many men were injured during the dominos of munitions crates that succumbed to the heat and explosions. They were brought into the hospital on stretchers, in wheelbarrows, and some limping slowly. The operating theatre ran the full day, the surgeon stitching limbs and abdomens back together. One man had a piece of shrapnel fracture his skull which needed to be trephined. That night, we were up to our armpits in dressing changes just when we needed to be organizing the unit for handoff. We ran frantically about, trying to settle the men for the night while at the same time getting things sorted and ready for our departure the next day. It was utter madness.

I sat on the edge of a hospital bed, changing the soaked bandages on the head of the skull fracture patient. I could feel the heat emanating from him, his hair stuck to his forehead. He looked me full on then, a dull sheen covering his gaze. I wondered how long until the infection took him. Tonight? Tomorrow perhaps?

"Do you think I might see my wife and children again before I sleep?" He looked slowly around the ward.

"Your family?" I asked. Of course there was no soldiers' families in camp.

"Yes," the man said, still straining to see them. "They were here earlier, but I haven't seen them since."

I tied off the gauze and settled the man into bed, pulling his blanket up over his shoulders.

"Do you think perhaps I will see them again?" the man asked, his eyes pleading with me to grant his request.

I drew in a steadying breath. "Yes, certainly you might see them soon," was all I could say.

The man smiled weakly and lay back against his pillow, his gaze wandering about and settling on nothing in particular.

I felt a tap on my shoulder then and turned to see one of the orderlies behind me.

"Sister?"

"Yes?" I asked.

"You're needed in the treatment room," he said.

"Oh? Surely we can't still be getting injuries from the accident?" I needed to start doing the inventory and certainly had no time to be bandaging more men.

"No," the orderly said with a shake of his head. "Two D&Ds—nothing to do with the accident. I was told it was a fight in the main strip."

"Ohhh," I groused. "Why do these men choose now to vex me with their antics? Such senseless injuries and all because of their drinking! What good has alcohol ever done anyone?" I shook my head. "Can a VA look after them? I have much too much to do with the handover in the morning and the other men already taking up my time. I've not even gotten near the patient reports for morning yet— and now there will be more of them!"

"Sorry, Sister," the orderly said, "I was told their injuries needed tending by a Sister."

"Then I suppose it will have to be me," I huffed, "but I can't guarantee those soldiers will not get a decent reprimand to go along with my care, wasting my precious time like this. Please take inventory of those shelves while

I'm gone," I said, gathering my skirts and marching off in a somewhat unladylike manner.

In truth, it was not the disruption I was angry about—that was simply typical for army organization. Rather, I was caught up in memories of John, what with his penchant for drunkenness and his ill behavior. Those thoughts drove all others before them.

These men were just like him!

I collected my basin and bandages and marched to the treatment room. Wasting no time, I went about my task quickly, setting up my equipment on the side-table before turning to the soldier who sat in silence on the exam table, head hanging low. It took a second or two before he lifted his face to mine.

My chest seized the instant I saw his face. I wasn't certain if it was my anger, my disillusionment, or the red-rimmed blue eyes staring out at me from a chalky face that made my heart start pounding in my ears—perhaps all three.

"You?!" I managed to get out.

How dare he? How dare he drink? How dare he be that sort of man?!

"*You* are the 'Drunk and Disorderly' I am to tend?!" I spat out from between my teeth.

Private Ryzak winced and closed his eyes. He leaned forward slightly, clutching his abdomen. A cold stillness descended, the two of us frozen as we were for a moment. After several long seconds, Ryzak lifted his head to look at me, his expression that of a man looking up from the bottom of a very deep well.

That look ought to have melted me like snow in late May, but just at that moment, I caught the scent of stale beer coming off the man and all I could see was John's face hovering much too close to mine as his body pressed against me and I could smell his acrid breath spilling over my face. I took a steadying breath, squaring my shoulders as I pushed back against the heavy bars of my cage, and went to work.

I was not gentle with Private Ryzak, thinking he deserved whatever treatment he received from me. I dismissed him when I was done my work and looked at him steadily, daring him to make excuses for his behavior. To my great surprise, he went down like a light-weight fighter in a heavy-weight match. The man at the bottom of the well stepped out of the small beam of light and back into the shadows, disappearing into a hole of his own making. Surprise, or perhaps something very like guilt, punched hard at my stomach and I sucked in a quick breath at the impact. Ryzak left the room and I told myself it was the liquor that made him walk unsteadily.

I cleaned up my equipment and got another dressing set then called in the other D&D.

Fury was still pushing forward its tight-fisted rationalization when the next patient entered the treatment room. I stood waiting by the exam table and watched as a muted scarecrow of a boy shuffled stiffly into the room, his eyes weighted to the floor as he stopped in front of me.

"You are the other 'Drunk and Disorderly'?" I asked. By the look of the frail thing, I would not have thought he could do much drinking before he passed out, nor did he seem capable of causing a disorder of any magnitude.

"Yes, Ma'am," the youth said, continuing to stare at the floor.

"How old are you?"

"Eighteen—regimentally speaking, Ma'am," the boy pronounced without hesitation.

"Of course you are," I sighed. "And you were truly drunken and disorderly, fighting on the main strip?"

"That was the charge, Ma'am."

"Hmmm… Well, come over here and show me your injuries. I don't see any wounds."

The boy lifted his eyes to mine then, their green depths translucent like an empty glass bottle. He studied me for a moment, his face twisted as though he were walking a gangplank rather than getting his wounds dressed. He began unbuttoning his shirt and slowly turned.

The back of the boy's shirt was a shredded mess of red-soaked strips that were barely holding together enough to be called cloth. He pulled his arms free of the shirt sleeves and let the shirt hang from the waist of his pants. Swollen jagged red lines crisscrossed his back in a torturous roadmap.

"What happened?" I asked. "How did you get these cuts?" I pulled the shirt loose from his pants and balled it up, throwing it into the garbage bin. The waist of the boy's pants, freed of the bulk of the shirt, hung askew on his hipbones.

The boy's head dropped. "A whip, Ma'am."

"A *whip*?!" I felt the air stop short in my lungs. "Was Private Ryzak involved in this?" I choked out.

"Yes, Ma'am," the boy said, and I felt my gut wrench. Then: "He took on the man whipping me."

I let out a sharp breath, the room spinning around me as my reality re-oriented itself.

"I see," I replied.

I pulled a stool over and gestured for the boy to sit down then went to work cleaning the gashes on his back. I could feel him flinch each time the wet cloth touched his back.

"I was told it was a drunken street brawl," I said, still trying to jam my assumptions into my new reality.

"I wouldn't 'xactly call it a 'brawl', Ma'am. Lieutenant Hastings was whipping me for not pulling the sledge along quick enough. I couldn't do it. It weighed three times a grown man. Just when I was about to go down under the whip, Ryzak got between me and the Lieutenant. He tore into the Lieutenant and set him on his backside."

I felt as though I had just dropped off a steep embankment, my stomach rising up in the fall—and I could see no way to halt my tumble.

"But… surely the Private knew better than to attack an officer? I am certain he only attacked the officer because he was drunk?" I asked. I knew he had been drinking—I had smelled the liquor on him.

"He'd been drinkin' right enough, but the man can hold his liquor. He sure weren't drunk enough to take on an officer and get himself in front of a firing squad. Ryzak knew full well what he was about when he stopped the man."

"But he could be executed for attacking an officer!"

"I know it. Ryzak knows it too I 'xpect. Didn't seem to matter—he just wasn't gonna let the man keep whippin' me."

"So what will happen to the both of you now?"

"Captain Drewe sentenced us to seven days on Fox Farm, half rations and hard labour for bein' 'drunk and disorderly'."

"I see," I said. This time, shame soundly trounced disappointment, and fury fell hard to the side, having no footing whatever. I had treated Ryzak shamefully and he now likely believed me to be the meanest shrew alive.

There was only one thing I could think to do.

I quickly bandaged up the boy and sent him off with the guard, giving the guard strict orders that the boy was to rest. I went back to the ward and issued a wheel barrow full of commands, assigning the orderlies and VAs a great deal of work to get done in my absence. I then spent the next three hours tacking down and generally irritating large army men whom I woke from sleep—not a good combination.

My first stop was at the tent of Dr. Cavers, the MO for the hospital. The man appeared at the tent door bleary-eyed and asking if there were more casualties as he pulled his shirt on. My heart was pounding in my ears, but I stood my ground, more terrified of my mistake than of anything Dr. Cavers might do to me.

"Are there more injured?" the doctor asked.

"No, Sir," I said, pushing papers containing orders at him. "I simply need these orders signed before I'm gone tomorrow."

The doctor blinked down at the papers as I held the hurricane lantern aloft for him to read. He looked up at me with one brow cocked. "This is what I'm woken at one A.M. for, Grieves?"

"Apologies, Doctor, but I've made a mistake and I must correct it before I ship out tomorrow."

The man sighed and disappeared into his tent. He returned and handed me signed orders, the ink still wet.

I opened my mouth to thank him, but he held up a silencing hand. "No, don't thank me—I'm not being magnanimous. This is simply the quickest way to get back to bed," he said. "Besides, I know better than to argue with you, Lieutenant. Heaven help the Germans with you over there. You have what you came for, now leave me to my sleep." He disappeared back into his tent without another word.

I might have deliberated the meaning of his words. I had no idea why the man would hesitate to argue with me much less what threat I might pose to the Germans, but I hadn't the time to think on it. It took me another forty-five minutes to track down Captain Drewe and deliver the signed doctor's orders prescribing rest and sufficient food for Private Ryzak and the boy during their sentence. It wasn't much of a gesture, and Ryzak would likely never know how I tried to make amends, but it did still the tumbling of my stomach somewhat to have done it.

August 12, 1916

War Diary

Private Henry Ryzak

August 12, 1916-September 30, 1916

Volume 2

Diary Text: 16 Pages

[August 12, 1916-September 30, 1916]

After spending the summer months training, our unit was called up. The *Sommes* battle was raging and reinforcements were needed. We left camp, bound for France and the front lines. I had mixed feelings about that. Yes, I was nervous about going to the front. I had no idea how I was going to keep Will safe in the trenches let alone on the battlefield. For my own sake, on the other hand, I was impatient to join the fight. I hated waiting, and waiting for a fight that would be coming to you, like it or no, was the worst. I was happy simply to get on with it.

We entrained at Liphook and travelled back to Southampton where our troops were divided among three ships: *The Lydia*, *City of Dunkirk*, and *Transport 886*. We began our crossing of the channel, but there was some delay. Evidently, there were German submarines patrolling the channel and we had to wait until it was safe to cross. A wise decision in my view. We eventually disembarked in *Le Havre* at noon on August 13th.

Women and children gathered around us as we made our way through town to our rest camp. The women called out, trying to sell their apples and baking while the children begged for chocolate. We mostly ignored them and marched on to our temporary camp.

[August 15, 1916]

Our unit paraded in the morning as the weather was fair, then undertook physical drills and training in bayonet fighting. That evening our battalion entrained for *Gare Des Merchandises*, leaving for *Poperinghe*, Belgium around midnight. We arrived to find our billets in a deplorable state. The tents were not level and there was mud everywhere from heavy rains the area had sustained just before our arrival. It was impossible to clean anything including our pathetic rations of bread and stringy meat. Will joked about the sorry conditions, but I could find no humour in the situation. I had a suspicion things were only going to get worse from that point on.

[August, 21, 1916]

The battalion was divided into sections and moved into the rear-most trenches. I had a bit of a scare when Lieutenant Eylon approached our unit just before we left camp.

"They need more men in C company so I will be reassigning three of your men to another unit," he announced as we stood with our kit, waiting to form ranks and move out. We all looked at one another then turned a sharp look on the Lieutenant who was continuing his instructions. "Galt, Stewart, and Will Ryzak are to attach themselves to C company."

"No, Sir," I said, immediately stepping forward. "We can't do that."

"Beg pardon?" Elyon asked in a *be-careful-of-your-next-words-son* tone.

"Forgive me, Sir, but I signed up on the condition my brother and I could stay together. We can't be split up."

Will cast me a glance then turned to the Lieutenant. "That's true, Sir," he added.

"And I'm not leaving either," Galt chimed in. "In fact, none of us ought to be re-assigned."

Elyon looked sternly at each of us in turn. "Gentlemen," he began in a cautionary tone, "one could construe this as disobeying orders…or even mutiny perhaps?"

"Hear us out, Sir," I said, pulling my full *negotiating* skills to the fore. "Each man in our group has a unique skill set. In plain terms, we've trained together and already know how to work well as a team using all of our skills together. If you split up our men, you will be losing a good fighting team. Surely there are other, shall we say, *less defined* units you could break up?"

Eylon pressed his mouth into a line, studying me as though he had just picked up the card he needed to complete his hand. He took a breath. "It would seem I have a group of 'inseparables' on my hands. All right, Private," he began in a calculating tone, "how about we made a deal?"

"And what would that be, Sir?" I asked, trying to get a read on what hand he held.

"I've watched you during raid drills and target practice. I know my predecessors have talked to you about leading raids or becoming a sniper and you've refused. I will leave your unit together if you agree to be one of our snipers and lead raids as needed."

I paused for a moment, considering. I was determined to get the most I could out of this little negotiation. "I will agree to your terms on one condition: *I* say who my second is during sniping duty and *I* choose who to take on raids with me. I will also plan the raids I'm leading."

"Done," the Lieutenant replied readily. "Excellent," he added, mentally raking in the pot. "All right then," he added, "I will seek out another unit to attach to C company. Make ready, men."

There was a chorus of "Yes, Sir"s from our unit and we saluted the Lieutenant as he moved off.

"You did good. *Ja*," Lundgren said, slapping me on the back.

"Nicely done," Ransley put in.

"Thanks, Henry," Will added, giving my shoulder a squeeze.

"You did the right thing," Galt began, "but it was a high price to pay. Sniping isn't a bad lot to draw, but you do know how dangerous raids are, don't you?"

I frowned. "Yes, I am very much aware. That's why I've refused in the past. However, the bargain I made might keep me one step ahead of command. If I were a betting man— and I am—I would be willing to bet our unit can conduct a better, safer raid if we plan the thing on our own—keep things fluid and deal with whatever comes at us as a team—

none of this write the script and stick to it nonsense. That's what gets people killed: not having any control of the situation when they're actually knee-deep in it. Of course, a script will have to be put in to the brass but how closely we follow it out in the field, well…that's another story and one best kept to ourselves." I looked at Galt with a raised brow and he responded with a grin.

"I'll lay that wager with you, lad," Galt said, hitching his kit onto his shoulders. He smiled and shook his head then marched off to join ranks. The rest of us fell in behind him, enjoying the warmth of the sun as we marched to the trenches.

[September 9, 1916]

We moved into the front-line trenches for the first time, relieving the 73rd Battalion. No one seemed very certain about the layout of the trenches and it took us some time and much marching through the lines to finally locate the 73rd battalion and relieve them. The 73rd moved out of the trench in the soaking rain and our lot was left to repair the trench as best we could—the area had sustained a great deal of damage from the ongoing rain and several bombings. The walls were collapsed in places, mud coating the duck boards and making them as slippery as drifting snow on a frozen lake. A few of the funk holes had caved in, their wooden plank floors broken, making the wall unstable and prone to further collapse.

We were to be assigned work details to repair the trenches, but first there was to be a church parade. Slater met with some difficulty on the point of church parades. He avoided them whenever possible through various excuses and cursed them when he had no choice but to attend. This time, the Chaplain came to us in the trench, so there was no getting around it for Slater. When he couldn't find a way out, Slater simply refused to join in.

"This is stupid," Slater complained. "I'm not going."

"Don't be a fool," Ransley replied. "You have no choice—it's orders."

"How can they force me to listen to such rot? I simply won't go," Slater responded.

"You'll go, like it or not," Galt said sternly, "or you'll get all of us in trouble again." Galt moved to stand in front of Slater as he hitched his rifle a little higher onto his shoulder.

"Don't care," Slater said, shaking his head. "I'm not going." Slater leaned over Galt, staring him down.

There were a few attempts to coax Slater into moving along, but he stubbornly remained where he stood.

"Fine," Stewart finally said as he moved past Slater and Galt's stalemate, "let him stay behind and get court martialed. I would find that outcome most agreeable." Stewart stopped a short distance down the trench and turned, waving the rest of us forward.

I looked at Slater and went to join Stewart.

"They don't court martial a man for not going to Church parade," Slater objected.

"Sure they do," Will replied, stepping up to Slater. "Come now, man, it's only a few words and a few songs. We had to sit through a lot more than that back home each Sunday, right Henry?" Will smiled over at me.

"Absolutely," I replied. "Mother saw to the salvation of our souls most devoutly." Will and I grinned at one another.

Will turned back to Slater and waited.

Slater let out a slow, heavy breath then turned and followed Stewart and I down the trench looking as though he had a lemon wedged in his mouth. He groused about the parade as we made our way down the trench to where the Chaplain was collecting men and he groused all the way back to our portion of the trench after it was done, but at least no one was court martialed. I had to agree with Stewart, however, I would not have been too broken up about it if Slater had been tried for his obstinacy. The man was certainly a loose cannon.

We worked on the trenches in six-hour shifts, resting and eating when we could. It was cold, tiresome work. The rain had permeated the ground, turning it to a slimy muck that sucked down boots and refused to stay where it was put. We re-dug the rain-laden trench walls, shoring them up with corrugated tin and sandbags. There was precious little material with which to make repairs and we fervently hoped for dry weather to harden the mud. The rain eventually stopped some days later and things began to dry—including our clothes and boots.

Our first barrage while in the front lines fell heavily among us. I heard a whistle then felt a simple, dull thud. There was a sudden burst of light that shattered the night sky and a blast of mud and debris toppled me off my feet. I quickly looked around for Will from where I had landed on the duckboards. He was safely tucked into a funk hole while the others crouched against the trench wall. I took shelter against the nearer wall and looked at the men around me. It wasn't fear I felt, although I could see it plainly displayed on several of the faces around me, including Tommy's. My mind did not entertain worries of the next bomb or a reliving of the still-ringing blast. These things were to be expected. My only thought was that, for this moment, Will was in the safest place he could be. There was nothing else needing to be done.

We sat through the next hour of bombing and sniping, keeping low and still. At one point, I looked over at the Kid. He was crouched against the trench wall, rifle in hand, a veritable jack-in-a-box ready to spring forward at the least provocation—or at none whatever. His eyes met mine and all I could see was the back-lit eyes of a trapped cat hiding under a box.

"Tommy," I called quietly, keeping the boy's attention, "there's room with Will." I jerked my head in Will's direction. Will immediately looked at the Kid and waved him into the small dugout. Tommy went quickly and silently to join Will, only lowering his rifle after a moment or two of sitting in the dark hole.

The next night the Lieutenant sent a runner with orders for me to go speak with him. I followed the runner down the trench until we found Eylon in a command dugout. I stopped in front of him and saluted.

"Ah, Ryzak, good man," Eylon began. He went on to explain he needed a scouting party to find out what the Huns had planned. His suspicion was that they would be on the move, given the covering barrage the previous night and he needed to know just what they were presently up to.

"Yes, Sir," I said.

"Now here's the sticky wicket," Eylon began. He showed me the map of where the Germans were last reported and the line of their trenches. "But that was two days ago. Who knows what their position is now. We need you to find out."

"Yes, Sir," I replied. "I'll form a party and we'll go out just after dark."

"I'm supposed to submit a plan," the Lieutenant said. "What have you got for me?"

I considered this a moment then pointed to a place on the map. "I leave the trench here with three men," I said, "then move up two by two leapfrog formation until we find the Huns' wire. That should tell us the location of the trench. We will follow it for as long as we dare and report back on our findings."

"That will do," Elyon said.

That evening, I gathered Galt, Ransley, and Lundgren and explained our mission.

"I'm coming," Will said.

"No," I replied. "I don't want too many of us out there. Ransley is good with maps. Galt has done this sort of thing before. I can shoot and Lundgren can fight at need. We have what we need to do the job."

Will looked at me like he had when we were kids and he had caught me kissing his childhood sweetheart, Becky Alastair, in the school yard.

"You'll be my second on sniping duty," I added.

Will gave me a grudging nod.

We had a token supper of bully beef and biscuits along with some tea for which we heated water on a small cookstove set into one of the funk holes. Our tea grew tepid as we waited for nightfall and the scouting mission to begin. The cook's assistant came around with the evening's ration of rum. I stared down at the amber liquid in my cup and inhaled its biting aroma. I very much wanted the warm numbing of it, the mild dulling of senses, the burning of the stomach that calmed and deadened it. Rather than those thoughts bringing me comfort, however, the scent of the brew only served to conjure up *her* eyes, lit by a faltering flame guttered low by a draught of disappointment and sorrow. I heard Galt's caution about rifles and alcohol not mixing and, as his words bolted through my mind, I heard the echo of my own hollow thought:

Would I have helped the Kid if I hadn't been drunk?

Another whiff of the bitter drink and my throat tightened. I swallowed past the knot in my throat and handed my cup to Lundgren who eagerly downed the deceitful drink in one swallow.

We stowed our kit and the four of us made our way to the starting out point in the trench. We had each been given two Mills bombs and extra bullets for our revolvers and rifles. I carried my rifle under my right arm, hanging by its strap and one hand on the butt, ready for quick firing.

As soon as it was dark, I climbed the small ladder leading over the edge of the trench, keeping low. I moved quickly to the right, taking cover behind a small patch of short brush, the others following in my wake as smooth as a silently flowing stream. I motioned for Galt and Lundgren to move forward while Ransley and I covered them. We set out next, leapfrog style, as we advanced from the brush to a nearby shell hole. Our two teams continued that way, darting between any form of cover we could find. Slowly we made our way to our own wire then traced a path to the break in the wire and moved out into no man's land.

Just as we all collected in a shallow crater, a graceful arch of light pitched high into the air to our right. It grew taller and taller, then burst into a spray of sparks. The sparks drifted down lazily, illuminating the area underneath their umbrella until they reached the ground and went out.

We stayed put, motionless, until the light of the flare ebbed. As soon as it was dark again, I went forward with Ransley close on my tail. We ducked behind a bush and waited there until Galt and Lundgren caught up. Ransley put his ear to the ground. He looked up at me then, and pointed in front of us. He shook his head in the negative then pointed back the way we had come. Galt and Lundgren crept up to our spot just then and I motioned for us to return to our previous hiding spot.

We turned to go and I felt something heavy on my shoulder. I froze and reached for the thing. I met with some confusion when my hand seized upon a square piece of metal. It took me a moment or two of manual inspection to recognize it as a cow bell. I eased it off my shoulder, reaching for the clapper and being careful not to let it come into contact with the frame. I felt along the bell and followed it to its peak where a string attached it to the bush. I left it there and followed the others back to our previous crater.[1]

In gestures and hushed whispers, Ransley reported he had heard a great drumming when he had put his ear to the ground and thought it was the product of marching feet. He felt surely there was a German trench or perhaps a post nearby, although we hadn't yet passed a wire line. I told the others about the bell.

Why was there a bell set as an alarm within footfalls of the Germans with no wire or guards present?

Ransley put forward the idea that we might have skirted their line of wire and were much closer to the German trenches than we had intended to get. Galt pointed to the likely fact that the bell was to serve as a warning for the Hun if someone was to approach. He suggested we trigger the bell from a safe distance to find out what the Germans' plan with it was. I agreed. I ordered Ransley to make a note of any landmarks.

I took out a bit of wire I had in my pocket and crept back to the bush. Locating the branch on which the bell was hung, I secured one end of the wire to it then made my way back to where the others were waiting in the crater. I handed the wire to Ransley and set my gun on the edge of the hole in which we were positioned, siting through the scope and aiming down the barrel. Peering over the edge of the crater, I watched as Ransley pulled the wire hard twice. The bell clanged and an instant later there was a burst of gunfire just beyond the offending bell and over to my right. I fired into the spurt of light with several quick rounds, the noise of my gun drowned out amidst the German firing.

Silence descended for the briefest of moments. Suddenly we heard and felt the clamor of movement a short distance ahead of us, followed by the thudding of booted steps. We ducked down into the crater.

"Ransley," I whispered, "any idea where we are?"

"I believe we are further to the left of our trench position than we intended to go—likely from hopping between craters. If I remember the map correctly, there should be a hill just a bit further to the left—we could get behind that and keep it between us and the Jerries. Besides, anything in that direction is further away from them at this point."

I nodded and motioned to the others to follow me as I crept out over the top of the crater. I could hear the scurrying of heavy feet off to our right mixed with whispered shouts in German. The voices and footsteps grew louder behind us and I quickened my pace. We reached a small hill and rounded to the far side of it.

The four of us crouched behind the hill and exchanged silent glances as we waited. The German voices grew quieter and the footsteps eventually receded.

Ransley motioned for us to go back, but I shook my head. There was something wrong about the whole thing. Besides, I explained in whispers, we still didn't know where their wire line or trench was and we had orders to find out. I motioned for us to go around the hill to the far side. Galt and Lundgren concurred and, after some hesitation and a well-deserved scowl cast in my direction, Ransley also nodded his head.

When we reached the far side of the hill, I went around cautiously with the others close behind me. Just as we came into the open, another flare went up and we immediately fell to the ground. As the sky burst into orange light, I could see the full layout of German wire and trenches some way off to my right. I pointed it out to Ransely and he nodded. There was something else I saw too: a large barn near the end of the German trench. There was a single guard just outside the open barn doors. I pointed, and the others looked on as the darkness descended again.

We ducked back behind the hill and had a bit of discussion as to what the barn was and what we were to do next. Ransley reasoned it must have some important purpose for the Hun to be guarding a seemingly deserted barn—a barn situated right at the end of their trench and readily accessible. Also, they had set the cow-bell alarm and had taken action quickly when it had been set off. Lundgren said he had seen a path from the barn to the trench. Galt speculated it might be a munitions supply.

"Let's blow it up," he suggested simply.

I agreed.

It took us some time to crawl further to our left and come up behind the barn, but after 30 or 40 minutes, we had made it to our destination seemingly undetected.

Lundgren and I left the others a short distance off and crept around the barn. We had to move at a snail's pace—Lundgren was definitely not light on his feet and had to move with great intent in order to do so silently.

Lundgren stood and moved soundlessly along the back wall of the building, coming up behind the guard. With a quick grab, he caught the German by the throat, cutting off any warning the man might have issued. Lundgren thrust his blade into the man's side and the German went limp in his hand. Lundgren lowered the body quietly to the ground and dragged the man behind the barn, dropping him in the mud. I looked at the dead body at my feet, paused to consider this, then looked up at Lundgren, feeling as though someone had turned my bunk over with me still in it. Lundgren only grinned at me, looking for all the world like a hound that has just earned his supper by retrieving his master's kill. I nodded, having no other response to offer. Lundgren motioned me forward and we went around to the doors of the barn.

Sure enough, stacks of crates filled the barn stamped in German words. I couldn't make out the words, but Lundgren nodded at me emphatically. I went to an open box and pulled a stick bomb out of the straw in which it lay. Lundgren and I exchanged a glance. We both grabbed for several more stick bombs, tucking them into our belts and pockets, then took up two more and activated them. We tossed them into the far corners of the barn and ran for our lives. I threw one more bomb into the middle of the stack on my way out the door.

We raced past Galt and Ransley who lost no time in following us on our retreat to the hill.

Far too soon, there was an enormous explosion. The sound shook the ground and we stumbled, but managed to keep our feet moving beneath us. I could hear nothing. I let myself drop back behind the others, pushing them past me to count them and make certain they were all still there. The direct route took us in front of the hill and back past the bush. We ran as fast as we possibly could manage, not bothering to take cover and hoping the commotion behind us would buy us some time. Just as we reached the bush where the bell was tied, gunfire opened up behind us. For some reason, I reached down to grab the cow bell as I ran past, holding it tightly so it wouldn't give away our location—something I thought was pretty well known by that time anyway, considering the bullets whizzing past my head. We managed to drop down into the crater from which we had started just as a bright flash lit up the sky. Another burst of noise and a shower of dirt and debris made us duck down to the ground.

Guns from our trenches opened up then, firing into the German lines. We collected what wits we had left among us—I had to give Ransley a good shove to get him moving again—and raced back to our trench under the covering fire. We threw ourselves down into our trench breathless and checking for wounds. Miraculously, only Lundgren was hit and that was merely a scratch on his neck. A near miss to be sure, but a miss all the same. I doused the reddened area with water from a canteen I grabbed off a nearby soldier.

The Lieutenant called for us about an hour after the barrage had quieted. We went through the entire story, complete with Ransley indicating the layout of German wire and trenches on the Lieutenant's map. When Eylon looked at us skeptically, I held up the cow bell. He immediately grabbed it from my hand and twisted the clapper out before it could make any sound and attract the attention of snipers. He handed the now harmless piece of metal back to me.

"This was to be a quiet reconnaissance mission, not a very obvious raid of a Hun munitions depot. I think I should plan the missions from now on," he added tersely.

"That wasn't our deal," I replied with a shake of my head.

"Nor was any of this part of our deal," Eylon put in.

"I think some rather significant gains were made both in terms of intel and tactical advantage," I countered. "A *smart* man would take credit for the added value of what happened here tonight…"

Elyon considered me a moment, his eyes narrowing then nodded and told us to return to our post.

In the end Eylon received commendations for the destruction of a strategic German artillery depot. He did and said no more about being involved in the planning of our missions.

[September 13, 1916]

On September, 13th we were relieved and our company moved back to the *Kemmel* shelters. A couple of men were wounded in the process of leaving the trenches and we watched as the medics carried them off to the dressing station. We rested over the next few days with only routine parades and drills. Our lack of work detail was rumoured to be the results of Elyon's good humour over receiving commendations.

[September 25, 1916]

We marched to *Arques*, reaching our billets just before four o'clock in the afternoon that day. Over the next few days, we were moved on to *St. Martin* and then on to *Eperlecques* where we were scattered into various billets both in the town and outside of it.

We were given box respirators. The contraption looked ridiculous with their celluloid eye pieces glued into the rubber-coated khaki material making the wearer look like a blind raccoon. The mouth piece that connected a person's breathing to a box filled with absorbent chemicals hurt the lips and cheeks. I had no idea if the thing would actually work nor how on earth I would ever get it on in time. Still, it was some measure of comfort to have it with me.

We received a draft of thirty men and later more men were added from the 90th Battalion to shore up our numbers. Among them was Russel MacLean, a burly Scott who took a liking to our unit. We let him tag along, mostly because he had an excellent singing voice that helped to pass the time during the cold evenings as we shivered in our billets—and Galt thought it great fun to harmonize.

June 19, 1916

June 19, 1916

Have landed at Le Havre and have taken over the Hotel Des Emigrants, presently being used as a hospital. It is part of the No. 2 General Hospital. Some of the Australian nurses there have been called on to take out-of-action soldiers back to Australia so they will hand over operations to our unit. It is a good hospital. We shall have very nice lodgings while we are here, having each our own room in the hotel. For that, I am eternally grateful as I have heard other units have been much less fortunate in their billets. We even have electricity! Although it is turned off promptly at dusk—just when it is most needed—so as to avoid being a beacon for enemy aircraft and, thus, becoming a bombing target. Then we have to light dim lamps and use torches to find our way in the dark. There is much tripping and barking of one's shins on sharp angles that no one can find again in the daytime so as to remove them. These vicious beasts seem to venture forth only in the dark and attack one from the depths of evening shadows. It is "the witching hour" as some say. The time when men cry out more and moan as their pain takes grip of them more strongly, the dark and the pain wrapping around them and binding them in the darkness. Nights can be long, even in a hospital as nice as this one.[29]

And it is nice here.

Hotel staff have been conscripted along with the hotel itself. Knowing naught else what they are to do, they have continued to run things as they would the hotel. The hospital staff are having an excellent time of things with our laundry washed, folded, and left on our cots by stewardesses and stewards. The orderlies have the help of porters sporting shiny brass buttons on double-breasted lapels to carry supplies up tall flights of winding staircases. All of this and saying nothing of the excellent meals the hotel kitchen prepares! Today they served us a tea of boiled eggs, anchovy and sardine sandwiches, plum bread with butter, and tea. It would be so much more dignified if I didn't want my supper tonight after eating all of that, but I'm afraid I am still famished what with all this moving about of everything.

This is the lap of luxury for us Sisters. In truth it seems self-indulgent and ostentatious. I cannot help but feel we will pay in-kind for these luxuries in due course.[5]

PS: I am very grateful to have received this new journal from mother in which to write down my journeys. I had just about filled the last.

Payment did come due, to be certain.

The workload was light enough to begin. At first, the patients we saw came to be there mostly due to their own mishaps: men injured in a wagon accident, or, one with even less brains, poor dear, had somehow managed to be on the wrong end of another soldier's rifle. There were also a couple of limb injuries from an ill-timed detonation of a grenade. All in the routine battles our men undertook.

Then, of a sudden it seemed, soldiers began to arrive at the station.

The trains pulled in, filled to the top with wounded men. They stopped to unloaded their cargo, then immediately moved out again to fetch more broken men from the front. At first, the wounded trickled into the hospital, brought from the station in threes and fours by a carefully organized convoy of ambulances. By noon, the wounded began to arrive on any form of transportation that could be found: wheelbarrows, carts, on the backs of bicycles, motor vehicles. Anything that could haul a human being was employed to move the wounded to the hospital. The front entry of the hotel was soon filled with wounded, the entire foyer floor covered with blood-stained khaki, the sounds of groaning filling the place to the ceiling.

I threaded my way among the soldiers to look outside, trying to sort what was happing and decide what needed to be done. I spotted one of the MOs talking with the Matron and went over to ask what assistance I might offer.

"What's going on?" I heard the MO ask a driver as together they helped a wounded soldier out of a horse-drawn cart.

"The wounded are coming in faster than they can be brought to the hospital. The men are stranded at the station," the cart-driver continued, "with more'n the ambulances can transport. They've put out a call for anyone what can to help get the men to the hospitals." The driver didn't say anything further. Rather, he hopped into his cart and, taking off at a brisk pace, went back the way he had come.

The MO and the Matron looked at one another then we all glanced around at the stretchers that were now lining the front walkway. We looked toward the road only to see a long line of ambulances, carts, horses, motorcycles, lorries, and other forms of transports threading their way up the drive to the front of the hotel.

"I'll get the Sisters and orderlies," the Matron said to the MO. "You get the theatre ready and call in all of the MOs to prep for surgeries."

"Right," he replied, already setting off at a run.

"What can I do?" I asked, turning to keep up with the Matron as she dashed back inside.

"Alert each ward and have them send out staff to help sort and bring in the wounded."

"Yes, Ma'am," I said.

I rushed to the first unit on the first floor and looked around for the Sister in charge.

"The wounded are beginning to arrive," I told her when I had finally found her. "Rather a great lot of them. They are being left outside in the yard. Every ward must send out their staff to bring them in and get them where they need to go."

The woman stared at me for the merest fraction of a second—only long enough to blink once for that was how long it took for her face to harden into a marble bust, her expression that of someone taking their final determined steps over the top of the trench and into the fray.

"Time to get to work," she said with a staid calm that could only be born from a match between infinite experience and a certainty in one's abilities. She turned a firm look on two VAs and an orderly who were nearby. "You three come with me," she ordered. I watched as she hurried down the centre of her ward calling directions to the other staff as she flew past. "You! Get these beds ready for patients! Andrews! We will need more morphia—set up a deposit of it in that cabinet. Vickers! Collect all the bandages we have! You! Get some hot water and fill as many vessels and basins as you can find!" That was as much as the woman had time for, sailing out the door and down the stairs, her troupe scampering to their assigned duties.

I blinked at the marvel of the woman, took a breath, then hurried to the next floor. I raced through the hospital, mobilizing each ward.

We soon had every ward in top gear. I went out to find the Matron and ask her what I was to do next. I took one step beyond the large double doors of the hotel entry and halted in my tracks. What had once been a vast and lush front lawn, neatly trimmed and contained within the confines of the curving hotel drive, had become a sea awash with the war's jetsom of mangled men.

An endless train of every form of conveyance stretched down along the drive and out the gates to the road, disappearing behind the wall. Each vehicle pulled in, stopped at the far limits of the field of stretchers, and deposited wounded men, some on stretchers and others set down in a heap of their own broken bones and open wounds. Others pulled closer to the front entry, bringing men who could barely walk, held together by scraps of bandages, their lips cracked and dry, their eyes hollow and dull, reflecting only that horror to which they had born witness.

The sound of groaning engines and clutches being jerked filled the air, rising above the cries of the wounded, carried along on the smoke and fumes of the motorized vehicles. The clamor of the vehicles was punctuated by the questions that rose above the din, all of them beginning with "where". Where does this go? Where are the extra stretchers? Where does this man belong? Where is the water?

Where are the dead to be put?[29]

I didn't move for several moments, for I had no possible means of making any semblance of order from the scene that greeted me. I simply could not come up with my first action. I was saved when one of the orderlies called me over to help unload an ambulance that had just pulled up.

He cast me a glance and whatever he saw on my face prompted him to say, "First, we sort the men: the walking go over there," he pointed to a group of soldiers sitting on the lawn some ways off. "The stretcher patients get lined up there," he pointed to the long line of stretchers waiting on the lawn. "Those who can sit, we help get there." He pointed to a third area on the stairs where men leaned askew on the steps of the hotel.

I helped unload the ambulances until I spied the Matron. I excused myself and went over to her. She was bent low over a man on a stretcher. She bent his head up and held a cup of water to his lips.

"Thank you," he whispered hoarsely as she laid his head back down on the stretcher.

I saw her breathe a sigh then stand. She looked at me without truly seeing me.

"I was wondering where I could be of most use," I asked quietly. I cringed inwardly as I hear the word "where" pop out of my mouth.

It took a moment for the Matron to answer.

"Help register the men," she said calmly with a confirming nod of her head. "Here," she said, handing me a clipboard and pencil. "First fetch more cloth sacks from the wards. Then come back and write down each man's name and number. Mark his personal items on the registry then put them in a sack. Leave the sack with the patient to be brought in with them when there's room inside."

"Yes, Ma'am," I said, taking the clipboard. I hurried to a few of the wards, finding quite a number of cloth sacks with drawstrings, made by women back home, then returned to the lawn. I simply picked a man at random and wrote down his name and number on the paper. I then pulled out all of the things he carried in his pockets and placed them in the sack: a pocket watch that was no longer working, a dog-eared picture of a woman with a baby, a box of waxed matches, a handful of bullets, a pocket knife, and a pay book. I listed the items beside the man's name then put them in the sack which I left with the soldier. He hugged the bag to him as though it were the most precious thing on earth.[29]

I went from stretcher to stretcher, writing down names and filling sacks. From the pockets of pants and great coats I pulled out any assortment of items, from loaded revolvers to tins of sardines to nubs of candle ends to small trinkets meant to be sent home as gifts. Each time I handed back the bundle of carefully logged items, the soldier would, without fail, clutch it to his chest as though the items therein were a lifeline to their home and their families. I realized at one point that whatever a man carried into battle would need to have such value to him as to be worth the work of carrying it and the effort of keeping it safe—these were the items the man could not bear to leave behind in the trenches while he went into battle.

After a time, the line of vehicles slowed to a trickle and finally, the last one pulled in.

"Is that all of them?" I heard the Matron ask the last ambulance driver.

"Not even close to all," the driver said. "But you're more than full. The rest have to wait."

"What about the other hospitals?" she asked.

"They're full too."

"But how many are still waiting at the station?"

The man shrugged. "More'n I can count and there's still more trains pullin' in."

From where I stood, I saw the Matron frown then swivel around, searching.

"Where's the one who asked where she would be most helpful?" Her eyes landed fully on me with the weight of a cannon ball. "Yes, you Grieves! Go back to the station with this man and see what is happening there!"

"But…" I stammered. "What exactly am I to do there?"

The Matron didn't even blink. "Whatever is needing to be done, of course! Move on now, there are wounded men without anyone to care for them! Take a VA to help you."

"Yes, Ma'am!" I called back. I handed my clipboard to a nearby orderly—the one who had steered me to my starting place.

"Take some supplies with you," he said leaning low to me.

"Yes, of course. Thank you," I said. "I'll only be a moment!" I called out to the driver. The man ground out some harsh and unintelligible words ending with, "hurry up now!".

I raced off to the closest ward. I had no time to search so I grabbed a bucket on my way past the door. I ran through the supply room and on into the pharmacy room, scooping up bandages, scissors, iodine, and morphia into the bucket along with anything else I saw that looked useful. I hurried back outside and almost knocked over Hanes in my haste.

"Oh! Do excuse me, Lieutenant," she breathed, "I didn't mean to run into you like that. Terribly sorry."

"It was my fault. Don't apologize," I said. Then: "Do you have an assignment or would you be able to come with me for a time?" I asked.

"I was just going to find Matron to see what needs to be done."

"No need to ask," I said, grabbing the girl's hand and hurrying down the steps. "Come with me to the station. We are told there are men who need tending."

"Yes, Ma'am!" Hanes said, trying to keep her feet under her as I pulled her along.

We found the ambulance driver waiting impatiently where I had left him and jumped into the back of his vehicle. To say we charged back through the streets would be akin to calling a trickle of water the MacKenzie river. The streets were jammed with vehicles and pedestrians and bicycles and motorcycles. The entire city was practically at a stand-still as the influx of soldiers poured into the city from the station, carried along its streets in all manner of transportation as they moved to the various buildings now set up as hospitals.

I could hear the driver shouting at people and blasting his horn to get them to move. Once he drove up onto the sidewalk for a time to get around several carts that were not moving, sending surprised pedestrians scattering to the side. Hanes and I clung desperately to the braces on the wall of the ambulance and steadied our nursing caps to keep them on our heads as the ambulance bumped and jumped over the curbs. Despite our best efforts, our hats never sat quite straight again that night.

We stopped after a time and the driver came around to open the back door of the ambulance.

"All right," he said brusquely, "out you go! I've more men to get to the 'ospital."

Hanes and I hopped down from the ambulance and took a few shaky steps. I felt as though I had just climbed off a merry-go-round that some mischievous boy had spun far too fast as he tried to get a girl's attention.

We stepped out from behind the ambulance and looked toward the train station. Hanes and I turned to look at one another then. I could think only of the Pilgrim's Progress for, if Christian, having traversed the River of Death, had just been told to turn around and cross it again, his expression might have matched Hanes' at that moment.

"Oh, my," Hanes whispered. "Wherever shall we begin?"

I could not falter or we would both collapse into irresolution.

"Matron said to do whatever needs to be done. We shall 'treat first that which kills first' and try to stabilize each man until they can be taken to the hospitals. One soldier at a time. But first, let's see what we have to work with inside." I gave Hanes' hand a squeeze and nodded firmly, then turned and walked as decisively as I could. I picked my way between the stretchers and men that filled the station platform, holding tightly to my small, woefully inadequate bucket of supplies as though it were a last, dim candle lighting my way.

Hanes and I carefully threaded our way among the men amidst numerous calls for water and a forest of hands reaching for our skirts. The men's tugging of our hems left filthy handprints, some of it dirt and some of it blood. I said many a "yes, just a moment please", and "I understand", and "we'll be back as quick as we can", as I tried not to look too closely at any particular man so I would not see why he might be reaching for the skirt of a woman he did not know.

Inside the station we found two nurses who had been sent from one of the other hospitals and a grey-haired man wearing a train cap. He stood stooped before the force that was the Nursing Sisters like a thick-trunked, wizened elm standing against a gale—just another of many he had weathered in his time. The Sisters were harassing the aged tree of a station attendant into letting them use the small cook stove that was meant to heat the station as they wished to boil water. Not only were the Sisters demanding the use of Tree-man's station, stove, and supplies, they were also pressing him into service, ordering him to chop more wood for the fire or, better still, find coal if he was able. The Tree-man took one look around at the wounded men that covered every square inch of his previously well-kept floor then looked at the Sisters as balefully as the situation allowed—which was to say, not very, but sufficient to let them know of his displeasure in the upheaval of what had once been his tranquil existence. The man nodded and moved off, presumably to find the requested fuel for the stove.

I went over and introduced myself and Hanes. It took only moments for the four of us to determine our course. One of the other Sisters—the one who had harassed Tree man—was named Wyndham. She was a blustery storm cloud of a woman with steely hair, the thick determined twist of it appearing to resent the confines of the nursing hat she wore. Wyndham set off to recruit women from the near-by church. Together with her make-shift army, she intended to beg donations from every shop, church, and private dwelling, with the intent of returning with medical supplies, food, and water—along with extra hands.

In the meantime, the other Sister—Guthrie—appeared rather like a broomstick dressed in a nurse's uniform so trim and tucked, one had no choice but to understand the woman must have dared to sport a corset under her livery. Guthrie and I would tend to the wounded as best we could with what supplies we had on hand, combining hers and mine. Hanes was to search out water and a means of getting the men the drink they were all calling out for and of which they were in desperate need.

We set off about our tasks, time becoming lost in the minutia of our ministrations. To say there were many men would have been only the beginning—the small grain of truth on which tall tales were built. There were not *many* men—there were 2000 men and more abandoned at the train station—the human waste of War's feast.

It struck me then: this—*this*—was war. This was the reality behind the term "the horrors of war" which people back home casually bandied about. These men—the dross and debris left in the wake of the marches and the battles was what remained—a filthy and odious business that needed to be cleaned up by those whose duties did not permit them to turn away from such ugliness. It was the dark underside the papers did not report so as not to scare those that might otherwise enlist and not distress their mothers' so they did not permit their men to leave.

The scene shattered images learned as a child—the tin-soldier battles of men set neatly in ranks and battalions, marching through the enemy in a single force to come out the other side in the same tidy rows with which they had begun. There was no such concept left in war's wake when one saw it for what it truly was. Any thought of order or conclusion was killed outright on the battlefield along with the soldiers. This war, these battles, lingered and seeped into these men's lives, tainting whatever remained of them and their futures. War did not *end* with the conclusion of the fighting.[29]

And it was our job to clean up the mess and return to these men what remained of the lives they once knew—and we set in to our task with determination.

Together, Guthrie and I handed out morphia and clean bandages to the men lying on the stretchers until our supplies ran out. Hanes had recruited the station hand, enlisting his help to divert water from the water stop that filled the tanks of the steam trains to a trough from which we could draw water in a few buckets that were found in the maintenance shed. She went around with buckets of water and ladles, giving the men drinks of water. The Tree-man returned with fuel for the stove and began heating water. He found a small supply of Oxo and we were soon able to hand out hot Oxo to the men.

In surprisingly short order, Wyndham returned, leading a veritable army of stern-looking and sturdy women, all of whom carried some heavy item: a basket of food, a box of bandages, hot water bottles hanging in line on a string like fish in the market. Four of the woman were, together, carrying a heavy wooden table. The group went into the train station through the back and set up shop. Sandwiches and soup were quickly prepared and were soon being handed around. Together with the other Sisters, I worked to sort the men and triage them for transport to hospital when there was room.

We spent the next several days tending to men on the platform and in the station. We had mercifully mild weather, Mother Nature seemingly commiserating with our situation and trying to help as She could. When more trains arrived, Wyndham would sweep in and demand hospital train staff help to sort the soldiers they were bringing in and move them to the areas we had set out: walking wounded, sitting wounded, and stretchers. Lastly, there was a growing area of dead waiting to be taken to the cemetery for burial. This method of sorting was the beginnings of our triage.

I had long since lost my last hatpin and in flagrant disregard of the rules of nursing conduct, removed my hat and went about with my hair in a bun and exposed for all to see. I could only pray I would not lose my hairpins as well or all semblance of professionalism would be lost.

We cleaned and dressed the men's wounds as best we could. We kept them fed and as comfortable as morphia and simple positioning would allow. I tended to the wounded, watching helplessly as some died by inches over several days. One man lay for twenty-four hours agonizing over each breath he took, trying to get enough air past the bullet lodged in his lung to eke out another minute among the living. I sat with him during those times when I needed to rest my sore feet. As much as I longed to do it, I did not dare to take off my boots for I knew with great certainty I would not be able to cram my swollen feet into them again if once released of their confines. In those moments, sitting with the gasping man, I was only too aware that my aching feet and legs were nothing compared to his agony and yet, despite my good intentions to the contrary, my feet monopolized my thoughts every few seconds.

Another young soldier with a stomach wound asked me to send for his mother as he thought he could not hold out much longer. I assured him word would be sent to his mother. He died within the hour, having never seen his mother again. I wondered then if any of us would see our mothers or our fathers or our friends again.[5]

The nights were a nightmare seen through the dim haze of lantern or candle light, the sounds of moaning punctuated now and then by a sharp cry of pain as someone rolled over in their sleep and disturbed an intractable wound.

We nurses slept in turns and only at need, falling into an exhausted oblivion for several hours only to wake with a heart-thumping start when a wounded cry finally managed to penetrate our exhausted minds. We would find ourselves suddenly on our feet and moving to the man, ourselves not yet fully awake and our stomachs turning from want of rest. We ate as the others did, the volunteers bringing us sandwiches and soup before doling out the food to the patients. We rested when we must, but there was no such notion of "end of shift" or "breaks". Our uniforms grew filthy, the starched collars wilting, but none had brought a change and so we wore what we had.

The stream of men slowly began to shift and change, reversing its ebb and flow, as men from the hospitals returned to the station, from there to be taken to boats which would carry them back to hospitals in England. This emptied beds at the hospitals and the men on the platform began to slowly thread their way to better accommodations and much needed care.

After three days and three nights, Hanes and I returned to the *Hotel Des Emigrants* on a clear, fine morning and reported to the Matron. We had, in the time we were at the train station, never been ordered back to our posts nor had MOs been sent to take over and give orders—as though they could be spared. It seemed the military expressed their appreciation for our work above and beyond our duty by simply not interfering.[31]

On arriving back at the hospital, Matron looked at us for several long moments, inhaled deeply, and slowly let out her breath. Her eyes were dull and rimmed with red.

"We all three of us need sleep," she said. "You have twenty-four hours to get yourselves rested, washed, and fed. Report to the ward for lower extremity fractures tomorrow morning. I will see you then."

I went to my room and collapsed for the next six hours, not even fully undressed. I got up, washed, ate, and collapsed again until I got up to report for duty the following morning.

War Diary

Private Henry Ryzak

October 1, 1916–February 28, 1917
Volume 2

Diary Text: 27 Pages

[October 1, 1916]

The army, in its infinite wisdom, decided to move us around a great deal over the month of October. *Bouloyne* to *Etaples*; from *Etaples* to *Abbeville*; from *Abbeville* to *Villiers*; from *Villiers* to *Beauval*; from *Beauval* to *Bonneville*; from *Bonneville* to *Herisart*. We moved through Camp Warloy where we camped with three other battalions, then continued through *Senlis, Bouzincourt,* and *Albert.*

We started out from *Albert* on October 12th in good weather, moving out in small groups at 500 yard intervals. I kept my gun in front of me and Will behind me. The others arranged themselves loosely in our wake. We encountered no resistance and arrived at the Tara Hill tented camp at approximately 13:30 hours that same day, having suffered no casualties in our battalion.

The term "camp" could be used to define the billets only in the loosest sense of the word. There weren't enough tents for the officers, let alone the soldiers. To us mere foot soldiers, they allotted tarpaulins, expecting the men to shelter under them. Rations were equally scarce.

Fortunately, we had Galt with us. A seasoned soldier, I was convinced he could have found provisions had he been trapped in a sealed tin box. Through his conjuring, we strung our tarpaulins together and into a make-shift tent with enough room for us all, but not so big as to have difficulty keeping the area warm. Stewart had the idea to set up one of our small cook stoves in one corner to add heat while venting the stove out the side.

As for food, Galt took care of that. Our small stove would never cook enough food to keep us fed, nor did we have any such food to cook. Galt had other arrangements in mind. He pulled Tommy aside and told him to load his rifle.

"What for?" Tommy asked, already standing and retrieving his rifle from where it lay on top of his kit.

"I heard geese down by the river we just passed. Ever do any hunting?"

"Well, sure, but even if we can bag one, we don't have anywhere to cook the thing in this rain," Tommy objected.

"Just come with me," Galt replied. Their conversation continued and faded as they made their way to the river. The rest of us waited.

A few hours later, Galt and Tommy returned, not with a goose, but with two packages wrapped in butcher's paper. Tommy also drew two long loaves of bread out from under his rain slicker.

"What gives?" Will asked.

"Break out your mess tins, boys, we've got ham, hot potatoes, and fresh bread!" Galt said in a stage whisper, a smile lifting the corners of his thick moustache. He set down the packages and cut the string with his knife, revealing a cooked shank of ham in one package and steaming potatoes in the other.

We all looked up at him.

"You shot a pig?!" MacClean whispered as he glanced at the door of our make-shift tent. "That'll get you arrested!"

"We didn't shoot no pig," Tommy said in a *we're-not-that-stupid* tone. "We shot three geese. But we can't cook nothing here, so we took 'em to the town just up the road and traded them for this."

We all paused for a very brief moment to take in the information, then immediately got down to the more important business of dividing the food. This was accomplished with only minor disputes as everyone knew we would get to eat more quickly if we weren't taking up valuable time arguing. Rations and cook wagons eventually caught up with the battalion, such as they were, but none could rival Galt's acumen for finding food and, while we never had quite enough to eat, we did not starve.

Work parties were sent out to assist the engineers in the building of trenches. Parties of 50 men went out in 300 yard intervals. We were fortunate not to be detailed for the business. Poor communication between the engineers and the guides leading the work parties caused some of the groups to become lost and wander within range of German guns. Eight men were killed and twenty-five were wounded. One officer went missing and was presumed dead.

Our battalion was kept in reserve, moving to the trenches at intervals for relief duty. The weather turned cold. The trek to and from the trenches became a race with frost-bite, taking longer than it ought as the guides, unfamiliar with rendezvous locations, often got men lost before finding their way back to camp. It was a cold and dangerous business, moving between camp and the trenches amidst the ever vigilant German guns. Extra rum rations were doled out to the men as they returned to camp, both to shore up the men's resolve and to warm them.

I was sorely tempted to keep my rum rations. Not only for the warmth I knew it would bring (false and fickle though it was), but for the momentary relief from mental strain as the rum numbed the mind for an hour or so. I sighed heavily and handed my ration to MacClean. He took the proffered cup, considered me a moment, then saluted me with my own cup and downed my rum ration in one swallow. He handed my tin cup back to me and I moved to the small cook stove to make a pot of weak tea. MacClean handed me his rations of sugar for my tea and I nodded a 'thank-you'.

Rain began a short while after our return to the trenches, adding to our cold misery. Galt sought out an old line of trench from which he and Stewart scavenged wood to keep our cook stove supplied, giving us at least some warmth. It was meagre at best and certainly not sufficient to dry our drenched clothing. We sat, huddled under our ground sheets, trying to keep the rain out and the warmth in, but water is a very malleable substance. The cold drops always found a way down one's collar or up his puttees, or into a man's boots, driving out what warmth we could still produce in our thoroughly chilled bodies. Will and I huddled together, using both our sheets to protect us from the rain and met with somewhat more success. The others eventually paired up and did the same.

The officers had a difficult time trying to find a place for bath parade—something which was badly needed. Both men and clothing were caked with wet, cold mud. A local hospital at *Albert* served as the solution, providing a place to bathe and to dry our wet uniforms. We took over the bath rooms, using the tubs and any other serviceable receptacle for holding water to clean away the better portion of mud we had carried back from the trenches. While we bathed, the VAs and Orderlies hung our uniforms near stoves to dry as best they would in the time we had. We were given clean shirts, socks, and underwear brought in on the supply wagon. Our own clothes were taken away to be laundered and would be handed back to some other soldier after being cleaned. I had never before considered the necessity of dry socks, but would never again take such a luxury for granted.[1]

I kept a sharp eye out at the hospital, wondering if I might see *her* again—hoping so desperately that I would. Sadly, I didn't and I left feeling rather like a limp dishrag. I shouldn't have. It was silly, of course. What were the chances of running into her ever again in the chaos of the war? Besides, she likely had little regard for me given our last meeting, and seeing her again would have availed me only of her disdain. And yet, I thought, I might have taken even that from her if it was all I could have.

It was foolish of me to hope and those lines of thought always ended with a low-voiced curse.

On return to the front line trench, Captain Crain came to where our unit was stationed.

"I need six men to volunteer for a patrol led by myself," Crain announced, surveying our faces. "We need to reconnaissance Hun activities in this part of the front line. I hear your unit is good, but the Lieutenant insisted I ask only for volunteers on this one." He looked as if he had just swallowed a sour grape when he added the last part.

Ransley, who was leaning against the wall of the trench beside me, immediately leaned away from the wall, but I set him back with a hand on his shoulder. He cast me a glance, but didn't say anything, and leaned back against the wall again.

I had heard of Crain. He was inexperienced and ambitious—a risky combination. He placed bets he couldn't make good on and I wasn't about to lay my money on any plan of his.

"Sorry, Sir," I said, "our unit just got into this part of the trench. You should look for a unit who is more familiar with the layout of the area. We'd only get you lost out there."

Crain studied me for a moment then moved further up the line without another word.

The others all turned to me.

"He's a bad bet," was all I said in response to their unspoken questions.

There were a few nods, but no one said anything further.

The next day, Stewart, MacClean, Slater, and I cobbled together a few pieces of wood into a loose sort of box and draped Slater's rain sheet over it to form a make-shift basin. We had just received water rations hauled to the trenches in empty gasoline canisters. We boiled some of it, trying to rid it of the gasoline and poured it into our basin. We set about having a nice shave, taking advantage of the slightly more moderated temperature of the day.

While we were shaving, Old Bill from the unit next to us came over and asked if he could use our set-up after we were done. Stewart said he was more than welcome to a shave if he didn't mind the wait. The older man agreed and sat down to boil more water and wait until we were done.

"Did you hear about the patrol party last night?" Old Bill asked as he sat, watching us finish up.

Tommy's head shot up. "What happened?" he asked from where he lounged in the funk hole.

"They were trying to suss out Jerry's movements when a German covering party found them out. Crain made it back, but all six of his men are missing. Crain got a blighty and was taken away by ambulance."

We all exchanged glances and shook our heads.

"I'll lay odds along with you any day," Ransley said, clapping me on the shoulder.

I only looked at him, then went back to shaving. I didn't always like being right—especially when others died because of it. I had saved the men with me, but had essentially gotten six other men lost, captured, or killed. It didn't sit well with me. I splashed water on my face, ridding it of shaving soap and pulled my towel out from where it hung in the waistband of my pants.

"It's alright, son," Galt said soberly. I turned to look at him. "It's not your fault," he went on. "Crain's gone now and won't be getting anyone else killed. You did the right thing and we all appreciate it." There were nods and affirmations all around.

I nodded and dried my face.

"You can have my spot, Bill," I said.

I walked down the trench a ways and found a patch of sun in which to sit. I sat, rested my head against the trench wall, and lifted my face to the sun. I let my mind go blank or, at least, I tried to.

· · ·

In November, we moved back to billets in *Bouzincourt* before returning to Tara Hill. We drew work details to cut bush along the road and clean out billets. There was another church parade, but this time, Slater went along quietly. We had just heard Private Walton had been given thirty days confined to barracks for a self-inflicted wound as a result of negligence. Those sorts of things tended to make Slater straighten up and fly right for a time.

We also heard Crain was being sent home for his wound and had received a Military Cross for his raid.

[November 20, 1916]

We moved back into the lines by the end of November, making our way in the rain and mist of France's winter. In some places, we had to wade through mud up to our hips as we moved through the rear fields and into the trenches. We were wet and cold every moment of every day. Barrages continued with heavy artillery fire constantly overhead. The sound grated on one's nerves, an incessant reminder of the death that stalked a person, walking unseen among the soldiers lined up in neat rows along the trenches. The unseen snipers made one fear any motion and we ached for want of movement. I made certain Will kept his head down at all times—and the Kid too.

When I could conjure a few hours of sleep, I often dreamt of the dry and heat of a prairie summer, the ground so desperate for water that it blew up in great gusts of dust, reaching pleading hands to the elusive clouds above, circling around me and choking off my air. Waking to the chill and the mist was like awakening into a nightmare rather than from it.

My mind often wandered to the rich, full light of Grieves' eyes and the way the sun had played on her hair during our ride back to camp. I drew every scrap of pleasure I could from the memory, conjuring it so often, I almost wore all sensation from it. Each time I thought of her, it warmed me in a way rum never would, and each time I pushed back against the memory, not wanting to insult her by the recall of that day. I had no business drawing forth her image here or dragging the idea of her through the mud and cold and unending blast of mortar fire that was mine to endure. I belonged there, it had been a thing of my own making—but she didn't. I was grateful she was far from those things, safe and still shining brightly somewhere.

Will received a package from mother and that helped—
a little—in a way it made things worse. Mother had sent
several pairs of socks, some cookies, a small amount of
money, and a very thoughtful number of matches along with
a few candles. She also sent two tins of Zambuk which we
had found was excellent at eliminating the ever-present lice
we had previously had to endure.[1] Accompanying the
package was a long letter recounting the harvest. It was good
to hear her words and be reminded of home as Will read it
out loud—right up until the last paragraph. There, she
confessed father had forbidden her from writing to me
directly and asked that Will share the things she sent, that he
tell me she loved me, and that she prayed for the safety of
both her sons nightly.

"Sorry, Henry," Will said after reading the letter. He
looked at me as one might study a wounded dog.

"Well," I began, "I wish I could say I'm surprised, but
that would be a lie."

I took my share of the socks, matches, candles, and the
Zambuk, but left the rest of the package to Will.

As bad as our lot was, we at times wondered if the
Germans had it worse. One day a Bosche simply walked into
our trench to give himself up. He couldn't have been over
twenty and was in bad shape: skeleton thin, bones almost
pressing through his face in places, hair thin and unkempt,
and he walked stiffly and uncertainly. The medics came and
laid him down on a stretcher to take him to the nearest
dressing station.

The remainder of November and all of December saw
us on the move again. It seemed as though the commanding
officers couldn't quite decide on a plan of action or where
they needed their men. We moved to *Varrens*, to *Louvencourt*,
to *Marius*, to *Sartan*, to *Amplier*. We continued to *Authieule*,
to *Doullens*, to *Neuvillette*. There, we had a bit of a break,
getting good billets in a school in the centre of town. We
were grateful to be in out of the cold and the wind for a
time. We had church parade but no training drills as it was

inclined to rain. We were served a breakfast of tea and porridge and bacon. In the evening, MacClean suggested we find an *estaminent* in the town and we ventured out in the sleet.

We found a small pub and had a supper of chips and eggs. The others bought copious amounts of the local brew. I thought about staying for a few drinks but imagined that could only end badly for me. I also suspected it would make it more difficult to forego the army's watered down rum once we were back in the trenches. I didn't want to go back to that. I was liking the way I felt without it: energetic with my thoughts coming quickly, piecing together information like putting together a puzzle at lightning speed. That wasn't always an advantage in this war, what with some of the things one saw, but as a betting man, I would have placed odds that it would keep me and Will safer longer. I excused myself and walked back to our billets, surprised when the Kid followed me out the door.

We walked in silence for a time before the Kid spoke up: "I didn't like you much at first."

I shot him a sideways glance with a raised eyebrow, feeling as though someone had just given me a hard shove. "I'm not sure what to say to that," I replied, my mind still scrambling to catch the ball from left field the Kid had tossed me.

"Wasn't *you*, exactly, just didn't trust anyone who drank like my uncle did."

Ahhhh…

"I like you better now. You're different. I can trust you." Tommy gave a definitive nod, affirming his own observation to himself.

There were several thoughts that pushed themselves forward in my mind, some objecting to being told I was a drunk and others working through the validity of the Kid's reasoning, but none of them could overcome Tommy's very simple, yet elegant, truth.

The Kid was right.

"Thanks, Tommy," I said simply.

Tommy smiled up at me and we walked the rest of the way in silence.

●●●

Our battalion continued on the move: *Maisnil, Cambligneul,* and finally arrived at *Villers Aubois* in the *Arras* Valley near Vimy Ridge on Christmas day, having marched through the windy morning to arrive just before noon. Two companies remained in support and were assigned to working parties while the other two companies moved to relief in the front line.

[January 3, 1917]

The beginning of the new year saw Fritz commence *einen strafe,* firing *minenwerfers* all day. Five men were killed in the strikes and eleven were wounded. Our trenches sustained heavy damage and many working parties were established to make repairs.

The next evening, Eylon came over to our portion of the trench.

"Private Ryzak," he said in greeting, nodding over at me.

I saluted as I pushed myself away from the trench wall to stand at attention, being careful to keep my head down.

"At ease. We need a sniper to protect our working parties. It looks like there will be a break in the rain tonight and we are desperately in need of repairs to some of our wire lines. There's a party going out at 01:00 hrs. We need you to make the Hun think twice about taking a shot at our men."

"Yes, Sir," I replied. "Any idea where the main barrage is coming from?"

"Come with me and I'll show you."

Eylon and I moved along the trench toward the end of the line where a short ladder allowed a man to get up over the top of the trench. The Lieutenant pointed to it.

"Just up there and to the left a short distance is a small barn. I think if you can get up to the hay loft you'll be able to spot a few of the main gunners in the Bosche's line that way (he gestured to the right) and, hopefully, pin them down. The barn's a bit further along, but still closer to the target than here."

I gave the ladder a wary glance. "I'll head over after dark," I said, somewhat reluctantly.

"Fine," Eylon replied. "Go pick your second."

I nodded and he moved off, back down the trench.

I drew in a deep breath. I had, of course, promised Will he could be my second, but wasn't exactly keen on taking him over the top. I wasn't interested in taking anyone with me for that matter—it was simply too dangerous.

Then I had an idea.

"Lieutenant Eylon," I called, and the man stopped, turning back to me. "I'll need some covering fire when I go over."

The Lieutenant glanced at the edge of the trench then nodded at me. "Fine," he said, "coordinate that with your unit."

I went back to where Slater and the others sat, some sleeping, Stewart helping Ransley mend his torn shirt.

"Will," I said and he immediately looked up from the letter he was writing. "I'll need you to come with me as my second tonight. We have to cover the working parties."

"Right," Will replied, looking as though I had just told him we would be dining at a fine restaurant rather than assigned a dangerous sniping detail. "Got it," he said, nodding.

"Thing is," I continued, "we have to go out past the end of the trench, over the top, and find an old barn some ways out in order to get a proper vantage point. We're going to need some covering fire to draw off the Hun's attention when we go."

I glanced around at the others, waiting for volunteers. I certainly wouldn't ask this of anyone directly.

"This I do," Lundgren replied solidly. "*Ja*, I do some shooting for you to get there."

After that everyone else chimed in. We cooked up a plan, synchronizing a start time. When it was close to zero hours, Will and I grabbed our rifles. We made our way to the end of the trench and the ladder that waited for us there, marking the outer edge of safety.

At the appointed time, we heard rifle fire open up. Explosions banged convincingly as grenades were fired from grenade rifles. There was an immediate reply from the other side of no-man's land. I catapulted up the ladder and ran, crouched low, toward the barn. I could only just make it out in the light of the half-moon as the clouds scuttled across the face of it. I glanced back and saw Will close on my heels. We lit out across a field of tortured corn, the stalks only just standing in the rain-soaked mud.

I paused at the end of the corn field, surveying the bare farm yard. When I saw nothing moving, I motioned to Will to follow me and we crept silently to the barn. We pressed our backs up against the side of the building and moved slowly to the open barn door where we stopped and listened for what felt like an hour. It wasn't that long, of course, and, hearing no sounds from inside, we shouldered our weapons and went in, letting ourselves be swallowed whole by the darkness inside the barn, the syrupy smell of hay pressing in on us.

A pale blue beam of moonlight could be seen high overhead in the loft and we climbed the ladder, emerging amidst the stale hay and dust of the upper barn. Will and I crawled to the opening at the side of the barn, lying on our stomachs and inching to its edge. We had a fantastic view of our front line trench and could see where our line of wire ran. There was a stretch of no man's land and another line of wire marking the front line of German territory on the far side of the field.

I pulled out the binoculars we had been issued (an item which I would conveniently forget to return upon completion of the assignment) and swept my view over no-man's-land. The entire field appeared as though it had suffered the ravages of small pox, with large and small craters covering the land. Debris was strewn about: planks and wire, fencing and bricks, filling the spaces between the holes. Most of the cavities were filled with water from the constant rains and in one I could make out several white hands emerging from the dark, reflective scum on the surface of the water, reaching as though trying to pull themselves out of the watery grave in which they lay.

I lowered the binoculars and handed them to Will as he lay on his stomach next to me in the opening.

"Okay," I said, keeping my voice low, "just like back home with gophers. You spot them and give me directions; I peg them off. We're watching for any enemy fire along their front line."

"Got it," Will replied.

"Oh, and warn me if you see our own men. I wouldn't want to hit them by mistake—can't always see the uniform with this scope at night."

Will chuckled low. "Will do," he said.

I looked at my watch: 23:50 hours. Our work party would be moving forward in ten minutes. I found some boards and piled them up so I had a perch for my rifle. The bottom border of the hole through which I was sighting was made up of short boards. I arranged things so the end of the rifle barrel only just sat squarely between two of them, covering my barrel with some burlap lying nearby. I was hoping to keep the flare of my gunfire as hidden as possible so the enemy couldn't locate our position.

"I can see our work party," Will whispered. He lowered the binoculars and pointed out their location to me. I could just barely make out the movement of a shadow at the near end of our front line trench as it intermittently emerged from the surrounding darkness. Will reported their progress and, for a time, they encountered no difficulties, setting to work repairing the wire in one section of the front line and rolling out more wire.

A loud report split the silence of the night, and star-shaped bursts of yellow illuminated the Hun trench, lighting up a pill box as the machine gun fire continued.

"Straight left then up their line 100 yards," Will said.

I lined up the shot, taking careful aim at the strobing bursts of light. Any success I might meet with would require a large portion of luck. I pulled the trigger and felt the kick of the rifle butt against my shoulder. The machine gun stilled and the night went dark again.

"I think you actually got him," Will said with an *I-don't-believe-it* tone. "I saw the gun fall forward and out the opening just before it went dark."

"Don't sound so surprised," I said with a small laugh, "we've been doing nothing but practicing since we joined up—and they had the entire area lit up—I could practically see the gunner."

"Still, getting a shot inside a box is downright incredible."

"It would be—if I actually hit him. We may never know."

Just then a German flare arched into the night sky in a graceful spray of red sparks. Will and I pressed down to the floor as close as we could, ducking behind some hay we had piled up on the edge of the opening. Will quickly surveyed the area below us through the binoculars.

"Yup, you got him—the gun is half-way out of the box and there's a body slumped on top of it." He swiveled the binoculars to our men. "Our men are scrambling for cover. Looks like the line of wire is finished. Not sure if they have more to do or not."

"Let's hope they're done—if we have to shoot again, they'll make our position for sure."

There was a barrage of gun fire from the German trench aimed in the general direction of our men. I could see some of our soldiers scramble for cover in a hollow.

"They're cut off," Will said urgently. "They're pinned down in the crater."

Then there was a burst of fire from our line. The men in the hole ran, crouching low, as fast as they could toward our trench.

A second later, the gun in the pill box came to life again.

"They're working the gun again!" Will said. "Our men won't make it back to our trench!"

"Yep," was all I said in response. "Get out of here— _now_." I said to Will as I lined up my shot.

"Nu, uh," Will replied, "I'm not leaving."

"Get moving. I'm right behind you as soon as I take this shot. _Go_!" I added when he only stayed, looking at me. Will shook his head at me and frowned, but headed for the ladder.

"One shot!" he called back.

"Yep—just one." I took careful aim and pulled the trigger, very much hoping Lady Luck had returned to my side. The gun barked out a command that hung in my ear. Again, the German gun quieted. When no further shots came from the pill box, I picked up my gun and ran, not wanting to be there when the bombing started.

I was half-way down the ladder, Will waiting anxiously at the bottom for me, when suddenly there was a heated flash and a blast that threw me from the ladder, and then…nothing.

I came to with Will and one of our soldiers lowering me down into our trench. Will and the soldier dropped down beside me where I fell.

"What happened?" I asked.

"They launched a rum jar into the barn and the whole thing came down around us," Will said, helping me to sit up. My head seemed as though it was splitting in two and I felt around in my hair for the hole I thought must surely be there. My hand came up empty. "A beam fell on you. I dragged you out and we met up with our men on their way back to the trench."

I heard his words, but couldn't quite keep them in any sort of order. My gut twisted, and I turned away, emptying my stomach of its contents.

"Medic!" Will called out. No one came. "Can you stand?" he asked, pulling me to my feet. My ears were ringing and the walls of the trench danced around me. Will sounded as though he were miles away and getting farther. I couldn't understand what Will wanted, but followed along when he pulled me to my feet.

I staggered down the trench, clinging to Will's shoulders, my ears ringing. I thought I would vomit again, but then Will was lying me down in a funk hole and I recognized it as the one Tommy had been using. I felt my body give in to the unearthly weight of gravity and was aware of no more.

[January 6, 1916]

I woke to a chill light with all quiet about me (or maybe I still couldn't hear properly). I looked up and discovered I was in a tent. I sat up, putting my feet onto the ground. I waited for the spinning to stop. The air was cool and it helped clear my head. I stood on shaky legs, feeling a drastic tilt of the earth beneath my feet before things settled to rights again. I made my way out of the tent but found myself greeted by a medic.

"Ah, you're up," he said in a clipped British accent and sounding pleased. "Very good—you had some people worried."

"What day is it? Where's my unit?" I asked. "I have to get back."

"It's January 6th best I can recollect," the medic replied. "They left a man from your unit here to take you back when you're ready. The rest of the company was relieved from the front line and went to their billets."

Okay, okay—that was okay: Will should be all right in the billets.

"Let's get you some breakfast and I'll tell the doc to come 'round and have a look at you—see if you're fit to go back." The man flashed me a black-toothed grin and pointed to my tent.

I nodded and went back to my cot to lay my head down. It felt heavy. Ransley entered the tent carrying a mess tin of oatmeal and a cup of tea. Before I could finish it, the doctor stepped in. He took one look at me, asked if I knew where I was and who he was then said I could go back to my unit. I finished my breakfast then Ransley led me to our billets.

"Some of the men said I was to be sure to thank you for them," Ransley said as we walked.

I cast him a glance, but turned back to watching my steps, afraid I might succumb to my vertigo. "Oh? What for?"

"For taking out the gunner so they could get back to the trench in one piece," Ransley replied as though it should have been obvious to me.

"I did what?"

Ransley stopped then and turned to look at me. "Don't you remember?" he asked, a frown drawing down his brow.

I shook my head. "Last thing I remember is going over the top with Will. I vaguely recall him helping me back into the trench—nothing in between."

"You didn't mention *that* to the doc…"

"Nope—I have to get back to Will."

"Okay, well, let's get you back and I'll fill you in along the way," Ransley said. He told me what had happened as we walked. I felt as though I were listening to a fisherman's tall tale: two impossible shots both hitting home against the odds. I wished I could have wagered on them.

We found the others in the billets. They told us of some German retaliation that happened on the fifth in which eight men were killed and six wounded.

We had paid a high price for our repairs after all.

[January 7, 1916]

Over the next several days there was church parade and bath parade. I started to feel a little more like myself after the bath. We then moved between support and front lines at intervals, relieving the 73rd battalion in turns. With the wet weather, we were given new socks immediately after coming off the front line. Again, warm dry socks and dry feet were most welcome. The weather turned colder, however I wasn't going to complain about that too much. The colder weather lessened the dull headache that had dogged me since the sniping mission.

In early February, our company was moved to *Arras Souchez* along with B company. We began hearing rumours of the Americans joining the Allies and later heard official word going around that the Americans had declared war on Germany.

Toward the end of February, raids were almost a nightly event. We dodged them when we could, but my fear deepened with each assignment. Luck had remained with us so far, but I did not trust to her loyalty, changeable as her moods were.

[February 19, 1916]

One day in mid-February, Lieutenant Barron commissioned our unit and three others to undertake a raid on German trenches, the intent being to drive them back a degree. They had been getting a little bold over the previous week. The general idea of the thing was for team A to lead a larger raid under the direction of Lieutenants Norton and Jones while team B, led by Lieutenants Barron and Haldane, would undertake a smaller raid to provide both fire support and distraction, and would then cover the retirement of team A. Barron was to be the commanding officer of the enterprise and I had enough faith in him that I reluctantly agreed to the plan.

I went with Barron along with Will, Tommy, Ransley, Galt, and MacClean plus three men from another unit. I didn't like splitting up our unit and would very much have preferred to keep Lundgren with me, but Barron said it would be best to distribute our best men within the two covering units. I couldn't much argue with that reasoning and allowed the unit to be split up. Lundgren, along with Slater, Stewart, and four men from another unit, formed a unit under Haldane. Lieutenants Jones and Norton each took eight men from other units to make up their larger raiding party.

It was 20:00 hrs on a misty and somewhat windy evening when our squad left battalion HQ for our jumping off point at Lime Street armed with hand grenades, rifle grenades, revolvers, and mobile charges of thirty and ten pounds.

We reached Lime Street on the outskirts of the town and formed into our units. Lieutenants Jones and Norton led their men off to the right, away from the edge of town, and into no-man's-land, moving quietly through the night. Our support units waited a bit then followed along a short distance behind. We stopped before the other team did, forming into a tattered line as men dropped into craters and behind any shelter we could find. Our first order of business was to provide a distraction.

On Haldane's command, Slater launched a rifle grenade, setting off a torrent of fire from both our line and the closest Hun trenches. We lost sight of the other party as they moved beyond the lights of the gunfire and bombs, heading for some bunkers that were to be their target.

We were quickly pinned down, shells whizzing past and bombs exploding unnervingly near, sending up dirt and projectile debris. That wasn't a problem *per se*—we were doing our job holding the Germans' attention while the other team reached their objective.

In the light of a flare, I saw Ransley pressing himself hard into the side of his crater, looking as though he was staring down a hungry grizzly. He looked over at me, his eyes wide. I gave him a firm nod and he nodded back. He shouldered his rifle, lifted it over the edge of his crater, and began firing.

Intent on covering our men, I turned back to the task at hand just in time to see Tommy racing toward a crater close to the German trench like some deranged cat loosed from a hot tin box. My heart stopped for a split second then started up double time.

"Will! Galt! Cover!" I yelled over the percussions surrounding us. I pointed to where the Kid crouched in a hole. We quickly started firing again, laying down a covering barrage so Tommy could get back to us—except he didn't come back. As the enemy ducked down from our fire, the Kid tore ahead to yet another hollow further out. The Huns opened fire again just as the Kid dropped into it.

"What's he doing?" Will yelled over the din as we ducked down into our hole, flinching away from the zinging noise of bullets that whipped past our heads and *thwumped* into the dirt behind us.

"I think he's trying to get to the pill box that's blasting the other party!" Ransley called out.

"He's insane!" I yelled. "Cover him or he'll get his head shot off!"

We all began firing again and watched as the Kid sprinted to yet another shell hole. We soon had a system worked out, Tommy advancing crater by crater under our covering fire, taking cover when the Germans were bold enough to shoot back. He reached the pill box and tossed in a live Mills bomb. We started shooting again and Tommy raced back, bent almost double against the bullets that peppered the air like the mist around us. He dropped into a crater several yards from the pill box and ducked down, covering his head. An explosion burst open the box, sending chunks of cement higher in the air than they had a right to be. Parts of the dismembered bulwark landed with heavy thuds, scattered over the field. Several seconds of silence ensued, and I watched anxiously, waiting for Tommy to reappear from the hole into which he had dived.[1]

I saw him pop up and out of the crater, running like he was being chased by all of the spirits of the dead that lay in the field around him. We opened fire again, keeping the Hun pinned down as best we could for both Tommy and the raiding party.

Tommy was about six or seven yards from our crater when the bomb landed. A grenade from a grenade rifle fell just behind him. Dirt, parts of dead bodies, and debris rose up in a cloud and engulfed the Kid. When the cloud settled again, Tommy lay on the ground, face down.

My chest seized.

"Cover me!" I yelled, jumping up over the edge of our shell hole.

Gunfire erupted around me, sending up a hailstorm of bullets. I tore across the field and slid to a stop beside Tommy like a baseball player rounding into second base.

"Kid! Kid!" I yelled.

Nothing.

"Tomasso!" I was screaming in his ear. He'd have to be deaf to not hear me or …

I crouched down beside the Kid, pulled his arm across my shoulder, heaving the rest of him along with it. I stood on legs that shook under the full weight of the boy, but braced them and gained a firm footing. I took off feeling as though I were trying to run through mud. I felt a hot sting on the arm that held Tommy's legs on my shoulder and ran faster, tumbling down into our crater along with his limp body. We both lay sprawled out on the bottom of the hollow and I stayed there a moment, trying to pull air into my spent lungs.

Will appeared over me and grinned in relief when I moved enough to wave him toward Tommy. I forced myself up and crawled over to where the Kid lay. There was blood seeping from a tear in his sleeve and he was moaning loudly, but didn't open his eyes. I took a deep breath, the first that went all the way to the bottom of my lungs since I had set out after the Kid.

"It's all right," Will said to him, and perhaps to me as well. "You'll be all right." He pulled out a bandage, wrapping the Kid's arm and tying it off tightly.

I picked up my gun again and got myself back to the edge of the crater. I saw a soldier from the other party run to the hole beside us and drop down beside Barron. A moment later, Barron was calling over to us above the noise of the shelling.

"We have to move further down the line! The other squad has met with heavy resistance at the Kennedy crater. They're getting slaughtered and we can't cover them from here!" He waved us forward.

"Leave Tommy here and follow me!" I ordered.

"Wait!" Ransley yelled. He quickly picked up a piece of wood and stuck it upright in the ground at the edge of the crater. "So we know where Tommy is on the way back!" he called out. I nodded at him.

We moved forward, shooting as we went.

I dropped to one knee and lit a mobile charge. I threw it toward the German line with everything I had, sending it just ahead of where we were going. A flash lit up the night sky and I turned away from its brightness, closing my eyes.

"Go! Go!" I yelled at the men still behind me, waving them past me.

We ran down the field. There were explosions and cries ahead of us and I figured we must be getting close to the other squad. I saw Galt drop into a hollow then reappear on its edge and open fire. Ransley fell in beside him. As I raced toward the crater, I saw MacClean veer off, closer to the German line. I could only just make out the top of a German dugout behind their trench. I saw MacClean toss something—likely a mobile charge—then turn and beat a hasty retreat to where we were positioned.

He never made it.

Tonnes of soil, mud, and clay lifted and fell again, a behemoth of earth opening up and swallowing the dugout, the Germans, and the trench whole, taking it back down into the abyss from which it had risen up. Dirt and wreckage piled high just beyond us—right where MacClean had been.

Seconds later, men from Norton's squad, came stumbling, falling into the crater about us. There were few men.

"Where are the others?" Lieutenant Norton yelled at one of the privates.

"Wounded, Sir! Still back there!" he said, pointing in the direction from which the blast had come.

"We have to go get them!" Norton yelled.

Norton and two other soldiers both jumped out of the crater.

"Covering fire!" yelled Lieutenant Haldane as he and Lundgren fell in beside me.

Every soldier who still could began firing on the German trench. We were close enough that a few of us were able to throw Mills bombs and mobile charges close to the trench, buying our men a few seconds as they pulled the injured soldiers into another crater. When they had recovered all they could, Haldane yelled, "Fall back!".

Men began scrambling back toward our line.

"Ransley! Take Lundgren and go get Tommy!" I yelled. They both darted off in the direction of the crater where the stick marked Tommy's location. "Will, you stay with me!"

Will, Galt, and I along with several men from the other unit laid down covering fire while the others retreated with the wounded men. When they were a good way back, we fell back too, divided into two groups, each covering the retreating group in turns.

As we neared our trenches, stretcher bearers came running, helping the wounded. I could see Tommy and Ransley running back toward the trench. Lundgren followed, turning every so often to fire back at the enemy.

We ran until we were out of breath then we ran some more, finally reaching our trench.

Tommy was taken to a dressing station along with the other casualties.

"You too," I heard a medic say from somewhere close by. "You!" he said again.

I looked up at him. "What do you need?" I asked.

"Get yourself to the dressing station!"

"What for?"

"To take care of that wound! Get going!"

Confused, I looked at Will who sat beside me, gasping for air. Breathless, Will could only point at my arm.

I looked at my arm and realized the sting I had felt when getting Tommy was not as slight as I had thought. Blood was still seeping from the area, a red stain spreading down the sleeve of my coat, tattered red threads sticking up from the centre of the tear.

"Come on," Will said, pushing himself up. "I'll make sure you get there."

I nodded and followed Will, tailing along at the end of the line of stretcher bearers, on their way to the dressing station.

[February 20, 1916]

Tommy and I were patched up and kept at the dressing station for our dressings to be changed the next day, while Will returned to our unit in the trench. After clean dressings were put on, the Kid and I were ordered to return to our unit, our wounds superficial enough to be deemed "a scratch".

We went back to our spot in the trench where the others were still on duty.

"Where's Slater and Stewart?" I asked Galt, looking around, but not seeing them anywhere.

Galt only shook his head, his expression that of a shipwrecked man watching the last hope of rescue sailing away on the tide.

I sighed and nodded.

Ransley filled us in on what had happened. The other team had been caught in a heavy barrage near Kennedy crater. Slater and Stewart had been killed along with seven other men. Fifteen men had been wounded and were brought back or had made their way back on their own, thanks to MacClean's bombing and our covering fire. As it turned out, MacClean had unknowingly bombed a dugout housing a mine shaft in which the Germans were storing munitions. The resulting explosion had formed a crater eighty feet wide and twenty-feet deep—now dubbed the Winnipeg Grenadier crater. While MacClean had been buried in the blast, he had saved many lives in the process.

"The Kid did some nice work himself," Galt added, pointing at Tommy.

Tommy nodded soberly and looked down.

"Yep," Will said, "Good work. Good, but insane."

Tommy grinned then, still studying the ground. He sobered and looked up at me. "Thanks for coming back for me."

I nodded, giving his shoulder a squeeze.

Tommy quickly turned away, looking as though he had just remembered that boys don't cry.

[February 22, 1916]

A few days later, raiding parties went out to avenge the deaths of their fallen comrades with an assault on Kennedy crater. They reportedly met with great success and tallied many kills. The Hun retaliated the next day with two separate thirty-minute bombardments, but no one was seriously injured.

We were relieved by the 73rd battalion on February 25th and returned to *Verdrel* where congratulations were received during our Commander parade.

July 10, 1916

July 10, 1916

We have no sooner sorted the handoff of the No. 2 hospital than the Army has given orders for some of us to move out again! Five officers and 34 Nurses and VAs, including myself have been sent ahead to Lezarde Valley to set up a 400-bed No. 7 Canadian Stationary Hospital. Four-hundred beds! Can you imagine all of them full?! I suppose they are expecting casualties from the upcoming Somme offensive, or so the gossip has it.

We arrived at Camp 19 in the Lezarde Valley yesterday. The officers and other men are setting up the tents while the Sisters and VAs are organizing supplies. There is so much to do! Everything must be taken into the tents and put in order: from beds to workstations to treatment areas to the surgical theatre to the pharmacy cabinets. Everything must be constructed, supplied, and organized—right down to the last syringe and needle! The work is unending.

I ought to have guessed at what was coming, ought to have been disabused of my naivety by what I had seen in *Le Havre*, but I was still new to the idea of war. Not yet able to anticipate its vagaries or read its nuances as its labile character changed in turns. There were signs enough had I recognized them. The rumbling of machines and the marching of heavily booted feet along every road as we struggled to make progress in our journey. There were the civilians scampering toward us along the road like rats fleeing a flood. Where once there had been singing, there was now sober expressions on the soldiers as they tramped along. Lorries rumbled to the front in an unending line, laden with soldiers: fresh fodder for the guns.[31]

The tidal wave hit us within days of our arriving, some of our preparations only barely in place. Ambulances came in long lines once again, depositing their burdens in front of the receiving tent and quickly returning to the clearing stations to fetch more wounded without even giving account of the patients they had dropped on our front door. Some scant information could be gleaned from the smeary grease-pencil scrawl on the men's foreheads indicating the time of their last dose of morphia and from the medical tag pinned to their collars. This would (or, rather, may) outline the soldier's wound, what had been done already, what diet to feed them and, most importantly, what their prognosis was—this pivotal piece of information was written across the top of the tag in large initials.

"What does *SI* mean?" Ashwell asked, crouched beside a stretcher and straining to read the medical tag of the man who lay there.

"*Seriously Ill,*" I responded, moving to the next stretcher and checking the time of the man's last dose of morphia. I handed him a pill from the bottle in my pocket and helped him wash it down with a sip from the canteen he still carried.

Ashwell hadn't moved. She only looked up at me, head listing to one side like a confused pup.

"Help the orderly to move him into that tent," I said, pointing to the resus tent. "They will see if they can revive him sufficiently for surgery." The girl stood and grabbed the nearest orderly, but did it with a twisting of her mouth.

"I've filled the buckets with clean water," Barnette said, coming up behind me. "Where shall I bring them?"

I glanced around. "Bring them out to the VAs who are making rounds. They can give medication and let the men have a drink as they go along."

Barnette gave me a nod and was off again.

I moved over to a man when I heard him let out a loud groan. "What is it?" I asked.

He only closed his eyes, clutching his arm to his side. I pried his hand free and looked at his arm, but could find no wound. Instead, I saw a small, round black mark on the side of his shirt. I opened his shirt and inspected the area underneath. A puncture hole marked where the bullet had entered.

"Can't breathe," the man gasped out and pulled at his side again. I quickly wet his shirt and pressed it to the hole. The man took in a small breath then.

"Orderly! Now!" I yelled to no one in particular. An orderly magically appeared beside me and together we hurried the man into the surgical tent.

I explained to the surgeon that I thought the man had a sucking chest wound that was slowly deflating his lung with every breath the man took. The surgeon nodded and pointed to an operating table that was just being cleared of another patient—one that was being carried away with a brown funeral blanket covering him. We set down our patient and the operating theatre Sisters took over, preparing the man for surgery.

Outside, staff were working to sort the chaos into some sort of order.

"Some of the men are asking for something to eat," Hutchinson said, coming up beside me. She stood looking at me like a stray cat waiting for scraps at the kitchen door.

Surely she can see how easily solved this problem is?

Evidently the child could not, in fact, conceive of the solution for she only stood on the spot and continued to watch me.

I sent Lathan, Hutchinson, and Ashwell to the mess tent to bring soup and biscuits to the men. "Feed those who are not going to surgery, but keep the surgical patients without food—they musn't have food in their stomachs during the procedure," I ordered.

"What do you want the rest of us to do?" Garvie asked. Middleton and Hanes had come up beside her and they all three stood watching me expectantly.

I suddenly had difficulty pulling in a full breath.

"Who am I that everyone is asking me all of these things?" I asked.

"Well," said Middleton, her tone implying the answer ought to be obvious to me, "You've done this sort of thing before—at the train station in *Le Havre*. Naturally we would come to you now."

"I simply made that up as I went along—and I wasn't in charge."

"But you *have* done this before," Garvie said.

"Well, yes, but that thunderous nurse was in charge there—she gave all the orders. I certainly didn't do that on my own."

"You're not 'on your own' now either," Hanes suggested quietly.

"But, Garvie, surely you have experience in this sort of thing…" I hedged.

"Sorry, Ducks," she replied with a shake of her head. "I can take charge of a nice neat ward, but not 'is sort 'o thing."

I drew in a full breath then, casting around at the seemingly endless array of stretchers and men.

"Very well, then," I huffed. "Short of a better, I suppose I'll have to do. Garvie," I said squaring my shoulders. "Since you can handle the wards, go about and check that each is in good order and working as efficiently as possible—we need to get these men cleaned up, fed, and into proper beds.

Have each ward send out one staff to escort men inside when they have a bed ready—and see if you can fit in more beds."

Garvie was off before she finished nodding.

"Middleton, you and I shall get buckets and fill them with supplies with which to tend wounds. We shall go 'round to the men and make certain old dressings are changed so the wounds do not get infected. Hanes, keep us supplied with buckets of clean water as we go and help restock our supply buckets."[31]

We all three nodded and ran for our things.

I went from soldier to soldier, cleaning and dressing wounds. Some had been left in the field for days before making it back to the clearing station. Their wounds were caked in mud and dried blood. Several of the men had maggots crawling under a filthy dressing—one that had been slapped on in the muddy field and not changed since. Others were only just beginning to realize they had a ragged stump where a leg or an arm used to be, too befuddled by dehydration and morphia to take note before. Several of the men were cold and silent by the time we could get to them.

We worked through the day and into the next before the receiving tent was cleared and all of the men tended to. We were just looking for anything remaining to be done when Garvie returned to tell us the wards were set to rights with only a handful of men remaining in the theatre.

"All right," I said. "Everyone get cleaned up and get some rest. Report to your wards for assignment when you have had some sleep and food."

Our group shuffled off, barely able to move now that things were quiet and calm.

"Middleton," I said quietly as we walked to the tent we shared. "I don't know if I can do this."

Middleton glanced over at me then turned away again, her eyes on the ground. "And yet, you just did—and very admirably too. I do believe you're made of sterner stuff than you might think."

"Maybe," I conceded. After a pause I continued. "I'm not certain I can rest. There are so many men still suffering. It is all so very sad. I feel I should keep working."

"It will be sad whether you are there to help or not. You'll do no one any good wearing yourself out. We will start again after some food and a rest."

I looked over at Middleton who gave me a nod that imparted *this-is-just-the-way-it-has-to-be* which I returned in kind.

Middleton was right, of course: I felt ever so much better after food and sleep. The next morning, I reported to the tent ward to which I was assigned: abdominal wounds. We had one Charge Nurse, three Nursing Sisters, and five orderlies to care for the one hundred acute cases that were now under our charge. The days were busy, all the beds filled with soldiers and each one with wounds to be cleaned and dressed and all of them begging for water every five minutes.[5]

They were an odd lot, the soldiers who survived—British and Canadian soldiers alike. They would grumble for want of sugar in their coffee while in their cots then, when all was healed again, they would be on their way without gripe, stepping right back into the fray to lay their lives down without a word.[29] One of the men explained very simply: "there's a job to do you see", as though that ought to explain everything right there.

July and August of that year went by in a blur of heat and wounded soldiers. I do recall walking out to a local church one sultry evening to sit in the cool of the cathedral and listen to the calming drone of the women praying. Another evening some of the Sisters attended a concert put on by the orderlies and one of the MOs. Most peculiar to sit in the cool evening air on crates and watch men stand in the middle of a hacked-together stage, listening to music as the tones drifted in and among the disorder of the place. Being out of doors with no walls to even make a pretext of being a theatre, the music darted about as though it were a curious draught, staying to linger here, but then moving quickly on.[5]

A most eccentric experience.

September 9, 1916

Construction has begun on wooden frames to move the hospital out of its tents and into huts. They are building a large mess tent too. When that is done, equipment shall be brought in from Le Havre to our hospital here near Harfleur. It is an incredible undertaking. Imagine moving an entire hospital! I have difficulty believing we shall ever have everything put to rights. However, one thing I have noticed in this war: a great many incredible things have been done that should not have been possible in peace-time. People are quick to work hard toward the war effort and governments are free-handed with funding. I wonder now, if such work is seeming easily done during war-time, why such efforts have not been made before to ease the plight of the down-trodden and less fortunate. But that is weightier stuff for a time and place when the war is over. For now, I am still wondering how on earth shall we manage the patients in the midst of all this turmoil?

And it was turmoil to say the least. In the middle of the construction the wounded continued to arrive. Occasionally we would get a large convoy of patients but mostly they came in an unending trickle from the front. The noise and the movement almost never stopped and one would have to get away from it all just to hear herself think.

One fine September afternoon Barnette and I had a half-day and decided to step away for a bit of quiet. We were walking in a companionable silence along a narrow dirt road, enjoying our solitude together when we heard horses behind us. We turned to see a carriage coming up the road looking much too fine to be out in the middle of a country that was at war. The thing belonged in a quiet English estate and had certainly not been built to withstand shelled roads.

If we had been surprised by the sight of an expensive horse-drawn carriage, we were astonished when the thing stopped alongside us and Lathan and Hutchinson, dressed in their afternoon tea dresses, smiled out at us from the open side windows.

There was a rush of giggles from inside the carriage.

"Grieves, Barnette," Lathan twittered, "fancy meeting you when we're out like this!"

"Indeed," laughed Lathan, "whatever are the two of you doing walking through all this dust? You'll be in a fine state by the time you get where you are going!"

"A thing which will not matter in the least as we are going no place in particular," Barnette replied, looking at the two girls in their carriage in the same way a schoolmarm would address children making a spectacle of a frog in a ditch.

"We are simply enjoying a quiet walk," I added, hoping to smooth over communications.

Hutchinson's face dropped into a pout. "Ugh! How boring! We are all on our way to a country garden for tea. You must join us! It will be ever so much fun!"

Hutchinson disappeared back inside the carriage but her voice carried far and wide: "Teddy! They can come along too, can't they? We simply cannot leave them walking in the dust! Surely we can make room?"

"But of course they are welcome to join us," a man's voice said. The tenor of it hung on my ear in a familiar way. There was an immediate rocking of the carriage as someone exited on the far side.

Hutchinson's face appeared in the window again. "You'll never guess who has arrived over on this side!" she gushed, sounding as though she had caught Santa Claus coming down the chimney. She turned her secretive gaze to the back of the carriage and we all followed suit.

Out from the behind the carriage stepped Sergeant Dunlevy—a rascally officer who had once escorted Middleton and me back to camp when we had been out walking at Shorncliffe! He had been much too forward for my liking, likely encouraged by the way the women of camp adored him.

His parting remarks sprung forward in my mind and I suddenly felt my cheeks light as though on fire. The Sergeant chuckled, his keen gaze fixed on my face, and my face burned hotter. Dunlevy laughed out loud.

"Well," he announced, loud and clear, "it seems the only time I meet you is when you are out walking and in need of an escort! Come ladies, Lieutenant Sathers is with us as well. We shall make a merry party at tea!" The Sergeant stepped forward and opened the door of the carriage, extending a hand to help us in.

Barnette and I looked at one another for a moment. Barnette shrugged then step forward to let the Sergeant help her into the carriage.

I followed Barnette inside, squeezing in beside Hutchinson and finding myself sitting opposite a rather narrow-framed man whom I could only assume was Lieutenant Sathers. He smiled and tipped his cap to me. I had no time for polite reply as Dunlevy dropped onto the seat beside me, pressing close in the narrow confines of the coach. He pulled the door closed and thumped the side. I heard the slap of the reins and we jerked into motion. I was jostled back against Dunlevy and felt rather than heard his low chuckle as it rumbled through my ribs. I straightened away from him as much as the close quarters would allow. Out of the corner of my eye, I could see a grinning Dunlevy watching me.

We drove along with unending conversation supplied by Hutchinson and Lathan as they plied the two men with questions about what they expected to find at the front and how long they would be staying before moving out and how many men did they have under their command and weren't they frightened to go and wouldn't it be much better to stay at the hospital—as though that were an option for men under orders.

I chose not to listen to the questions overly much nor to the answers as neither seemed to quite ring true. I was tired of chatter and noise and stories from the front—the wounded brought those with them by the bucketful for anyone who took the time to listen. Instead, I watched the countryside passing outside the carriage window, mesmerized by the blur of early fall colours. For no reason other than perhaps the similarity of the situation, my mind drifted back to the ambulance ride I'd shared with Private Ryzak and the clear-water scent on his very warm jacket. I gave my thoughts free rein.

When the carriage turned up a curving drive and stopped, I checked my wandering thoughts, bringing them back to present day. Dunlevy quickly hopped out of the carriage, helping each of us women out in turn. I stepped down from the coach, watching my step closely to find the small metal footplate. When I had successfully navigated my way onto the step and had firm footing, I looked up to see a large chateau rising tall and splendid on its own pedestal of a hill.

"Do you like it?" Dunlevy asked, stepping up beside me and looking down on me as I stared at the structure. It appeared as something out of a fairytale—a castle, hidden at first, then emerging from the woods as one neared.

"It's very grand," I said. The statement was true enough, although I kept other thoughts to myself. What I didn't say was that, had I stumbled down that lane on a dark night, the edifice before me might well have sent me running as quick as my legs could carry me as if in a nightmare more than a fairytale.

"It is, yes," the Sergeant replied. I turned to see him smiling down at me.

"Sergeant!" Hutchinson demanded, coming up alongside Dunlevy and linking her elbow in his. "Which way to the gardens? I'm simply famished!"

Dunlevy smiled good-naturedly and replied, "Right this way." He moved off, Hutchinson clinging tightly to his arm. Lathan did the same with the Lieutenant while Barnette and I found ourselves trailing after the small group without a clue as to where we were going or what exactly it was that we were doing there.

Barnette and I exchanged a small smile and walked along, taking in the impeccably manicured grounds.

We rounded the back of the chateau and entered a large, precisely kept garden with a picture-perfect cottage set off to one side. There were tables set out on the lawn, circled round by flower bushes and small trees.

Dunlevy went to one of the tables and held a chair out for Hutchinson. He looked up at me then. "Lieutenant Grieves, why don't you join Katherine and I at this table?"

I nodded and went to sit in the chair he presently pulled out for me. Barnette joined Sathers and Lathan at a near-by table.

"What is this place?" I asked as I took in the gardens. "I mean: how is it we are having tea here? It appears to be a private residence."

"The owners of the chateau have removed themselves to a safer location," Dunlevy explained. "They have given the caretaker and his wife leave to do what they can to maintain themselves until the owners' return. He and his wife make their way by serving tea to the officers and their acquaintances before they are moved to the front."[5]

The caretaker's wife came by to greet us then left again to bring us our tea. We were soon enjoying fresh bread with butter and jam, boiled eggs, coffee, and two types of liqueur. It was a marvelous thing to sit quietly out of doors enjoying the warm September sun, everything stillness and quiet and with air that was ever so much more breatheable than the air heavy-set with the fumes emanating from the incinerator back at camp.

It was still early when we had finished our tea and the caretaker came over to collect payment. Sathers asked if we might tour the gardens and the caretaker was most accommodating. We were left to wander about, taking in the rolling hills, trees, and bushes. I lingered behind on the walk, collecting some autumn leaves and enjoying what solitude I could until Dunlevy dropped back to walk with me and forced me into polite conversation. As always, he was charming enough and his conversation full of descriptions of the surrounding countryside, such that I could not possibly remain aloof for long.

November 5, 1916

Had I known how cold it would become, I should have taken much more care to enjoying that last, warm outing! The weather has turned piercingly cold and we have resorted to sleeping with our uniforms and socks on for it would be much too cold to strip off our clothing in order to get into bed—and heaven knows how much colder to dress in the morning! Hot water bottles are in very short supply so that one can often not find a bottle to take to bed. Barnette and I are taking turns keeping the stove burning through the night, but it is a bitter pill to have to leave one's warm bed and trudge over to the thing to put in more wood. I find myself racing back to my bed to reclaim some of the warmth I left there. I simply cannot conceive of how our poor Tommies are getting on out in the trenches! They bring back terrible stories of the cold and trying to warm themselves when all is wet and open air. I am quite certain I would freeze quite solidly if ever I should have to trade places with them. Even their stories make me shiver.

But I am saved. I received a birthday package from Mum yesterday and am ever so grateful for it! Woolen petticoats, stockings, and pyjamas right when I shall be in need of such things. I wonder if I might fit my pyjamas under my uniform like woolen underwear? Mum is such a dear, always making certain I am well-stocked.

I may have had the luxury of a dry bed and warm clothes, but the soldiers certainly did not. Men came in from the front with feet blackened, rotting from frostbite and trench foot. The smell was almost more than we could bear until we got them cleaned up and sorted. Most often the limb would have to be amputated for there was no salvaging a foot once it had blackened. One man came in with his toes solidly frozen so that they simply fell, dead and black, into the basin with a loud *clink* when the MO tapped them with the reflex hammer—no anesthetic nor surgery required. I shall never forget that sound.

The cold created problems for us when caring for the men too. Ink would freeze solid so we could not make our notes and we would have to thaw the ink wells on the stoves in the tents. Oil for the lamps froze too and if we did not think to thaw some of it before night, we would have to make do with candles. The candles would blow out, often at the most exasperating times, blotted out by the draughts that leaked in around the tent flaps. Food and milk froze if we did not keep it near the stove. Overall, we would all go to bed cold to the bone and unable to generate enough of our own heat to warm ourselves—no matter the heavy bedding. I often thought of Ryzak's warm jacket that winter. I was glad I had returned it to him—he would be in desperate need of it.[31]

War Diary

Private Henry Ryzak

March 1, 1917-April 4, 1917

Volume 2

Diary Text: 7 Pages

[March 1, 1917]

Ours was one of two companies from our battalion that were moved into billets just behind support lines at *Arras* near Vimy Ridge. Rumours were rampant: the Huns were in reach of Paris; *Passchendaele* had been recaptured; and our area was surrounded by the Germans. Some said there was preparation underway for another large offensive and the way resources were being mobilized, we thought at least some of the rumours were likely true.

We took on force with Private Robert Barlow and Private Alastair Tulloch joining our company. Barlow was a well-meaning man and very pragmatic. He had a knack for getting to the bottom of a problem and tackling it directly. He had joined up when hail had wiped out his crops back home. He said he needed an income to support his family and thought the war would guarantee work.[39] Ever practical he added that, in the likely event of his death, his wife could sell the farm and remarry, so it would all work out for his family regardless of what became of him.

Tulloch was an outspoken Scotsman who could be a little too straightforward at times. I didn't mind, thinking there was simply something lost in translation in the way he spoke, but others didn't take well to it. He was a member of the 42nd Royal Highlanders known as the "Black Watch". When they were told their unit was being split up to shore up numbers in other units, Tulloch had immediately asked to be assigned to our unit. Apparently, he had heard of MacLean's feat and felt, as he put it, "ye cannae be withoot a Scot among ya ta be savin' yer hides now an' agin".

On March first, we were moved to billets in *Verdrel*. It was cold and snowing as we made our way along the road. The wind whipped at our faces and whisked away any heat our greatcoats might have held. There was a constant stream of locals flowing past us in the opposite direction, moving farther from the front and making me feel like a fish swimming upstream. The people moved as if in a chain, carrying their meager possessions. Some items were borne in large sacks slung over their shoulders, others in wheelbarrows stacked high with pots, jars, clothing, and food if they were lucky. On occasion we would see a cart being pulled along by some bony and woe-be-gotten creature—usually a horse, but I once saw one pulled by a large, ragged mongrel of a dog.

I had tied my spare shirt around my head, hoping to shield my face from the stinging snow. Snow alone would have been nothing, but the tossing of the wind had the effect of sharpening each flake to a razor's edge so that it battered our faces like a hail of shattered glass. I would have thought our lives on the Canadian prairies had inured Will and I to such weather, but I was wrong—one did not simply "get used to" biting ice driven before a maniacal wind. Will elbowed me, interrupting my morose musings. I turned to him and he pointed to the side of the road on our left.

A stick of a woman knelt in a ditch, surrounded by a few possessions that lay scattered around her in the snow, among them, an empty wooden box on its side. The woman huddled low to the ground, trying to pull an infant to her and tie it to her with a long piece of thin, colourless cotton. The baby was howling but could not be heard above the cry of the wind.

Will gave me a look and I nodded. We stepped out of ranks and made our way over to the woman. She startled as we approached and her head snapped up. I could see a thread of tears frozen to her cheek. She quickly pulled her baby to her, holding it tightly. Will held up his hands as if in surrender. The woman hesitated, casting Will a cautious glance, then went back to her wrapping. Will knelt and held the infant in place for the woman while she swaddled the baby against her chest. When she had secured the infant, she pulled her coat closed about them both, hiding the child from the winter wind. She looked down at the detritus that lay at her feet: threadbare clothes—both the woman's and the infant's; a couple of diapers, a pan, several small sacks presumably containing meager rations.

Suddenly, a gust of wind kicked a gauzy kerchief into the air and I grabbed it on impulse as it tried to make its escape, snatching the fabric out of the air. I looked down at the feeble piece of cloth, the wind still trying to tear it from my hand. The embroidered red and pink flowers along the kerchief's edges clung tightly to my fist as if struggling to hold on to the only secure footing it had found. I tucked it into my pocket. I went over to the box, set it upright and, together with Will, we began picking up the woman's flotsam and depositing it back into the box while the woman watched, holding her baby through her thin coat.

I carried the box over to the woman and held it out to her. She looked down at it then glanced at the infant inside her coat, now quieting. She looked up at me as though I had just asked her to choose how she would like to die. She sighed heavily then pulled two of the small sacks from the box and started forward, a sack in each hand. I was left standing there, box in hand as she rejoined the thin thread of refugees walking along the ditch.

Will and I exchanged a glance.

We heard the sound of cart wheels and turned to see a two-wheeled farmer's cart moving toward us. Both the horse pulling the cart and the elderly couple in it appeared to have seen better days. Will elbowed me again and waved me over to the cart.

When we reached the couple, Will began talking and gesturing to the woman with the baby, by then some distance away. He pointed to the box, and he pointed to the back of their cart.

The couple only stared at Will with reluctant eyes that bulged from their sunken depths.

Will pulled out ten francs and held it up to them and their reluctance immediately turned to accepting nods. I set the box in the back of the wagon and Will went to retrieve the woman and infant. We left the elderly man to help the woman and baby into the cart, a weary smile on her face as she thanked the man over and over again. Just before the cart pulled away, I pressed another five francs into the woman's hand and handed her the gossamer handkerchief edged in flowers. She stared up at me for several seconds before scooping the coins from my palm. She pushed my other fist closed over the piece of cloth and held it tight for a moment. She let go, casting me a watery smile. She stayed like that, just staring at me until Will and I turned and walked away while the cart rejoined the stream of refugees and set off in the opposite direction.

I reached into my coat, tucking the handkerchief into my shirt pocket for safe-keeping.

We reached the billets of *Verdrel* and found them to be in bad shape. They had no heat in the huts and the wind howled between the feeble structures. Snow had blown in under the door creating a small drift in the entry. This time, it was the Scot that came through for us.

I heard him talking outside our hut as the rest of us were reluctantly dropping our kits onto various bunks.

"Hold up there, lads," Tulloch boomed as he poked his head into the hut. "Pick up yer gear an' follow me."

The others all turned to look at me. I shrugged, picked up my kit, and followed Tulloch outside. The others fell in line behind me.

"This way," Tulloch boomed, waving us forward.

He led us to an abandoned bunker where several other men were in the process of packing up their kit.

"It's all yours," one of the others said, clapping Tulloch on the shoulder as he passed by.

"Many thanks, lads," Tulloch called after the group. He turned to us then, "We can stay here," he told us, descending the stairs into the bunker. "Much warmer they said."

We followed him inside. It was a large, concrete bunker with bunk beds lining each side of the room. At the end was a wood stove, still warm from the small fire flickering inside.

The warmth surrounded me, driving back the cold of the winter wind in degrees.

"How did you manage this?" Ransley asked.

"Always scout out the billets when ye get whar ye're goin'," Tulloch replied. "T' best ones empty last as those before us are in no rush to leave 'em. I found those gents just packing up to go when I was looking 'round. They said we could take over the place as soon as they were oot."

"Nicely done," Will said, nodding and dropping down onto a bunk bed.

"I'll go find some more wood," Barlow said, setting his kit down on a bunk.

"I'll help," I said.

We were soon settled with a nice supply of firewood drying by the stove and cups of strong tea warming our hands.

For the next several days, our unit was assigned to a work party repairing the other billets, digging ditches to allow for drainage of melting snow, and re-building bombed roads. The road work was the heaviest. We set up an assembly-line to collect rocks from the fields and move them to fill the shell craters in the roads. By the end of each day, we were physically tired, but our minds were still busy with thoughts of where all this preparation was taking us, the efforts providing ample grist for the rumour mill while the men worked.

We moved into the front line again. Preparations were underway for more raids on the German trenches. The units assigned to the raiding parties were from the 72nd and 73rd battalions, so we were not involved. It was a good thing too. The raids did not go well and the parties returned with men killed, missing, or wounded.

We spent long nights in the trenches, each night ending with the order to "stand to" in the blurred and weary hour just before dawn. That was when the Germans liked to attack—in those moments when men were most prone to dozing off and when many had already done so. Invariably, some officer or another would wind his way through the trenches hissing the command to "Stand to!". We would rouse ourselves and take up our guns as best as still-sleeping hands and chilled minds could, then line up against the trench walls with rifles at the ready. There we would wait, the ice-fogged air swirling about our faces, our stomachs turning over from hunger or lack of sleep or both. We stood through the first hour and sometimes the second, silent as death in those still moments just before a frozen sun broke through the black ice sky, knowing the world might crash down on our heads in an instant.

Those were the moments I wished I still drank.

December 16, 1916

December 16, 1916

We are making the best of things for the men in our care, far from their families and with Christmas on the way. There is a bit of a competition amongst the units to see how well-decorated they can make their wards. We have all of the able patients making paper chains to put up along the walls and to hang from the ceiling. Pity we don't have entirely the colours we need, but the chains are quite festive even if they are of pink or blue. One of the orderlies went out to the woods and brought back several small fir trees. Middleton helped me get each tree into a pot of dirt and we set them about the ward. Now all the patients are working up decorations to hang on them. Some are really very lovely like the star one soldier carved out of wood. He said for me to keep it after the tree was taken down and I shall be glad of it.

December 24th, 1916:

Have only just enough reserve to write this brief entry before bed, I am so stuffed with cake, crackers, mince pies, pastries, and carrot pudding from the Sisters' dinner! I had not planned on attending—it seemed to me rather self-indulgent. But Ashwell, Lathan, and Hutchinson had convinced Barnette to go and she insisted I come along so she had someone with whom to sit. It was, after all, a bit of all right. The officers had got together a few songs to sing for us during our dinner and I very much enjoyed the music.[5]

December 25, 1916:

Marvelous day, even though we are all far from home. I went to the early service of church before shift. Sadly, it was not much of a service. The Padre is not much of a figure among the men. And yet, it was a pleasant sort of way to start Christmas morning.[5]

Later, all of us Sisters raided the store-room and made quite the feast for the men. We served them tea of iced cakes with little candles on them, mince pies left over from the Sisters' dinner, and even found some claret. The VAs and orderlies pulled together acts and made a talent show then we set out games for the men to play. While they were busy, we went around and gave out small stockings stuffed with handkerchiefs and shaving soap and even a few bits of hard candy that the church women back home had sent.[5]

After we were done for the day, the Sisters were invited to the officers' mess. It was a merry gathering with games and music around the tree. Dunlevy is really a fine singer, although I do wonder if it was me at whom he had winked during the singing. I think it was, for when I blushed rather inconveniently, he laughed. His behavior after the singing was not at all better. The scoundrel!

However, I arrived safely back in my room by midnight and was asleep almost before I lay down!

It was scandalous really. After the singing, Dunlevy came over to where I was standing and talking with Middleton. Middleton politely moved off (even though I tried to get her to stay), leaving Dunlevy and I on our own at the side of the room. He lifted his glass of claret and said, "To the New Year and a much better one it shall be!"

I clinked my glass to his and toasted with him. "And what makes you believe it will be better?" I asked. Personally, I could not see the war ending so quickly as all that.

"Well," Dunlevy said, one corner of his mouth twisting up into a grin as he inched toward me a half-step, "for starters, I'm quite hoping you and I can become better acquainted."

"Well, I must disappoint you on that front," I said, looking down, but keeping watch of the man's feet.

"Disappoint me? Why ever would you do that?" he asked. I looked up and his grin had lessened a degree.

"Because I am engaged," I replied. "You and I getting better acquainted would not be appropriate."

Dunlevy's grin widened again. "Oh, is that all?" he asked. "I shouldn't think a little thing like that need get in our way."

"Sergeant!" I scolded. "That is truly an improper thing to say!" I frowned and shook my head at him. I set my glass down on a near-by table and turned to walk away, but the Sergeant's hand quickly reached for my own and I found myself being pulled back.

"Oh, no you don't!" He said. He had set down his glass and wrapped his other arm around my waist, pulling me close. I could smell the claret on his breath and my mind flashed to the barn and John's face close to mine.

"Sergeant, you have had far too much to drink!"

"I have. Yes."

"Let me go."

"I think not. You're much too beautiful for me to let you get away. The manner in which you blush is quite beguiling."

Recalling a useful trick an orderly had taught me one night, I reached for Dunlevy's hand where it gripped my wrist and caught his thumb. I bent it backward until his hand let go of my wrist and kept pulling until he had no choice but to sink to his knees to lessen the pain of it. I gave the man a sharp look which he likely wouldn't remember when he sobered up, but it felt good to give it none the less. I stepped past Dunlevy where he knelt on the floor and left for my room.

As I lay warm in my bed, I had two thoughts about the incident: the first was to be appalled at the man's behavior, insulted that he would think me like all the other women with whom he amused himself; the second was to feel quite pleased with myself at the way I handled the situation. I thought that, just perhaps, I might be able to manage John sufficiently after all…

December 31, 1916

The Hotel des Emigrants was handed over to the No. 2 Hospital staff and the remaining staff of the No. 7 Hospital will be joining us in our little tent hospital at Harfleur. I am pleased with how well we have set it up and am certain the others will find it well-organized and running quite efficiently.

February 27, 1917

Our small tent hospital has expanded to 400 beds, and none too soon! The Germans have been using gas on our men. It is ghastly what gas does to a body. Infernal beasts! Their

consciences shall die a martyr's death and leave them with
naught but their own hollow hearts to guide them![8]

Never did I feel worse for patients than when they suffered the gut-wrenching grip of poison gas. Columns of gassed soldiers could be heard a mile off as they trudged slowly and breathlessly along the road, walking double file and each holding the shoulder of the man in front, each one blind and choking from the fluid in his lungs—a train of chalk-covered, pale ghosts who did not yet understand they were dead. We would immediately strip them of their clothes and wash them down to stop the poison's effect as it eeked in through their skin. Why this had not been done earlier was never quite clear—perhaps lack of water or time or understanding. Regardless, it was left to us to do and the men to suffer under the rough treatment of the gas residue along the entirety of their trek until they could be rid of it. If the gassing had been mild, it would appear as a pneumonia while the more severe victims were blue and gasping or worse, gurgling in their own secretions and blood, unable to breathe past the fluid in their lungs. Some, more fortunate than others, simply died instantly.[31]

One cold morning I watched a soldier in the yard behind the hospital. He had been blinded from gas. His eyes were bandaged tight against the light. He fumbled with an axe as he tried to feel where he had set a log in order to chop it. He took a swing and missed the timber wildly, the axe landing very near his foot.

"Stop!" I shouted, and started off toward the patient. "I shall have an orderly chop the wood if it is needed," I said, coming up to the man and reaching for the axe.

"No, he will do it himself," Middleton called from behind me.

I turned, trying to parse out her words for they did not quite fit. "But he could hurt himself," I objected.

"He could," Middleton said, "but best to have that done with here where there are people to tend to him. This man

221

will not be getting his sight back. He lives alone on a farm. He must be able to chop wood or he will freeze to death in winter. He will learn how to do this here and now or it will be on your own head if he's to freeze when he gets home."

"She's right, Miss," the man said quietly. "As maddening as this is, it's gotta be learned. Stand clear, Miss. I don't want to hit you by accident."

"Of course," I said. I stepped well out of the way. "All right, I'm away."

The man nodded and knelt to feel for the wood and set it up again.

"Call out if you need us," I said. The man nodded and took a swing at the wood. He struck it dead-on that time and a small smile lined his mouth when he heard the crack of the wood.

April 4, 1917

War Diary

Private Henry Ryzak

April 4, 1917– April 9, 1917

Volume 3

Diary Text: 12 Pages

[April 5, 1917]

We knew something big was coming. Battalions were on the move in full force. Long rivers of munitions-laden army vehicles moved along the road like icebreakers leading a fleet, streams of soldiers following in their wake.

[April 8, 1917]

We moved to our appointed positions along Vimy Ridge—A, B, and C companies as well as HQ moved into Vincent Tunnel while our company was positioned in a dugout further south along the ridge, grateful for the shelter from the misty rain.

[April 9, 1917]

We were roused by the Sergeant at 5:30 the next morning. The weather had turned chill overnight and I could see my breath hanging in the air as I breathed. The snow and rain fell silently down, creating an ephemeral cloak about us, separating each man from the others. We were given tins of whale oil and told to put it on our feet to keep the water from them lest we succumb to trench foot.

We watched from our dugout as A and B company went up over the top of the trench, hunched down against the rain. The men went forward in waves, each unit pausing and dropping down to shoot while the men behind moved forward. Lines of our soldiers swept along without waiting for covering fire from our side. They gained a fair amount of ground before the enemy put up any resistance.

The Germans finally moved men forward toward our line, rifle fire and bombs going before them. Our men fell one by one as they advanced until our own machine guns opened fire and drove the enemy back. The dead from both sides sank down, into the reaching mud that pulled them to itself, reclaiming its own.

Will and I crouched at the edge of our dugout, watching the slaughter and blinking at the thundering noise of the blasts. The others sat in a shared stony silence, men reconciled to their fate and wearing their resignation like a veil to hide their desolation.

Suddenly several men jumped down into the opening of our dugout and all therein immediately put their hands to their rifles. The men were our own, others from another unit. Their unit had been cut down to a quarter of its strength and they had come to join ours.

"Over there!" the Captain yelled over the rifle fire raging around us. He pointed to the ridge on the right.

Through the blurring rain, I could see a row of German soldiers at least two-hundred and fifty yards long just emerging from their trench, followed by row after row of more grey-coated men.

"Come on, men!" Captain Drewe called out. "We can't let them get past our line or they'll have us surrounded!"

We all raised our rifles and began firing on the advancing enemy wall, blinking against the rain as we tried to aim our rifles.

Then, further to our right, one of our Lewis guns made its presence known, cutting down the Germans as they swarmed forward. The German advance was torn like tissue paper in water, the pieces falling where they stood or flying back to the German trenches.

The German attacks continued. The enemy advancing and our men driving them back time and again. They were focused on our right flank, trying to chip it away so they could skirt our lines and get behind us, hemming us in.

More of our men fell with each repelling of the enemy and reinforcements were sent in. At some point, Drewe ordered Galt, Tulloch, and Ransley to shore up a unit to our left, leaving me, Will, Barlow, Lundgren, and Tommy in the dugout along with several men from the other unit.

We were losing men quickly and our right flank was weakening despite the reinforcements. Tommy elbowed me and jerked his chin toward the right. I looked over and saw a group of Hun running toward the far edge of our trench, crouched low and throwing grenades before them as they ran. The men in the trench fell under the blasts and I saw an arm fly up then lost track of it in the dirt and debris that billowed up. One of our soldiers was blown up and out of the trench. I heard his neck give a loud snap as he landed head first in a crumpled heap.

"Follow me!" I yelled, and hurried out of the dugout, intent on charging at the Germans and keeping our line intact. I blinked against the heavy snow that pelted my face as I ran.

I ran toward the advancing German soldiers, firing as I went and trying to aim in the murk of an unlit day. I didn't have time to see if anyone followed. When I was quite close to the site where the bomb had exploded, I jumped down into the trench and found myself face to face with several German soldiers just entering it from the far side. Bodies lay at the bottom of the trench, slowing the influx of the Jerries as they tried to wade through the dead and dismembered.

I dropped to one knee feeling the soaking of my pants where I knelt, and fired as quickly as my gun would allow. I heard shots from behind me and saw the Germans go down one at a time while I reloaded. When they had all fallen, I turned to find Lundgren and Tommy behind me.

"Where's Will?" I asked, looking around frantically.

"He went with Barlow and the other two—they stayed up top," Tommy replied.

I raced back to the ladder and up out of the trench. I looked around frantically, trying to find Will.

"There!" Lundgren pointed with his gun.

Some distance off, several Germans were ushering Will and the others back toward the German line, aiming rifles at their backs. Will staggered and fell to one knee. One of the Germans hit him with the butt of his rifle and Will scowled back at him. Will stood and began limping forward, his hand to his thigh.

I tore forward, full speed, mud splashing up and fleeing my feet, the sleet stinging my cheeks. I couldn't fire, worried I would hit Will or one of the others. Just before we reached the Germans, one of them turned.

"*Achtung!*" he yelled, and all of the Jerries with him reacted. Will and the others had been stripped of their weapons and could only watch or dive for cover as we advanced on the German squad, shooting as we went.

Shots rang out from both sides, a bullet coming so close to me that I heard the whine of it as it whistled past my ear. I stopped and lined up shot after shot, feeling the gratification as one by one, a German fell with each shot I fired.

When all of the Hun were down, Will and the others hurried back toward us, hunched against the wet wind and the assault of enemy fire from their line.

I moved forward to help Will who, by that time, was limping badly and running doubled over as he clutched his left thigh. I could see a stream of watery red running between his fingers and down his leg. I pulled his arm over my shoulder and moved him forward as fast as I could, half carrying him as we ran.

Just ahead of me, I could see Lundgren helping one of the other soldiers whose foot was torn away. Lundgren had flung the soldier across both his shoulders as though the man were a slab of meat, the man's destroyed foot dangling from his leg by a strip of ragged flesh and a piece of puttee.

We hurried forward in a disjointed group, Tommy and Barlow covering our rear as we moved back. We were about 50 yards from the safety of our dugout when I felt the ground shudder then drop out from beneath my feet. It was as though time stopped and the laws of gravity were suspended. I felt Will's weight lift from my shoulders. I turned to see him seemingly float away into the wave of fragmented light that billowed up around us. A cloud of dust and brightness surrounded us, cutting us off from all else. All around was a pressing silence. I looked at Will as we floated there and, for the briefest moment our gaze met. I saw in his eyes a man searching, trying to find a foothold in a foreign world. Will disappeared then, swallowed whole by the engulfing cloud.

Then I was falling, time and gravity firmly reasserting themselves while I still hung upside down in the air. I landed on my shoulder, feeling the harsh reality of wet earth as it drove the air from my lungs. I heard a crack like that of river ice breaking in spring thaw and felt a stab of heat shoot through my shoulder. A jolt shot up the same arm and I quickly rolled off of it, sinking into the cold mud as I tried to escape the throbbing burn that lingered in my arm. It was a moment before I could draw in enough air to clear my head, the rain caressing my face as I lay there. The cloud that enclosed me settled to the side and I pushed myself up, sitting and pulling my right arm to me. It wouldn't lay against my chest properly, sticking out at an angle. I glanced down and saw that the entire arm hung oddly down at the shoulder. There was blood seeping into the fibres of my coat about half-way down my upper arm. The hot coals that seemed settled in my arm began to burn in earnest then and quickly spired into a flame. I winced, pulling my arm to my side as best I could.

I looked around and saw Will lying not far away. He was not moving.

No, no, no!

I pushed myself to my feet and staggered over to him then dropped down beside him.

"Will! Will!" I yelled. I could feel his chest rise and fall, but he didn't open his eyes. I checked him over quickly, searching with my good hand, looking for his injury. All I found was the same bleeding wound to his leg.

I glanced around and, while I could see several bodies surrounding me, I saw no movement from any of them. I forced myself to my feet, ignoring my arm as it screamed out at me from where it hung limp by my side. I grabbed

Will's coat collar—the best I could do—and started dragging him back to the trench. He was lighter than I would have thought, but then, I realized, rations had been thin for some time. I stumbled once, the mud sucking at my boots, but managed to stay on my feet and kept my death-grip on Will's collar. Step by halting step, I jerked Will back, my right arm dangling loose and swinging by my side with a tooth-aching pain that made my stomach roll like a ship in a storm.

We were several yards from our trench when the barrage began. I ducked at the cracking of shots. One of our machine guns opened fire then and I got up, pulling Will with what strength I had left.

I passed another body and cast it a quick glance to make certain Will's legs would clear it on our way past. My feet stopped of their own accord when I saw Tommy laying in the mud. He lay on his side, eyes closed and blood seeping from his head mixing with the snow and rain and mud. My chest seized for a time and I had to work to start breathing again. I quickly looked around, searching for something to use as a marker. I snatched up a fallen bayonet that lay in the dirt nearby, the metal cold and stinging my hand. I thrust the point of it into the ground beside Tommy, then scooped up Tommy's helmet and set it on top of the bayonet.

I grabbed Will again and looked to where our trench was.

Just a few more steps.

The edge of the trench. I threw myself forward, using all my weight to haul Will over the sandbags that guarded our line. A launching of myself as a bomb exploded not far behind me. And finally the drop and landing as Will and I fell in a heap at the bottom of our trench.

A couple of deep gasps of air to breathe down the pain and I was screaming for a medic. They came running with a stretcher and I pointed to Will.

"Take him!" I yelled. "I have to get the Kid!"

"You can't. You're injured!" one of them yelled at me. "You can't go back out there!"

I met the soldier's gaze for the briefest of seconds then turned and pulled myself back up the ladder with my good arm, stepping up and over the top of the trench. I set off back in the direction from which I had just come, staggering in the soft, wet ground as I searched for the bayonet and Tommy's helmet.

I didn't have to go far. Tommy lay beneath the bayonet and helmet and it struck me rather forcefully how very much it appeared a grave marker. I shoved at him several times, trying to rouse him. He groaned, but didn't open his eyes. I took hold of his collar too and, just as I had done with Will, I pulled Tommy back to our trench. The rain was falling harder by the time we reached our line, small snowflakes driven amongst the large, wet drops, a broken screen to hide us from the enemy's sight.

We reached the trench and this time the medics were waiting for me, helping to lift Tommy down into the trench. I sat on the edge and let myself slide down the muddy wall, landing in a crouch against the wall amidst a small avalanche of dirt and water. There I stayed for several minutes, pulling my arm to my side and trying to breathe while the rain dripped off the brim of my helmet.

Another medic was running past with a stretcher. He stopped and squinted down at me through the rain.

"Can you walk?" he yelled over the rain. I only looked at him. "You're injured. Can you make it to the dressing station on your own?" He pointed down the long stretch of trench.

I looked down at the blood seeping from my torn sleeve and watched as it ran down my arm in a river of red finally dripping from my fingers. I looked down along the trench then back up at the medic and nodded.

Dressing station. Will would be at the dressing station.

Pushing against the trench wall, I stood on shaky legs.

"Down the trench, first right, then up and out the end," the medic indicated, pointing again.

I nodded and began my stumbling trek along the duckboards, water squelching in my boots. I tried to keep my arm from moving, but met with little success. Each time it shifted, it sent a jolt of pain up my neck and through my chest. I lost control of my stomach at the side of the trench. I spat out the acid taste in my mouth and forced my feet forward again.

I turned where the medic had directed me to and saw lanterns far ahead at the end of the walkway. I staggered along the line then up the ramp at the end of the sap and out the far end. I emerged from the trench as though I were walking up out of the sucking sea, finding several small canopies erected there. Beneath them, lanterns were hung and men lay on stretchers, partially sheltered from the rain.

I wandered among the stretchers looking for Will. Maimed bodies were laid out in rows. A hushed conversation caught my ear and held me firmly in place. A doctor was speaking to a private who was holding a medical box.

"Give him four times the usual dose," I heard the doctor say.

"But, Sir—"

"I know. Look at him, man. What else can we do?"

The private looked down and I followed his gaze. At the Private's feet lay a man on a stretcher. The soldier's eyes, nose, and mouth has been blown away. His face was a pulpy mass of ragged flesh. And yet his chest rose and fell as he turned his head back and forth. His tortured grip on the boards of the stretcher spoke of his agony more loudly than any scream he might have been trying to issue.

The Private took a bracing breath then knelt at the soldier's side. I couldn't see what the Private did, his back shielding the business from my view, but the soldier on the stretcher calmed, his breathing slowed, then stopped all together. His grip on the stretcher loosed, silencing his unspoken torment. The Private stood and looked down at the man on the stretcher. After several long moments, he waved over two stretcher bearers who came and bore the soldier away.

I turned and redoubled my efforts to find Will, finally locating him on a stretcher toward the back of the dressing station. I sat down on the ground beside him, my legs crossed and supporting my limp arm on one knee. Will lay silently, eyes closed, a tourniquet on his leg. The blood on his pants and puttees was hardening and turning a deep coffee colour. I watched as his chest rose and fell several times, even and smooth, then closed my eyes and let my head drop.

"This one next!" someone yelled and I jerked out of my doze. I pulled back against the pain in my arm as it reverberated through my teeth and into my head. A doctor dressed in a white smock covered in red from top to bottom stood at Will's feet, pointing down at him.

I forced myself to my feet and moved back as two medics hurried over to pick up Will's stretcher.

"Where are you taking him?" I asked.

"Surgery. Got to get that shrapnel out of his leg before he loses any more blood." The doctor paused, glancing at my arm. "Have you been looked after?"

I shook my head.

"Follow us then," he ordered.

I fell in line behind Will's stretcher. I watched as a surgeon injected Will's back. Within moments, Will's body went limp and the tight lines in his face were smoothed into tranquility.

"What did you give him?" I asked.

The surgeon glanced at me then returned to his work. "Stovain into the spine," he said as he began cutting Will's bandage and pant leg. "It anesthetizes his legs. Someone attend to this man," he added, jerking his chin in my direction.

A near-by medic came over and led me to a stretcher lying across two wooden saw horses. "Take off your coat and shirt and lie down," he ordered.

I carefully stripped down to my sleeveless undershirt, fumbling, having to use my left hand. Every movement pulled at my useless arm, flaring the pain into white-hot fire that engulfed my body entirely.

I lay down, dizzy and clammy, and carefully guided my arm down by my side. I tried not to look at it.

The medic inspected my arm and shoulder. "You've fractured your collarbone and dislocated your shoulder. You have a bullet wound to your upper arm, but it's gone clean through. Still, we'll need to give you something for pain if we're going to re-set your arm."

"Will it put me out?" I asked.

"That's the idea."

"I don't want it then," I replied.

The medic stopped short and cast me a frown.

"Why not?" he asked.

"I need to keep an eye on my brother and make certain we're not separated. Can't do that if I'm out."

The medic paused, considering me. "Well," he said, "you haven't much choice. I can give you something for the pain and you can sleep through the procedure or we can go ahead without it and you'll pass out from the pain. Either way, you'll be out."

I considered the odds, wondering if I could stay awake through the pain.

"I know what you're thinking," the medic went on, "and no, you won't be able to last through the procedure—I've seen others try. Everyone passes out." I only looked at him and he went on. "All right, look, I'll make certain the two of you are put on the same ambulance to the train. Can we get on with this?"

"I'll hold you to that promise." It wasn't enough. "Just one more thing: swap my ID disc and card with my brother's. I have mine memorized. I'll be able to track him down if we do get separated."

"Are you mental?" the medic huffed. Then, "Fine. Whatever it takes to get this done—there are a lot more waiting and I don't care who you say you are." He took my disc off my neck and took my card from my shirt pocket. He went over to Will, swapped the items, then returned Will's disc and card to me. "Ready?" he asked irritably.

"Ready," I said, letting my head fall back on the stretcher.

The medic picked up a small phial from a tray on a nearby stand. He drew up some of the liquid into a metal syringe. Reaching over to my good arm, he plunged the needle in and pushed the plunger in a swift motion.

It was pure and instantaneous relief.

The pain was gone. My exhaustion was gone. The war was gone. My worries were gone. My memories were gone. My father's voice was gone, stricken from that part of my mind where it endlessly lurked. Finally, I was free from its ceaseless drone.

"I'll need to give you a mask to put you out," the surgeon said as he came to stand beside my stretcher.

I nodded. With the relief the injection had given me, had he told me he intended to saw me in half I would not have objected.

I smelled the cloying odour of the mask as the medic held it just above my face. After a few moments, he traded the mask for another and I smelled the sickeningly sweet scent of the medicine he dropped onto it.

Then all was still as I fell into a dark and confining rest.

April 10, 1917

War Diary

Private Henry Ryzak

April 10, 1917– April 12, 1917

Volume 3

Diary Text: 14 Pages

[April 10, 1917]

I woke to the rattling rhythm of metal wheels on rails, rocked back from unconsciousness into a distant dream that I could not grasp. I felt myself slowly rising up out of the dark then and into the dusk of a shadowy awareness.

I resisted. There was pain down that road—I could feel it buzzing at the edge of my thoughts, a fly against a window.

The rising continued despite my intentions and I eventually admitted defeat and opened my eyes. Through the dim lantern light overhead, I saw cots arranged in bunk style lining the walls and every one of them occupied. The few windows in the sides of the train were black, reflecting the flickering lights of the train's lanterns back on its occupants.

Will!

I recalled my arm just in time to stop myself from jerking upright in my bunk. I felt around with my left arm. I was still in my undershirt under the scratchy brown blanket that covered me, my right arm held firmly against my chest by cloth wrapped tightly around my arm and body. I slowly lifted myself up on my good elbow.

To my great relief, Will lay on a cot just down from my own, unconscious or still asleep or, perhaps, sleeping again.

I lay back down, my arm throbbing in time with the swaying of the train. I knew I ought to stay awake to keep an eye on Will, but even with that thought, the pain in my arm would not fully release my waking mind, pulling me back into the dark nightmare in which the pain lived. I thought of the heavenly relief of the injection at the clearing station and waved down an orderly.

"Yes?" he asked, kneeling beside my bunk.

"Do you have anything for pain?"

"I do. I'll draw it up."

He drew up a syringe of the same restorative potion I'd been given at the clearing station and injected it into my good arm.

I lay back as the grey shroud of deceptive relief wrapped around my mind, covering over pain and memories. The troubles of the battle left me as the blood-spattered images were wiped away with the fabric of forgetfulness. Once again, the static of my father's ever-present censure was silenced. One last thought filtered through my mind just before it closed the door to reality, contained within the confines of the potion: this was like the sensation of drinking only so very much *more*.

My breath caught with a momentary panic at that realization just before the concoction engulfed me and I knew no more.

• • •

A groan awoke me.

My head was splitting in two. I felt as though an anvil were weighing it down from the inside. My stomach heaved and I fought it down. I thought perhaps I lay wounded on the battlefield but then realized there were no sounds of battle around me.

Dead, then.

I tried to open my eyes, but my eyelids were too weighty to lift. It was worse than awakening from an all-night bender. I forced my eyes open and was met by a lighter shade of darkness. I wondered for a moment if I had managed to open my eyes after all. I tried to roll onto my side to find out where I was, but had forgotten about my arm. The pain stopped me almost before I had begun to move. I heard another groan and let my muscles settle more firmly into my cot.

It was then that I saw it: a light breaking through the darkness, drawing nearer and brighter. In my cluttered mind

I wondered if it were a star reaching down for me, but despite my clouded thoughts, I knew that not to be the case. Still, the light hovered, floated, drawing nearer and nearer. Then it was settling beside me, coming to a rest just by my head—a guiding star.

Beyond it, swept up in the light of the star, I saw her: the angel that attended the light, her face drawn with concern as she peered down at me, a frown marring her perfection while somehow leaving it without flaw.

"I'll give you something for the pain," she said and then was gone, taking the light with her.

I breathed in short punctured gasps until the light returned, and the angel once again stood beside me, standing between me and the hell of reaching dark and pain.

"Let me have your good arm," the voice said, velvet and still.

I saw the syringe in her hand, reflecting the light and my thoughts coalesced into a single intent.

My hand shot out and grabbed her wrist as though of its own accord, halting the coming villain with its vile poison.

The angel looked down at me, her expression that of a school girl trying to solve a puzzle.

"Don't ever give me that stuff again," I choked out past the desert that was my throat. "No matter how much I ask or how much you might think I need it. Once more and I'll never be rid of it."

The angel studied me and I watched the pieces of her puzzle fall into place. I released her wrist only when she nodded her agreement.

I breathed a jagged breath, feeling the full reality of my arm reflected in the rise and fall of my chest. Still, pain was better than the dim and unclear thoughts I'd had with the morphia—at least the pain was real.

"Where am I?" I asked, keeping my eyes closed.

"You are in a stationary hospital in *Harfleur.*"

"Where's that?"

"Two or three hour's train ride from the front."

"Where's my brother?" I asked.

"What's his name?"

"Will Ryzak."

I felt a deliciously cool cloth on my forehead and breathed in the damp scent of it.

"There's a Ryzak just a few beds down the row. Here," the angel said tilting my head up with her hand, "have some water."

I drank in large gulps when she put the cup to my lips. The cold veracity of the drink helped clear my head. When the cup was empty, the angel lowered my head back onto my cot and I found I could breathe just a little easier.

"Thank you," I said, looking up at the angel.

It was then that I saw it—that same flickering light reflected in her burnt umber eyes, just as I had seen so many months ago.

This is not real.

No. This was still the vestige delusions of the elixir that had not yet fully released me from its grip.

I have no right to think of her in the state I'm in.

I closed my eyes again and let myself fall into a stale and restless repose.

[April 11, 1917]

I woke the next day to the bright daylight that only early morning can display. It magnified on the canvas of the tent, dispersed in the tent's fibres, and spread itself through the air, reaching for me with warm fingers. I took a deep breath, feeling the weight of my arm where it lay across my chest, held tightly by the bandage wound around my body. I moved to sit up, holding my arm lightly as I swung my feet to the floor.

The room spun about me as a lightning bolt crack split my head in two. I winced and dropped my head into my hand. I waited until the pain dulled to a vicious roar at the back of my head.

"Water helps."

I opened my eyes, squinting against the light, noting the soldier in the cot next to mine. He pointed to the small table that sat between his cot and mine. I looked over to find a pitcher and tin cup on the bedside stand and quickly filled the cup. I pounded it back, feeling the full weight of it as it dropped into my stomach all at once.

I set the cup down and looked around. Before me stretched row upon row of cots filled with men in all states. Some talking together, some moaning in pain and writhing on their beds, others shaving or combing their hair, some had orderlies helping them dress. This one thing they had in common: each one bore the evidence of a battle that raged miles from our present refuge.

"Where are we?" I asked, my mind void of anything but my own name.

"Stationary hospital in *Harfleur*. They're trying to make more room—men are starting to come in from Vimy. Seems more beds pop up every night with more men to fill 'em. What's going on at the front?"

I didn't answer. My mind had checked out after the man had reminded me where I was. I searched through my dim memories of the conversation I had with the angel who attended the star, finally finding the piece of information I needed in a shadowed corner of my hung over mind.

"I'm sorry. I'll fill you in later. I have to find my brother."

I stood on shaky legs and looked around, spotting Will several cots down in the same row as me. I hobbled over to check on him.

"Will," I quietly called to him when I reached his cot. He lay silently, eyes closed, but his chest rose and fell in an even rhythm. I put my hand on his shoulder but stopped myself from giving it a shake.

Will looked up at me then with clouded eyes shrouded behind heavy eyelids. "Henry?" he mumbled.

"Yeah, it's me," I responded. "Are you alright?"

"He's injured and in need of rest, which you will allow him," a stern voice said from just behind me.

I turned to see a workhorse of a nurse standing over me, one hand on her generous hip. She was looking at me as though she might impale me with the large, metal needle she currently held aloft.

"That applies to you as well. Back to your bed, Private, and stay there until you've dressed and had breakfast!" she barked.

I looked down at Will and saw one corner of his mouth turn up. "Better follow orders," he said in a muffled voice. His eyes fell shut again.

I moved off to my bunk, the Clydesdale nurse hard on my heels. "He's my brother," I began. "Why isn't he more awake?" I asked, settling myself back into my cot. "How badly was he injured?"

"He has a concussion and blood loss from his leg wound and we've given him something for the pain," the nurse replied. "He won't wake properly for some time. Now lie down and rest as you're meant to. I won't be chasing after you to tell you again. I have patients to tend." She gave me a curt nod and turned to leave.

"Will he be all right?" I called after her.

"If you let him rest he will be. Stay in your bed!" She marched off.

The soldier next to me rolled over in his cot. "Best not ta vex thet one," he said with a grin. "I heerd she wrestled an ox an' wun."

I couldn't help a chuckle. My mind flashed back to the angel.

"Was there a different nurse here last night?" I asked, sobering.

241

"Expict so," the soldier said easily. "Thir are some on the dai sheeft and some 'at work at night and then they chainge their sheefts 'round every now an' ag'in. You might see one for a few dais but it's 'ardly the same one twice."

"Huh."

"Name's Walker—Ryan Walker," he said, rolling over in his cot and offering me his hand.

I took his hand and shook it. "Where are you from?" I asked.

"I'm with the Austri-li'n boys. All the units got pritty mixed up in the end thir an' I got sint 'ere along with you Tommys," he said with a grin.

"You'll do alright then—we make for good company."

Walker smiled and nodded. "So I've bin told."

The hefty nurse walked by and cast us a cautionary glance. "Orderly!" she barked, still looking down at us. An attendant rushed over and stood waiting for orders. "Get these men washed up and given them some breakfast!"

"Yes, Ma'am," the orderly said, scurrying off. The nurse glanced between Walker and me then trudged off.

Walker grinned at me then lay back in his cot.

The orderly returned with a folding stand and wash basin which he set in front of me as I sat on the edge of my bunk. The water was steaming hot and smelled deliciously soapy. The orderly handed me a cloth then set to work unwinding the bandages that held my right arm snug against my side.

"We'll wrap that back up after your dressing is changed," the orderly said, then went off in search of a basin for Walker.

I looked down at my upper arm. It was wrapped in layers of gauze, a thick dressing underneath. A dark stain had seeped through front and back, coalescing in the middle as though someone had spilled coffee on it. The fabric was stiff and I had to resist the urge to yank it off. Instead I focused on the basin of hot water before me and set to work, taking full advantage of it. I had long since forgotten the feel of hot water on my body.

When my washing was done, the orderly set my arm in a sling then directed me to a line of tables that ran down the middle of the room, between the rows of bunks. I took a seat at one of the tables and Walker joined me, hobbling over with the help of the orderly. The orderly left then returned with two bowls of steaming oatmeal along with hot tea and toast. Walker and I looked at each other for the briefest of moments before laying in to the feast before us. Hot food was a luxury—no matter what it consisted of.

When I was done breakfast (and after taking a moment or two to revel in the sensation of feeling truly full for the first time in recent memory) I went over to check on Will, despite Walker's caution about the nurse—she was busy with another soldier's dressing for the moment.

Will lay, sleeping quietly. I looked down at him for several moments, wondering why he appeared different to me. I finally realized that this was the first time in a very long while that peace had settled on his features. I drew in an easy breath and turned to head back to my cot.

I stepped right into the iceberg expression that seemed permanently carved on the Clydesdale's face. She stood, both hands on hips, looking as though she was measuring my weight and wondering if she would need one arm or two if she were to toss me back into my cot from where we currently stood.

I might have been worried but through my long hours spent at the card table, I had learned that I was not without some degree of charm and could wield it when I had need to. I grinned at her, catching her gaze and holding it just until I saw her fight a smile.

She forced her mouth into a line. "Back to your bed, soldier! I'm coming to change that dressing and I'll not be delayed by you."

I gave her a wink and a nod then casually made my way back to my cot.

The Clydesdale arrived moments later, carrying a tray topped with various dressing implements and cloth bandages. She laid it across the folding stand which had held my wash basin then pointed to the chair at the end of my bed. I sat as I was directed.

"You'll need something for the pain," she said. "I'll be right back with it."

She turned on her heel.

"No," I said, causing the woman to halt mid-step and round on me. "I don't want the morphia." She only studied me through narrowed eyes. "I can't have any more of it," I asserted.

The nurse tilted her head and studied me a moment longer, finally taking a breath. "Very well," she said, her tone that of someone taken by surprise by a turn in a story. "But you've stopped bleeding now so you will take Aspirin." Her tone and her immediate departure let me know there would be no debate on that.

The woman returned with two small white tablets and held them out to me along with a glass of water. I swallowed the powdery pills and prayed they would dull the ache building in my arm and shoulder.

The Clydesdale glanced at my face repeatedly throughout her ministrations. She softened the hardened gauze with warm water then slowly peeled it away. I closed my eyes and turned away from the burn of it. While I hadn't time to feel the full weight of the pain when I had been shot, I certainly was feeling it as the woman changed my bandages. I may have groaned once or twice as she worked. The nurse cleaned the wound with the warm water then dried it carefully. She re-bandaged my arm then secured it to my side and across my chest with another roll of cloth around my body. When the work was done, she looked down at me for some time before taking away the bowl of rose-coloured water.

"Rest for a time and let the Aspirin work," she said in a tone that had softened around its edges.

I simply nodded and went to lay down in my cot. My arm stung and ached all at the same time and I clenched my teeth. The pain eased slightly when I let the weight of my arm settle into the bed and I was able to drift off for a time.

My day passed in a succession of rest, walking about the ward, checking on Will, and meal times. Will woke at intervals but largely rested throughout the day. Despite a day that felt positively like a vacation compared to a day in the trench, I was still exhausted by the time the makeshift hospital darkened.

Around seven in the evening, there was an overall atmosphere of upheaval as the night staff took over, but it settled quickly. I took advantage of the distraction to check on Will one last time before I went to bed. He woke long enough for me to give him some water then he was out again. I went to my cot and found an orderly setting up a basin for me to wash up for night. When I was finished, I lay down and fell into a peaceful sleep, albeit with the underpinnings of pain from my arm—I dreamt I was kicked by a horse.

I woke to a flash of light, the image of Will lying silently in the mud, and my father bellowing that it was all my fault. I sat bolt upright in my cot, my damp hair sticking to my forehead. I looked around frantically, trying to see where my father was and felt a slow dawning of reality settle on me.

I'm in the hospital. Will's all right.

I looked over and could just make out Will's form several cots over. My heart was still pounding high in my chest when I saw the light floating toward me. A small beacon of reality in the darkness of my errant thoughts, held aloft by its attendant. She came closer, her white gown floating up about her as she moved, her face hidden behind the star she carried before her. She set the light on the bedside stand and spoke quietly:

"You're safe," she said in a tone that would not have suffered anyone to disbelieve her words. "You are in a hospital and your brother is resting nearby."

I only stared up at the flickering flame in her coffee-coloured eyes, the brightness of the light that shone there beckoning me as if to a home I'd never known, yet understood it was home all the same.

"Here," she said, pulling a small glass bottle from her apron pocket. "Hold out your hand," she said in a soft whisper. I did as she asked. She touched the bottle to my hand and when I looked down there were two white tablets in my palm. By the time I looked up again, she was holding out a glass of water. "Aspirin," the keeper of the light said quietly.

I swallowed the pills and washed them down with the water. "Very good," her whisper-soft voice said and I felt as though I might do anything to hear her say those words again. "Now lie down and rest."

Again, I did as she bid me.

The angel hovered over me, watching for a moment from just beyond her circle of light, then was gone, vanishing into the darkness. My breathing quickened and I glanced up at the star where it still sat on the table. Surely she would not leave it behind. I had just determined to look for the angel when she appeared over me again. I felt her lift my shoulder then settle it against a coolness that drove away the burn of the wound. I closed my eyes and took a full breath.

"Try to sleep now," the angel whispered and I felt the light move off. I let myself drift out along a calm river of darkness and stillness and ease that carried me into the morning light.

[April 12, 1917]

I woke early to the noise of the changing of the shift and turned over, trying to return to the forgetfulness of sleep. Just as I was dozing off, my mind thrust forward the memory of Tommy lying deathly still in the field by the bayonet left to mark where he lay. I sat up with a jerk that stabbed at my arm. I searched around for the Clydesdale but didn't see her. I spied a volunteer aide nearby and waved her down.

"Yes?" she asked as she stood at the end of my bed. Wisps of hair escaped her cotton mop cap and her collar was lined with wrinkles. Her dress hung loose at her waist, lagging behind the turning of her frame as she moved within it.

"I lost track of my friend," I began. "He was injured and I'm wondering if he was brought here along with the rest of us from our unit. Is there a Tommy Cor—Colbert here?"

"I'll have to check," the wisp-girl said in a voice barely above a whisper. She scampered away as if driven by a gust of wind and I lost sight of her. After some time, and long after I had given up hope of seeing her again, the girl reappeared, seemingly brought back by the same breeze that had carried her away.

"He's here," the girl said breathlessly, "but in the next tent over."

"Can I go talk to him?" I asked.

Wisp-girl shook her head. "Matron says you're on bedrest for now—you've not been here even 48 hours. I'll go over and let him know you're here."

"Thank you—that's kind of you."

The girl nodded and blew off again.

My day moved on apace just as it had done the day before. After the chaos of the trenches, I didn't mind the dullness of the day's motion. I dozed throughout the day, time marked in the coming and going of the nurses performing their duties and punctuated by the trolleys that brought lunch and then dinner. I checked on Will several times and was relieved to find him more often awake than not.

I chatted with Walker, updating him on the progress of things at the front. He had been at the hospital with trench foot for more than a week, his feet propped on pillows and the nurses changing his dressings endlessly. Their unit had not had the benefit of the whale oil. Walker asked endless questions about how we were getting on but by the end of the day I could see that he was tired and I told him we would talk some more the next day.

I settled into my cot that night eager to sleep, and very much hoping to see the angel who attended the star during the dark watch of the night.

She never came.

April 13, 1917

War Diary

Private Henry Ryzak

April 13, 1917– April 24, 1917

Volume 3

Diary Text: 31 Pages

[April 13, 1917]

I woke the next morning feeling stiff and suspecting I hadn't stirred at all through the long dark hours of the night. I was again made to wash and have breakfast, having thrown a hospital shirt around my shoulders to cover myself until my dressing could be changed. I ate quickly then snuck over to check on Will.

I was pleased to find Will sitting in a chair beside his cot, a small folding table and a bowl of porridge set before him. He was making quick work of his breakfast and paused only long enough to cast me a grin. A cloth screen had been erected between his bunk and the next and I could hear the next man over talking. His conversation led me to believe he was having his dressings changed. I took advantage of the cover to sit on Will's cot and stay with him a while, thinking the odds were good I would not be discovered so long as the nurse was busy with the other patient.

"This is so good," Will said between mouthfuls. He jammed a bite of toast into his mouth before he had swallowed the oatmeal and washed it all down with a swig of tea.

"Take it easy," I said. "You might want to actually taste that food. In this war, you never know if you'll see more of it."

Will shook his head and continued attacking his breakfast while I watched. When he was finished, he sat back in his chair and looked over at me. His eyes were vaguely unfocused. He looked at my bandaged arm and sobered.

"Are you in pain?" I asked. "Do you want me to fetch the Nurse?" I asked.

Will shook his head. "No. They're keeping me well supplied with pain medication." He paused and considered me. "What happened?" he asked.

"You were hit when the Hun captured you—I don't know how—I didn't see that bit. We came to get the lot of you then high-tailed it back to our lines. A mortar hit close to us just before we reached our trenches. I pulled you back to our trench and we both wound up here."

"When were you hit?" he asked, gesturing to my arm.

"I don't quite recall. I didn't really notice it happen. I did land hard when the Mortar got us."

Will's brow furrowed and he looked down into his empty bowl. He looked up at me then and my breath caught slightly. Once, when we were children in school, Will had broken the school house window playing ball too close to the building despite the teacher's frequent warnings. I had told the teacher that it was me who had broken the window and had gotten the strap for the deed. Will's expression was the same now as when I had come out of the school after being strapped.

"It's my fault you got hurt," he said quietly. "You wouldn't be here if it weren't for me and on top of that, you wouldn't have been hit if you hadn't come for me when I got captured."

I shook my head. "Might easily have gotten hit doing anything else. For all we know, I could've been killed if I *hadn't* come to get you. You don't know what might or might not have happened."

"Still, I got you into this. I'm sorry."

"No. I chose to come. This is what I came to do. No— that's not right. This is what I *ought* to do and I'm doing it."

Will looked away, his eyes red. After blinking a few times and swallowing hard, he said, "I owe you. I'll make this up to you." He nodded firmly to himself.

"You don't owe me anything. I wasn't there for you or our parents before—I always did as I pleased. Father was right: I was reckless and irresponsible. This is the least I can do to make things up to all of you."

"Father shouldn't have said the things he said."

"Maybe not, but that doesn't make him wrong."

Will considered me for a moment. "Things will be better when we get home."

There was a fair chance we wouldn't be getting home alive let alone live to see Father change—so I said, "Yeah, things will be better."

"Ryzak!"

Will and I both turned to our name. An orderly stood at the end of Will's cot. He gestured to me. "You need your dressing changed. You're off bedrest now so you can go to the treatment station. The Sister will change your dressing there." He gestured to a corner of the building partitioned off by cloth screens. "You," he said, gesturing to Will, "will remain on bedrest for now. The Sister will come by later to change your dressing."

"Yes, Sir," Will and I chorused.

I turned to Will, gave him a half-smile and a nod, then left, heading for the dressing change area.

I went around the screens but found no one there. A table brimming with bandages and other supplies sat in one corner of the partitioned area. There was a long examination table along one side with a wash basin on a stand in front of it. I sat on the table and waited for the nurse.

Within moments, a familiar figure rounded the corner and came to stand in front of me. I found myself looking down into eyes lit to hazel as they claimed for their own the diffuse sunlight that filtered in through the tent walls. Before—in the trenches—I had believed her eyes to be less than their recalled beauty, thinking surely I had conjured the vision out of excessive desire and a need to shore up my failing morale.

I was wrong.

Her eyes were every bit as beautiful as the feast my memory had served up—perhaps more so.

"Lieutenant Grieves," was all I could manage before my thoughts escaped me entirely like stallions set loose from the corral. I stared at her blatantly, fearing she might vanish if I looked away but for a single second. I hardly dared to blink.

"Private Ryzak," she replied with a sort of nod. Our gaze met for a moment before she turned her head away and stood motionless for another moment. She turned back to me. "How are you—that is, how is your arm doing?"

I could have sworn her cheeks were pinker than they had been a second earlier and her eyes took on a translucence I hadn't seen before.

"You must be in pain. Did someone bring you Aspirin this morning?" she asked when I failed to speak.

"Yes. No." I shook my head to clear the muddle. "I mean—it hurts some. No one brought me anything."

"That will never do." She vanished then and I was left staring at the spot on which she had stood. She returned a minute later with Aspirin and a glass of water, both of which she extended to me.

I took the proffered items and swallowed down the bitter pills, never taking my eyes from her face. She looked down then back up at me as I handed the glass back to her.

"Does this help?" she asked. I paused, thinking: of course her presence helped; but when I didn't answer right away, she asked again: "The Aspirin. Does it help?"

"Oh, that," I said, having finally deciphered her meaning. "Some."

"You said you didn't want the morphia. I wish there was more I could give you. I'm sorry."

"That was you? The one I saw in the night?"

"Yes. I've just gotten off nights and am starting a stretch of day shifts." When I only stared at her, she pointed to my arm. "I need to change your bandages if that's all right." I could only nod, feeling as though my dreams had collided squarely with reminiscence at the intersection of Reality and Fancy. I wasn't certain as to where I presently stood.

Lieutenant Grieves unpinned the edge of the bandage securing my arm in place and began unwrapping it, rolling the cloth as she went. She had to reach around my back to pass the roll from one hand to the other and in doing so, leaned in close. My head exploded, filled with the smell of roses and the same sunlit scent I had embraced in the ambulance. I had to remind myself to breathe then took in several deep breaths as she continued undoing the wraps.

"How is it?" she asked when my arm was free of its bonds. Again, it took me a second to understand, my thoughts fixed squarely on her.

I stretched out my arm then made a fist and bent my arm back on itself, testing it. I grabbed at the bandaged wound in my upper arm when it suddenly caught, sending a hot-poker jab up my arm and into my jaw.

"I see," she said, not waiting for any further response. "Let's have a look at it, shall we?"

I nodded then proceeded to study her as she unwrapped the bandage from my arm. I wanted to memorize every curve and line of her face—storing up memories to keep me alive when I was back in the trenches.

Lieutenant Grieves tossed the strip of cloth into a basket then turned back to study my arm. She took my arm in both hands and turned it over, peering at the wound from both sides. Her small hands flexed with a tiger-like strength and I wondered at the juxtaposition. Still, they were warm and my sore muscles relaxed under her touch.

"It is healing well," she said, taking up a cloth from the basin in the stand and washing the wound. I glanced at the ugly brown hole in my muscle, but didn't waste time on it.

Something occurred to me then. "How long until it's fully healed? When do I go back to the front?"

She looked up at me with a *why-would-you-want-to-do-that* sort of expression. Her brow turned down, whether in confusion or hurt I couldn't have said, although I very much wanted to believe she was disappointed by the thought of my leaving again.

"Anxious to get back?" She crooked one eyebrow up.

"Quite the opposite—now," I said, watching her expression closely.

Her brow smoothed. "Gun shot and shrapnel wounds generally take about three weeks to heal."

"And you'll be stationed here for that time at least?" I asked.

Her eyes flicked up to mine as she dried my arm then focused on the re-bandaging of it. "Yes and much longer I expect. We have been told this will be a lengthy offensive."

At least a couple of weeks with her then.

The pain in my arm began to dull and I found my breathing easier. I nodded, still studying her.

Lieutenant Grieves stepped back, having finished wrapping my wound. "That should do. Let me know if it is too tight and I can rewrap it."

"It's fine."

"I believe your collar bone will be all right with a simple sling now. Your shoulder seems quite set back in place and ought not to pull down on it anymore." She turned and retrieved a clean shirt from a nearby cupboard and handed it to me.

I took the shirt and gingerly slid my right arm into it then tucked my left into the other sleeve. I tried to do up the buttons, but found my left hand uncooperative in taking on the task by itself. Grieves quickly stepped forward and began buttoning my shirt for me. I let my hand fall to the exam table and simply watched her hands as they slid along my buttons. They reminded me of the hands on a porcelain doll I had once seen in a shop window.

Grieves did not look up. When she was finished with the buttons, she placed my right arm in a sling then reached up to tie it around my neck. I took the opportunity to breathe in her scent again. I must have sighed as she immediately asked, "Are you tired? Were you up in the night again?"

"I slept well enough."

Grieves nodded then paused as she looked down at my arm, fussing with a fold in the sling. "I owe you an apology," she said, her tone that of a sergeant telling his men to surrender.

"Whatever for?"

She stopped playing with the sling and looked fully at me. "I made assumptions that night at camp even though you tried to explain. I thought you to be only a selfish and reckless drunk. I didn't realize what you had done until I spoke with Private Colbert. He explained things. I'm sorry for what I said and how I treated you."

There were so many things wrong with her apologizing to me.

"You don't need to apologize—you were right to think that about me. I deserved what you said and it was good that you said it."

Grieves only frowned up at me. "It was still wrong of me to do that to you."

"I think this is a disagreement that can't be won by either side so I will simply thank you for saying so."

She nodded then. After a pause she said, "I—I'm done with your dressing. You should rest now."

I sighed and slid off the exam table. I went to leave but stopped just at the end of the screen and turned back. "I must tell you—I need you to know: I'm trying to change."

She looked at me with wide eyes lit to a burnt-sugar. "Yes. I do know that. I can see you've changed already."

I nodded, took one last look at her, then turned and went back to my bunk.

I rested and sat with Will at intervals throughout the day. Despite the nights of comfortable sleep in the warm, dry bed, I was still exhausted. I wondered how much more sleep it would take before I would feel normal again.

I kept myself happily occupied by watching Grieves as she went about her duties around me. At one point, she came to check Walker's feet. I saw her face sober and heard her call for an orderly to set up screens around his cot. The doctor was called in and there was a hushed conversation that was easily heard no matter how one tried not to listen.

Walker's feet were worsening and the discussion turned to amputation.

"Not on yer life!" Walker insisted. "I tind sheep beck 'ome. Can't make a livin' wi'out my feet!"

"You'll not make a living if you're dead either, Private," the doctor said plainly.

"Right enough, but if I'm dead I won't be needin' to," Walker insisted.

In the end, the doctor ordered Grieves to make the man comfortable and keep his feet as clean and warm as possible—and pray they would improve.

Evening came and I settled into my bed after checking on Will. The evening staff came around with my Aspirin dutifully on time. I dropped into a sleep unlike any I'd had since signing up.

[April 14, 1917]

In the morning, I found myself in the same position as when I had settled into my cot. It took me a few movements to loosen my joints and work the kinks out of my muscles.

The day fell into the same routine as the previous day, but for one thing: I was disappointed when the orderly said I didn't need my dressing changed that day as it was no longer bleeding and could wait until the following day. I had to content myself with mere glimpses of Lieutenant Grieves and an occasional brief "hello" whenever she brought my Aspirin.

By afternoon, I was bored and didn't feel like resting. I asked the VA if I could go find Tommy and was granted permission "provided I return by tea time". The directive made me smile: there was certainly no "tea time" where I had been the last few months. I agreed easily and made my way into the adjoining ward where I asked after Tommy. I was directed to one of the bunks and found him there sleeping. His chest was wrapped in gauze and his forehead prominently displayed a stitched gash. I didn't want to disturb him, so I asked the orderly to let him know I had stopped by, then returned to my bunk.

Walker and I had just been served tea seated in our cots when Tommy appeared at the end of my bunk. He pulled up a chair and joined us for tea.

"How are you?" I asked, wondering just what had happened to his head.

"I got knocked on the head pretty hard and they tell me I broke a couple of ribs, but I'm comin' around," he said, taking a sip of his tea. "Just a bad headache now and my ribs ache if I move the wrong way." He fingered the stitches on his forehead. "This looks pretty bad though. Pretty sure it won't ever go away." He made a face.

"Not to worry: girls find that sort of scar very manly. They'll be falling at your feet."

Tommy grinned and looked sheepishly down at his tea.

"Do you r'call whit 'appened?" Walker asked.

Tommy shook his head. "Nope—just know I woke up in the clearing station." He turned to me then. "I thought maybe you'd know," he said, pinning me down with a heavy look. "They told me you went back out and pulled me off the field."

Walker cast me a look then glanced at Tommy.

I shrugged. "Sorry—I don't recall that. I don't know what happened to you out there or how you got off the field."

Tommy looked at me with the look of a kid whose older brother tells him he's not allowed to tag along with the big boys.

I met his gaze evenly and held it—bluffing.

Tommy squared his shoulders then and raised his chin a bit. "Well that's what the medic said at the clearing station so I'm bettin' you came back for me," his tone a leap-of-faith assertion.

"Couldn't say," I replied with a shake of my head.

The conversation turned to Walker and his unit and Tommy left after a bit saying he was tired.

When Tommy had gone, Walker turned to me and studied me for a moment. "Why did you till 'im you didn't remimber?" Walker asked. It was more an accusation than a question.

"Last thing I need is some kid depending on me out there and thinking I'll save him every time he gets in trouble. I have enough work keeping my brother alive. I can't look out for everyone."

"Seems to me yer lookin' after the boy lik it or no. Might as well tell 'im you've got 'is beck. He'll do be'er knowin' thit."

I looked at Walker, trying to swallow down that feeling of knowing someone is right when you don't want them to be. "Maybe." I finally said. "Maybe not."

I did think about it—thought about telling Tommy the truth as I drifted off to sleep that night. What if I didn't have to look after Tommy out there? What if he'd never signed up—what if they hadn't believed him when he lied about his age...

I drifted off into a sleep filled with memories disguised as nightmares.

[April 15, 1917]

I spent the next afternoon with Will. He was coming around and getting back to his old self. His leg wound was healing well—they had been able to get the bullet out of it— but his concussion would take longer to resolve. Between the orderly and myself, we got Will up on crutches and I helped him through a short walk about the ward and over to visit Tommy. It didn't take long for Will to tire, and we soon returned to one of the tables to play cards. Cards, however, gave him a headache and we had to stop that too. So we sat, simply enjoying a hot "cuppa".

"Have you gotten her name yet?" Will asked, grinning behind his cup as he peered over the edge of it at me.

I turned to him, trying to rein in my thoughts and steer them in the right direction. "What was that?" I asked.

Will jerked his chin in the direction of Lieutenant Grieves. "You've been watching her this whole time. Seems to be your new favourite pastime. Has she told you her name yet?"

I turned back to watching Grieves and sighed. "No. I haven't asked again. I don't want to put her in a bad position," I replied with a shake of my head. "I can't figure her out. She's always doing the extra things for her patients—making sure they're comfortable. Very gentle too. But in the next breath, she'll face down a belligerent soldier twice her size. She looks like a strong breeze would break her in half, but I've seen her help big men to their feet and carry heavy bags of laundry over one shoulder. She's like steel wrapped in tissue paper and perfume."

Will grinned. "And the fact that she's prettier than a rose has nothing to do with it?"

It was my turn to grin then. "Certainly doesn't hurt."

A runner came onto the ward then, waving an envelope, and all eyes fixed upon him as he spoke with the staff. Will and I watched as the runner was directed to Grieves. There were several seconds of conversation between the two of them before Grieves looked up and scanned the room. Her eyes connected briefly with mine. She turned to the runner and dismissed him then made her way over to where Will and I were seated.

We both looked up at the Lieutenant as she came to stand beside the table. Grieves' expression was that of a woman watching the army telegram carrier walk up to her front door.

"This was just delivered for you," she said soberly. Her brow creased as she slid a brown envelope across the table to me. The word "ORDERS" were stamped across it in large, red letters along with "HENRY RYZAK".

I read the envelope then looked up at Grieves. I could see the faintest flickering of light in her chestnut eyes, a glow just beginning to lighten them in the centres.

I took a breath and reached for the envelope. I pulled the paper open and read the type-written note on the intimidatingly official army letterhead. I took a steadying breath and laid the paper on the table between Will and me feeling as though I had just won the biggest jack-pot of my nefarious gambling career—and then lost it again. After a solitary second in which I stuffed temptation into a small box and lit it on fire, I slid the paper toward Will and watched his face steadily as I said, "Looks like you're going home."

Will's eyes darted up to mine. His brow creased and he picked up the paper.

"What does it say?" Grieves asked quietly.

"Our father is unwell and can't keep up the farm. The government has priorized farm work. They need farms running to supply the army, so they're sending home one son to keep up the farm," I explained as Will read the note.

"But this says the *youngest* son is to be sent home… *You'll* be the one going home," Will said, looking up at me.

"It says *Henry Ryzak* is to be sent home," I replied. I reached across the table and picked up the ID tags that hung around Will's neck—the ones with my name on them.

He read them then turned back to me. He said nothing, only stared at me with an expression like he had suddenly found himself looking at a different face in a mirror.

"W—how?" Will asked holding up his ID tags to me.

"Doesn't matter," I said. "*You're* going home."

"No," Will said. "You're supposed to be the one going home."

I shook my head. "Come on, you know that won't work out well for me. What do you think will happen to me if I show up on Father's doorstep having left you here?" I let the vision of that hang in the air between Will and me for several seconds until defeat settled in Will's gaze. He sighed. "Besides," I continued, "I promised Father I would get you home safe. *Please*. Let me keep my promise. Let me be *that* man for once in my miserable life."

Will's face twisted and he shut his eyes, giving me a reluctant nod.

I looked up at Grieves—the only witness to our deception. "*Henry Ryzak* will return home as ordered," I said to her while pointing to Will.

Grieves looked between Will and me. She reached for our ID tags and read them in turn. She studied me for a long moment, looking at me as one might watch snow in July. Her brow flicked down and her eyes lit to a russet colour for the briefest of seconds just before she gave a silent nod, her eyes darkening again.

"I'll have the Sergeant make the arrangements," she said quietly. "We can send *Henry* home with the other injured soldiers." Grieves picked up the note and turned to leave. She cast me an ephemeral smile as she passed—a smile that was much more sad than happy.

Will stared down at the table, glaring at it as if it were his own personal enemy. His jaw clenched when he finally looked back up at me just before he turned away again.

Will said nothing further about the arrangement nor did I, fearful that if I mentioned it again Will would argue and insist I go home. He changed after that. Gone were the school boy grins and easy smiles. In their stead were the eyes of a man who had dug himself a hole from which he had only barely managed to climb out—a man determined to fill in the hole again.

Will's condition slowly improved over the next several days while he waited for his transport home to be arranged. We spent the time talking about war and home and visiting with Tommy. We could feel the sun growing warmer each day as it filtered through the canvas of the makeshift hospital, a still-cool breeze wafting in through an open window.

Unfortunately, Walker's condition deteriorated during that same time.

I found him one evening soaked through with sweat, his eyes reflecting a light that was not there. His cheeks had sunk down around their bones, shrinking to fit his skull. His lips were dry and cracked.

"Walker?" I asked, bending to look at him.

"I'm cold," he said with a shudder.

"Orderly!" I called and pulled the man over when he didn't come fast enough for my liking.

The orderly took one look at Walker and told me to fetch the Sister while he stayed to help Walker change into dry bedclothes. I scanned the ward, finally locating Grieves.

"The orderly asked me to get you," I said when I reached her. Grieves was just replacing a dressing that sat precariously covering one eye of her patient.

She looked up at me waiting to see what I wanted, her cheeks warming to a sunset pink.

"Walker's not well," I said.

The flame in Grieves' eyes guttered, darkening them to coal. "I'll be right there."

I went back to tell the orderly the Lieutenant was on her way. By the time I got back to Walker, he had paled several shades to an ashen colour, his chest rising and falling in uneven waves.

The orderly told me to go to my cot, then he set up a curtain screen between Walker and myself. It was a visual barrier only.

Grieves came and I could hear her moving bedclothes as she checked Walker's feet.

"I'll get the surgeon," she said.

"No!" Walker called out.

"You're feet are black. The doctor says we cannot save them," Grieves said, her voice like heavy footsteps in soft grass.

"I can't lit ya tek 'em. Who 'uld I be without feet? Some beggar in the gutter? A burden on my family? No."

"I understand," Grieves replied, "but at least let me get the doctor so we can talk about how to keep you comfortable."

I heard Grieves leave and return with the doctor. I heard the hushed conversation with the doctor about the patient's suffering and I heard one last attempt to convince Walker to let them take his feet. In the end, Walker was given laudanum and a very solemn doctor walked away.

I settled into my bunk for night while Grieves tended to Walker just on the other side of the screen. I felt rather than heard her soft reassurances. After a time, Grieves appeared on my side of the screen.

"Are you settled for the night?" She held out Aspirin and handed me a cup of water from my bedside table. I nodded and swallowed down the pills.

"All right," she said, "try to rest."

"You're back tomorrow?" I asked.

"I am," Grieves replied.

"Sleep well," I said.

I saw the candle light reflected in Grieves' eyes and watched as it flamed to life momentarily then darkened again. It rekindled to a low flame in her dark-as-onyx eyes just before she turned and walked away.

When I woke in the morning, the screen was gone and so was Walker.

He had slipped away quietly in the night, aided by heavy doses of pain killers, administered by a reluctant yet benevolent hand.

[April 18, 1917]

A couple of days later, I was eating breakfast at a table opposite Will, brooding over the loss of someone I barely knew. It could so easily have been Will or Tommy, or even Galt or Lundgren. Will, at least, would be leaving this unending hell, but the others would remain—and there was nothing I could do about it.

Well, perhaps there is one thing...

Later that morning, I was sent to have my dressing changed. I went eagerly, anticipating a private exchange with Grieves.

I was not disappointed.

She came around the screen with a dressing tray in hand, studying the tray diligently as she set it down.

I sat on the exam table and slid off the shirt I had draped over my slinged arm to cover up for breakfast.

Grieves worked silently, glancing at my face often. When our eyes met for the fourth time I asked, "Did you sleep well?"

Her hands halted in their task of unwrapping my arm. After a second or two, she continued her work. "Yes," she said simply. "Thank you." Then: "I'm sorry about your friend."

"Me too," I replied with a nod. "I don't quite know what to make of his decision. I can't decide if the man was very brave or very frightened. You've seen these things before—what do you think?"

She glanced up at me then turned away to fetch a washbasin. "I ought not tell you what I think—it isn't my place," she replied.

That will never wash.

"Well now you simply must tell me: what do you make of the man and his decision?"

She put the basin down on the table and considered it for a moment or two. She looked over her shoulder as though she thought someone might be listening, then said, "I feel the man was selfish."

"Selfish?!" I exclaimed before I could stop myself. I lowered my voice. "How so?"

"He chose to make his family deal with the loss of someone they loved rather than do the hard work of remaking himself if he were to go home different than the way he had left. He ought to have taken on the work of the thing rather than making them do it."

"Don't you think he rather spared his family the burden of caring for him?"

"He could have looked after himself had he but taken on the challenge of learning how. We all of us will return different. We will all have our work cut out for us upon arriving back home. What if we all made the same decision Walker did and never returned to our families simply because of our own fears of who we had become? Where would that leave them? Where would that leave the country we are fighting so desperately to save?" she asked, looking up at me as though daring me to do less.

"You do make the finest of points."

Grieves set aside the wrappings and began washing my arm, the touch of her soft hands easing the pain in my muscles and sending a warm sensation up into my chest.

I watched her face. "My brother is scheduled to go home day after tomorrow." The Lieutenant cast me a sideways glance then returned to the drying of my arm.

"Yes," she replied. "And are you still letting him go?"

"I am not only *letting* him go, I am sending him with a heartfelt prayer of a safe return."

"I don't understand why you are doing this," she said, her lips settling into a tight line.

I took a deep breath. "Could I ask a favour of you— before my brother leaves and I'm sent back to the front?"

She stepped back a half step then, looking at me with her brows drawn down. She handed me a shirt and I slipped my arms into it.

"And what would that be?" she asked cautiously.

I began fumbling with my buttons, trying to do them up with my left hand.

"Help me write a couple of letters," I replied, holding up my injured arm for illustration purposes. "I'm right handed."

Her features smoothed. "Oh, yes, of course I can do that," she replied as she took over buttoning my shirt.

"Thank you," I said simply, watching her small hands deftly manage the buttons. She looked up at me as she did up the last button, her hands slowing. She took a step back. I slid off the exam table and found myself much closer to the Lieutenant than even I had intended. Grieves took another quick step back. I fought a grin when her cheeks reddened.

"Tomorrow then?" I asked, turning to leave and very much enjoying the notion that perhaps I had seen her breathing quicken. I made certain to curb my smile as I stepped out from behind the curtained screen—I certainly didn't want to cause the Lieutenant any trouble. I turned back, waiting for her reply.

She nodded. "Tomorrow. It should be a warm day. Why don't I meet you just out back after lunch? There's a table in a sheltered spot that should give you some privacy for your dictating. I'll bring paper and pen."

"Thank you," I said and went to find Will.

[April 19, 1917]

I woke the next morning and looked around eagerly for that now-familiar face, but saw no sign of Grieves anywhere. I spent the morning looking for Grieves and worrying she had been unexpectedly shipped off.

"Stop worrying," Will said in an easy tone as we ate lunch together. "I'm sure she's around somewhere. Go meet her—I'm betting she shows up.

I glanced out the open door at the bright sunshine as I tried to screw up the courage to take that risk.

"As a gambling man, I'm not certain I like the odds."

"For crying out loud, man, just go!" Will said. "You'll hate yourself if she shows up and you're not there."

I frowned at Will then stood and made my way outside. I stepped out into a sunlit grassy area and saw a table and some chairs set there. The sun shone down with a welcome warmth. I took a seat at one of the tables and waited, my fingers worrying at the edge of my cuff.

I didn't have to wait long.

Moments later, I saw a figure walking toward me from the far end of the small field. I recognized her even across the distance that separated us. I sucked in a full breath. To my surprise, Grieves was not in her Bluebird uniform. Instead, she wore a simple ivory muslin dress tied with pink satin sash at the waist. The skirt was long, but not quite long enough to keep her ankles covered as she walked, and I caught a regrettably brief glimpse of delicate ankle as she made her way toward me. Out of long habit, I stood when she neared the table at which I sat.

Grieves smiled at me then came to sit in the chair beside mine, setting out paper, pen, and ink well as she took her seat.

"You're not in uniform. Are you not on duty today?" I asked.

She smiled up at me easily. "No. I am off this afternoon. I return to nights tomorrow."

"Then...you shouldn't be helping me with this," I insisted.

"Why ever not?"

"Because I don't want you to waste your off-duty time on me. Surely you have better things to do when you're not working than to help your patients." I didn't want to think that she may have a picnic planned with some officer, but the idea barged through my head, steamrolling over any coherent thought I might otherwise have had at that moment.

"I have nothing else to do—my break isn't long enough to take in any sightseeing so I am staying in camp."

"But..."

"It is quite all right, Private Ryzak, I am happy to spend my afternoon helping you," Grieves interrupted, casting me a patient smile.

I sighed in defeat. "Well then, I will accept your help gratefully. I truly would prefer not to bring more people into my little deception of sending Will home—that is why I asked you to help me write the letter I need to send to my father."

"I see. Still, you must be careful of what you put in it. The censors will be sure to read it."

"I won't be mailing it. I plan to send it home with Will personally."

"I see." Grieves opened the ink well and took up her pen. "All right. This letter is to your Father, then?" she asked, looking up at me with pen hovering over the paper.

"Yes, but, one last thing: won't you get in trouble for fraternizing with a private while off duty?"

"I think helping a patient write a letter in full view of everyone cannot be too damning, hmm?"

I looked around at the buildings and the handful of people surrounding us. "I suppose not. Fine then—yes, the first letter is to my Father."

"All right, tell me what you would like me to write."

I dictated in a halting manner, tripping over thoughts which seemed scattered about my head. I tried to sort them and string them together in some semblance of order. There was simply too much to say. In the end, I had Grieves write the following letter:

Dear Father,

I feel badly over the manner in which we parted. I know I have disappointed you tremendously in the past. I now understand what it was you saw in me that caused you dismay and angered you. I am sorry I failed to live up to the standards you set for me. However, if you are reading this letter, I have managed to send your son home to you safely as promised. Perhaps this act may, in some small way, begin to make amends for the wrongs I have done you and our family. I am hoping that, if ever we meet again, you might see me in a new light, having kept my promise for Will's safe return.

My throat tightened and I could say no more. I stood and walked around the table, trying to breathe and unclench my throat. In truth, I didn't want Grieves to see the unshed tears that pricked at my eyes. I worked desperately to blink them back as I paced.

After several moments Grieves asked, "Is that everything?" Her voice was the quiet hum of a mourner at a funeral.

"It is not nearly everything that needs to be said, but it is all I can bear to write."

"How shall I sign it?"

I cleared my throat, made certain my eyes were dry, and resumed my seat. "Sign it *Your Son, Henry*," I said.

"Right," she said, and penned the closing line in a flawlessly artful script. She sat, looking down at the letter for a time. After a moment or two, she said. "I'll not fold it just yet. It may not be dry." She moved the paper aside and drew forth another, dipping her pen and holding it poised to write. "You had more than one letter to write if I heard correctly. To whom is the next?"

I shook my head to clear the fog of memories and thoughts that clouded my mind.

"I do have another letter to write, but the other one can be written by anyone—Will or a VA or an orderly. I don't want to take up any more of your day off. Surely there's someone with a claim on your time? An eager officer perhaps?"

Grieves' eyes darted up to mine, burning to a deep topaz. She blinked and looked down at the paper that lay on the table in front of her. "I have no one waiting for me—not here, anyway."

"Back home then?" I asked quietly.

"That wouldn't be appropriate for me to discuss."

"I suppose that answer tells me all I need to know," I replied.

"No," she said, quickly looking up at me, "you don't understand."

I said nothing. I simply watched as her mouth twisted down on one side and she frowned at the paper.

"It's all right," I finally said. "You don't owe me an explanation."

She took a deep breath and looked up at me again. "But I do. You're obviously aware… It wouldn't be fair to you if I let you think… It's just that… Well, I'm engaged you see."

"Oh," I said, the air escaping my chest as though someone had just punched me in the gut.

"It's not as simple as all that—a rather long story I'm afraid."

"I'm not going anywhere."

She looked at me as though I had asked her to climb out a second story window. After several moments of watching her eyes dance from deep brown, to golden, and back again, she set down her pen and began to speak.

"My father, Walter Grieves, wasn't a very good farmer. He needed help to prove up on our land on time or he risked losing everything he had invested in bringing his family to Canada. He hired a man to help, giving the man, his wife, and their young son a place to live in exchange for labour. The hired man helped worked the farm alongside my father under a gentleman's agreement that he would be entitled to an even share in the farm, provided they proved up and got possession of the land. By the time they had earned the land, the man's wife had died. The man remained on our farm along with his son, John. John helped worked the farm when he was old enough and he and his father became part of our family in a way. John's father and mine later agreed that it would be ideal for me to marry John and join the two halves of the farm, keeping it in one family. I became engaged just before we each shipped out."

"A marriage of convenience?"

"That's rather presumptuous of you. You don't know I'm not in love with the man."

"And yet you didn't object."

"I beg your pardon?"

"If you loved the man, you would have immediately objected to my assumption that yours was a marriage of convenience and would have gone on to assert your love for your fiancé. You did neither."

She frowned at me.

"It's true: it is more of an arranged marriage."

The conversation had me feeling like I was swimming in open water, the waves rising and falling around me. I never knew when it was safe to draw breath or when I would be pulled down in the undertow. I chanced a breath.

"You don't like him much," I stated matter-of-factly.

Lieutenant Grieves looked up at me as though I had entered her room while she was dressing. "How on earth would you know what I think of him?"

"Because, again, you did not correct me."

"My father says John has a right to a share of the farm given all the work he and his father have done. Father says John will settle down and that love and respect will come later. Besides, a lot of marriages that begin with love do not end that way."

"That sounds rather cynical—*and* self-serving, given your father's agenda."

"It matters not at all. I promised and I cannot break my promise."

"That's a pretty big promise…"

"So was your promise to keep your brother safe," she said, her eyes meeting mine and refusing to let go.

I felt another kick in my gut. "Well…I certainly can't argue with that." I finally admitted defeat and looked down at the table. "So…you'll return home to marry the widower's son when all of this war nonsense is over?"

"I have to. I cannot go back on my promise. Besides, I also made a deal with my father: he would allow me to go into nursing and enlist—my last bid for freedom—and in exchange, I would return home and get married as planned."

"Where is John now?" I asked, preferring to torture myself rather than accept the reality of the situation.

"He joined up too and was assigned as the batman of a Colonel currently posted in Buxton."

"Pretty far from the front. Lucky man in many respects."

There was a heavy silence as though a thunderstorm were closing in. While the sun still shone down on us, I did not feel its warmth.

After a long time, Grieves said, "I am happy to write your next letter if you are ready to begin. To whom are you wanting to write?"

My mind snapped back to the present with a horrid whiplash sensation. "To a woman named Trinette Edgard who works at the *Hotel de Ville* in Montreal," I said. Grieves looked up at me then, her brows raised. "I need some information and I'm hoping I might enlist your help in the matter," I explained.

"All right," the Lieutenant replied with an *if-you-say-so* tone. "What do you want me to write?"

[April 20, 1917]

Will left the next day.

Tommy and I walked him to the lorrie that would take him to the train station. He was to go by train to *Le Havre*, cross over to England, then catch a boat that would take him back to Halifax.

Will tossed his gear onto the back of the truck and turned to me.

"I still don't think this is right."

"I do. Besides—it's too late now."

"You have to promise me you'll be careful. You take too many chances. How do you think I'm gonna feel if you die over here because you stayed when it should have been me?"

"I will certainly do my best to stay alive," I replied with a grin. I pulled the letter from my shirt pocket and handed it to Will. "This is a letter to Father." Will studied it for a moment then looked up at me with brows raised. "I want you to deliver it to him personally—make sure he reads it. It's a simple apology, but you can read it if you like."

"I'll make sure he gets it. I have something for you," Will said with a grin. He reached into his pocket and pulled out a small, white book. He handed it to me.

"A Bible?" I asked, looking down at the white leather volume in my hand.

"I was talking to Lieutenant Grieves the other day and mentioned my struggle with going home and leaving you here. She lent me her Bible. Guess she thought I might find some answers there. She was right. Seems all that time mother made us sit in church was not in vain. Anyway, I said I'd leave it with you and have you get it back to her. Be careful with it though—it seemed pretty important to her."

"I will certainly see that she gets it."

"You might want to have a look at it first," Will said with a grin. "There's an interesting inscription in the front." His smile widened.

Will turned to Tommy then. "Look out for him, will you?" he instructed, giving my good shoulder a shake without looking at me. "He's a gambling man and he likes the excitement of trying to beat bad odds. Don't let him gamble on the battlefield."

"No, sir," Tommy replied solemnly. "I'll keep watch on him."

"Thanks. And when you get back to Canada I expect you to come find me. Got that?"

"Yes, sir," Tommy said with a small smile. "It'll be the first stop I make."

"I'll hold you to that."

Tommy nodded.

The truck driver honked the horn and Will pulled me into a firm embrace, being careful to avoid my bad shoulder.

"Bye Henry."

"Good-bye Will."

Will turned and headed toward the truck.

"Stay above decks on the boat," I called after him. "And let me know when you've arrived back in Canada!"

"Will do!" Will waved then ducked into the cab of the truck.

Tommy and I watched as the truck pulled off, disappearing into the cloud of dust it sent up.

We returned to our bunks. Will had asked an orderly to move Tommy to the now-empty cot beside mine and I was grateful he had. I sat down on my cot, aimless and out of sorts.

What am I supposed to in this stupid war now that I'm not looking out for Will?

The war and the fighting seemed a large and endless void ready to swallow me whole if I didn't have a solid reason to be there.

I fingered the small Bible in my hand and opened the cover to the dedication page. My gaze immediately caught the first line: *Presented to Miss Abbigail Grieves.*

I smiled to myself.

Abbigail! Thank you Will!

The small stamped note went on to list Abbigail's address and indicated the Bible had been presented as a graduation gift from the Saskatoon City Hospital School of Nursing. It indicated the date of graduation and the fact that Abbigail had graduated with Great Distinction (naturally).

I flipped through the pages of the small book and saw Abbigail had underlined verses here and there throughout the text. I went to sit a table, laid the Bible down in front of me, and began reading, trying to figure out why she had underlined the verses she had and just what they meant to her. It was a frustrating but endlessly fascinating endeavor.

When Abbigail came on duty that evening and made her rounds, I dutifully handed back the Bible.

"Here," I said, "my brother gave me strict instructions that I was to return this to you."

Abbigail smiled. "Thank you." Her brow turned down. "I can lend it to you for a time if you'd like."

"Thank you but, no, I can't take it from you—it's important to you. I spent the day going through it. I think I got what I needed from it."

Abbigail smiled. "I'm glad." She paused then asked, "I was told your brother shipped home today. How are you doing?" in a tone one uses when addressing a widow at her husband's funeral.

"I'll be all right. Besides," I said, jerking my chin toward Tommy who lay in the next cot. "Will has assigned Tommy to look after me. What can go wrong?" I grinned over at the Kid.

Tommy grinned back. "I'll make sure he does fine," Tommy responded resolutely.

Abbigail smiled. "Very well then. I shall let you both get ready for bed." She cast me a quiet smile and left.

Tommy and I settled ourselves into our cots and the lights were turned off on the ward. Only the odd candle or lantern remained to drive off the engulfing darkness. The light from the scattered lamps bounced about the large room, sentinels over the bent and broken souls on the ward.

I thought about Walker and what he had said about Tommy and felt a sharp jab of conscience stick between my ribs.

"Tommy?" I whispered through the dark.

"Yeah?" he replied.

"I do remember coming back to get you off the field."

There was a pause, then: "I thought it would come back to you."

. . .

Tommy and I recovered and were given exercises to restore our injured parts to functionality again. It was good to have use of my arm again, but it tired easily. Tommy's ribs did not always pain him, but he said they were still "tight" when he slept in one position too long and would wake him with painful jabs.

I didn't see much of Abbigail. She worked nights for the rest of that week, keeping vigil while I and the others slept. She told me the hospital was soon to be moved to the *Chateau d'Arques*. It seemed our time together was coming to a close, the army and our obligations moving us along our separate paths.

The time came for Tommy and me to return to our unit. As much as we wanted to see the others whom we had left behind, we had obvious misgivings about leaving our warm dry beds and the reliable supply of food. We packed our few things into our duffels slowly, prolonging our time in the relative safety of the hospital.

We stepped out of the hospital door and into the bright, full sun on a warm morning late in April and made our way to the transport truck that stood by, waiting to take us to the train.

Tommy elbowed me in the side and I looked at him. He grinned and pointed in the direction of the truck. Abbigail stood beside it, picture-perfect in a light pink wisp of lace and muslin. My heart beat high in my chest as she stepped forward.

"I'll wait for you in the truck," Tommy muttered.

"Good-bye, Tommy. Take care!" Abbigail called after him as he disappeared around back of the vehicle. Tommy gave her a wave, but said nothing.

Abbigail turned to me. "I came to see you off," she said, looking at me with eyes the colour of iced tea on a sunlit porch. "And to assure you I will attend to that task."

"I would be ever so grateful if you would," I said. Then, "Thank you for taking of us. You are very good at what you do."

She gave me a weak smile. "Thank you. I…" she made a face and looked down.

"I suppose that, under the circumstances, it would be inappropriate for me to write to you—for at least a couple of reasons."

She lifted doleful eyes to mine. They shimmered and turned a deep walnut. "Yes, I suppose it would." She looked to the side.

After a time, she said, "I truly cannot say 'good-bye'. I thought I could do it, but it is proving too difficult."

"Then let me do it," I offered. I put my hands on her shoulders and pulled her a step closer. I leaned down and kissed her forehead lightly. I stepped back, holding her at arms' length and studied her for a second or two—just long enough to secure the memory of her face once more.

"Good-bye Abbigail," I said.

Abbigail's gaze shot up to mine and her fingers flew to her quivering lips. Tears rimmed her darkened eyes then spilled down her cheeks.

I took a steadying breath, wondering how on earth saying 'good-bye' could be more difficult than setting off across a battlefield. After another quick breath, I stepped past Abbigail, forcing my feet forward. I walked to the truck, climbed into the back, and sat down heavily on the board that served for a seat. I pounded my fist on the box of the truck twice and the vehicle lurched forward. Tommy watched me for a moment, took a quick glance at Abbigail as she grew smaller in the distance, then turned back to me.

"You made her cry! What did you do?" he asked, giving me a hard look.

I leaned my elbows on my knees and dropped my head into my hands.

"I said 'good-bye'," I choked out, forcing the words past the lump in my throat.

Tommy fell silent and I was left to brood in peace.

About the Author

Wendy Fehr holds a Bachelor of Science in Nursing and a Masters of Nurse Practitioner. She and her husband have raised four children together.

Wendy has a long-standing interest in World War I and the pandemic which followed at the end of that war. The origins of this story dates back to a story told by one of the characters in the Renate Saga, initially published as the Shifters series in 2014. Her research into this part of Canadian history surfaced again in 2018 while researching a presentation, and continued over the years, with more directed research beginning in 2019. When re-deployed to the COVID Assessment and Testing Centre at the beginning of 2020, Wendy began to write *The Light Attendant*, drawing on her Masters-prepared research skills and her experience as a nurse during a pandemic. The work culminated in two interwoven novels, with the series spanning three books.

All titles are published by ShiftersPress, an independent publisher, and are available in print and all popular eBook formats.

If you have enjoyed this book, please consider leaving a review on Amazon or Goodreads.

You can find other works by Wendy Fehr at www.ShiftersPress.ca

Reference List

1. Bird, W.. *Ghosts Have Warm Hands: A Memoir of the Great War 1916-1919*. CEF Books, Toronto, ON, 2002.

2. *Canada and the First World War*. Visit Canadian War Museum, October, 2019. https://www.warmuseum.ca/firstworldwar/history/.

3. Canadian Nursing Sisters. Visit Canadian Great War Project, http://www.canadiangreatwarproject.com/Regimental/NursingSisters.asp.

4. Champ, J. (January, 2003). *The Impact of the Spanish Influenza Epidemic on Saskatchewan Farm Families, 1918-1919*. Saskatchewan Western Development Museum's "Winning the Prairie Gamble" 2005 Exhibit. https://wdm.ca/wp-content/uploads/2018/08/WDM-1918SpanishFlu.pdf. Accessed July, 2020.

5. Cowen, R. (Ed.). *A Nurse at the Front: The Great War Diaries of Sister Edith Appleton*. Simon and Schuster, London, 2012.

6. Crewdson, R. (Ed.). *Dorothea's War. A First World War Nurse Tells her Story*. The Orion Publishing Group Ltd. London, 2014.

7. Cumming, E., Gillings, J. & Richards, J.. *In all those lines : the diary of Sister Elsie Tranter 1916-1919*. Newstead,

Tas. 2008.
https://throughtheselines.com.au/research/etaples#elsie

8. Dawson, R.. *Some fast facts about the 1918 Spanish flu pandemic in Moose Jaw.* Moose Jaw Today, 2020. https://www.moosejawtoday.com/local-news/some-fast-facts-about-the-1918-spanish-flu-pandemic-in-moose-jaw-2371661.

9. Drugs. 1914-1918. Online: International Encyclopedia of the First World War. New Articles RSS. Kamienski, L. (2019). Accessed May, 2020. https://encyclopedia.1914-1918-online.net/article/drugs.

10. Fitzgerald G. J.. Chemical warfare and medical response during World War I. *American journal of public health*, vol. *98*, no. 4, 2004, pp. 611–625. https://doi.org/10.2105/AJPH.2007.11930

11. Fowler, T.. *The Canadian Nursing Service and the British War Office: The Debate Over Awarding the Military Cross, 1918.* Canadian Military History: Vol. 14, no. 4, Article 4, 2005. doi: https://scholars.wlu.ca/cgi/viewcontent.cgi?referer=https://www.google.com/&httpsredir=1&article=1358&context=cmh .

12. Government of Canada. *Military History*. Accessed October, 2019. https://www.canada.ca/en/services/defence/caf.html.

13. Halifax Explosion. Canadian Encyclopedia: https://www.thecanadianencyclopedia.ca/en/search?search=halifax+explosion.

14. Halifax Explosion. *The Canadian Encyclopedia.* Kernaghan, L. & Foot, R., 2017. Retrieved August, 2020 from https://www.thecanadianencyclopedia.ca/en/article/halifax-explosion.

15. *Halifax Explosion*. Wikipedia: The Free Encyclopedia. Wikimedia Foundation, Inc., July, 2020. https://en.wikipedia.org/w/index.php?title=Halifax_Expl osion&oldid=969366292. Accessed August 2, 2020.

16. Hodd, Thomas (Ed.). *A Soldier's Place. The War Stories of Will R Bird*. Nimbus Publishing Limited, Halifax, NS, 1972.

    https://www.arcgis.com/apps/MapJournal/index.html?a ppid=6b1f4fecb5504f3abd6ca2de3bfb445c.

17. *Imperial Limited*. Wikipedia: The Free Encyclopedia. Wikimedia Foundation, Inc., February, 2021. Accessed March, 2021. https://en.wikipedia.org/w/index.php?title=Imperial_Lim ited&oldid=927671729.

18. John A. Hayward. M.D., F.R.C.S. 1914-1915. Assistant-Surgeon (rank. Captain) British Red Cross Hospital, Netley. 1915-1917, Medical Officer, Queen Alexandra Hospital, Roehampton. April to November 1918, Temporary Captain R.A.M.C., B.E.F. *First World War. com*. (August, 2009). Retrieved September, 2020 from: https://www.firstworldwar.com/diaries/casualtyclearings tation.htm.

19. Kelly, J.. Last Call to Dinner. Classic Trains. *Kalmbach Media*, February, 2001. Retrieved August 3, 2020: https://ctr.trains.com/railroad-reference/operations/2001/02/last-call-to-dinner.

20. Lang, B.. *"There's nobody. The streets are empty": City archivist gives a look at Saskatoon during the Spanish Flu*. March, 2020. 650 CKOM. Accessed July, 2020. https://www.ckom.com/2020/03/26/theres-nobody-the-streets-are-empty-city-archivist-gives-a-look-at-saskatoon-during-the-spanish-flu/.

21. Library and Archives Canada (2019). *Canadian Army Medical Corps*. Government of Canada. Accessed

October, 2019. https://www.bac-lac.gc.ca/eng/search/Pages/search.aspx.

22. Library and Archives Canada. *78th Battalion War Diary*. Accessed October, 2019. https://www.bac-lac.gc.ca/eng/search/Pages/search.aspx .

23. Library and Archives Canada. *Caregiving on the Front: The Experience of Canadian Military Nurses During World War I*. Government of Canada, September, 2020. http://www.bac-lac.gc.ca/eng/discover/military-heritage/first-world-war/canada-nursing-sisters/Pages/caregiving-on-the-front.aspx.

24. Library and Archives Canada. *Infantry*. Government of Canada. Accessed October, 2019. https://www.bac-lac.gc.ca/eng/search/Pages/search.aspx.

25. Library and Archives Canada. *Soldiers of the First World War: 1914-1918*. Image retrieved September 14, 2020 from: https://www.bac-lac.gc.ca/eng/discover/military-heritage/first-world-war/first-world-war-1914-1918-cef/Pages/image.aspx?Image=632874a&URLjpg=http%3a%2f%2fdata2.archives.ca%2fcef%2fgpc016%2f632874a.gif&Ecopy=632874a.

26. *List of named passenger trains of Canada*. Wikipedia: The Free Encyclopedia. Wikimedia Foundation, Inc., September, 2020. https://en.wikipedia.org/w/index.php?title=List_of_named_passenger_trains_of_Canada&oldid=962783771. Accessed August, 2020.

27. Lornic, J.. *How the 1918 Spanish Flu Epidemic felled nearly as many Canadians as the war*. Canada's History Magazine, September, 2018. Retrieved January 25, 2021 from: https://definingmomentscanada.ca/the-spanish-flu/themes/peacetime-killer/.

28. Lyman, H., Fenger, C., Jones, H., Belfield, W.. *20ᵗʰ Century Family Physician*. Charles C. Thompson Co., Chicago, 1912.

29. MacNaughtan, S.. *A woman's Diary of the War. Life of a Nurse at the Front*. Lume Books, London, 2016.

30. Maritime Museum of the Atlantic. *Halifax Explosion, Explosion in the Narrows: The 1917 Halifax Harvour Explosion*. Nova Scotia Museum, 2019. Retrieved August 3, 2020 from: https://thestarphoenix.com/opinion/columnists/history-matters-1918-spanish-flu-led-to-saskatchewans-first-female-mla.

31. Mayhew, E.. *Wounded: From Battlefield to Blighty, 1914-1918*. The Bodley Head, London, 2013.

32. Mitchell, A.. *The outbreak and its aftermath: The little-known story of the 1918 Spanish Flu and how we're preparing for the next great pandemic*. Canadian Geographic, August, 2018. Retrieved January 25, 2021 from: https://www.canadiangeographic.ca/article/outbreak-and-its-aftermath.

33. Nicholson, G.. *Official History of the Canadian Army in the First World War: Canadian Expeditionary Force 1914-1919*. Queen's Printer and Controller of Stationery, Ottawa, Ontario, 1962.

34. Oxford, J. and Gill, D.. *A possible European origin of the Spanish influenza and the first attempts to reduce mortality to combat superinfecting bacteria: an opinion from a virologist and a military historian*. Human Vaccines and Immunothrapeutics, vol. 15, no. 9: 2009-2012. Published online 2019 May 23. doi: 10.1080/21645515.2019.1607711.

35. Provincial Archives of Saskatchewan. (2011). *The Spanish Flu in Saskatchewan*. Retrieved August 3, 2020 from:

https://www.saskarchives.com/collections/exhibits/spani
sh-flu-saskatchewan/spanish-flu-saskatchewan-
newspapers.

36. *Pullman Sleeping Cars add Comfort to Overnight Travel*.
Rails West (2002-2010). DigitalNetExpress.com, Burbank,
California. Retrieved August 3, 2020:
http://www.railswest.com/pullman.html.

37. Redekop, B.. *The Great Pandemic. WAVE* Winnipeg's
Health and Wellness Magazine, December, 2018.
Retrieved August 3, 2020 from:
https://www.wavemag.ca/2018/11/the-great-
pandemic.php.

38. *Regina Spanish Flu Memorial.* Retrieved January 29, 2021
from: https://reginaspanishflu.ca.

39. Reid, M. (Ed). *Canada's Great War Album: Our Memories
of the First World War*. Harper Collins Publishers Ltd,
Toronto, ON, 2014.

40. Reiger, S.. *100 years ago a train carrying Spanish Flu
pulled into Calgary. Within weeks, Alberta was in Crisis*.
CBC, December, 2018. Retrieved January 25, 2021 from
https://www.cbc.ca/news/canada/calgary/spanish-flu-
alberta-history-1.4948081.

41. Report On The Work Of The Australian Army Nursing
Service In France. *E. M. McCarthy, Matron-in-Chief,
British Troops in France and Flanders, Headquarters,
31.7.19*. Retrieved January 10, 2021 from:
https://throughtheselines.com.au/research/etaples#air-
raids.

42. Rutty, C. and Sullivan, S.. *This is Public Health: A Canadian
History*. Canadian Public Health Association, Ottawa,
Ontario, 2010.

43. Saskatoon Public Library. Local history collection.
Accessed August, 2020:

http://spldatabase.saskatoonlibrary.ca/ics-wpd/exec/icswppro.dll?AC=SEE_ALSO&QF0=CLASSIFICAT
ION&QI0==%22HOSPITALS%20-
%20SASKATOON%20CITY%20-
%20SCHOOL%20OF%20NURSING%22&XC=/ics-wpd/exec/IcsWPPro.dll&BU=&GI=&TN=LHR_RAD&SN=A
UTO27241&SE=2203&RN=0&MR=20&TR=0&TX=1000&E
S=0&XP=&RF=www_Default+Canned&EF=&DF=&RL=0&E
L=0&DL=0&NP=4&ID=&MF=&DT=&ST=0&IR=0&NR=0&N
B=0&SV=0&SS=0&BG=&FG=&QS=.

44. Smulders, M.. *The Dalhousie Stationary Hospital No. 7: Dalhousie overseas*. Dal News, November, 2008. Retrieved January, 2021 from: https://digitalexhibits.library.dal.ca/exhibits/show/lives-of-dal-volume-1/chapter-1-9/dalhousie-stationary-hospital.

45. Spanish Flu Themes. *Defining Moments in Canada*. Retrieved January 31, 2021 from: https://definingmomentscanada.ca/the-spanish-flu/themes/.

46. St. Paul's School of Nursing Alumni Association. *The Great Canadian Catholic Hospital History Project*. 2005

47. The MacMillan Company. *A War Nurse's Diary. Sketches from a Belgian Field Hospital (1918)*. New York, 1918.

48. Thomas Lecky, 78th Battalion, Winnipeg Grenadiers:

49. Van Emden, R.. *Tommy's War*. Bloomsbury Publishing Plc., London, England, 2014.

50. Waiser, B. (November, 2016). *History Matters: 1918 Spanish Flu led to Saskatchewan's first female MLA*. Saskatoon StarPhoenix, November, 2016. Retrieved August 3, 2020 from: https://thestarphoenix.com/opinion/columnists/history-matters-1918-spanish-flu-led-to-saskatchewans-first-female-mla.

51. Walker, J. (2014). *Trench Talk: A Guide to First World War Slang*. The Guardian*, 2014*. Retrieved September 8, 2020 from:
https://www.theguardian.com/education/2014/jul/23/first-world-war-slang-glossary.

52. Wurzer, R.. *Saskatoon City Hospital 100 years 1909-2009*. Saskatoon City Hospital, 2917. Retrieved April 29, 2021 from: https://vimeo.com/179516785.

Made in the USA
Monee, IL
15 February 2022

91301930R00164